The Copper Connection

Lesley Elliot

The Copper Connection

This is a work of fiction. Names, characters, businesses, places, events and incidents are either the product of the author's imagination or used in a fictitious manner. Any resemblance to actual persons, living or dead or actual events is purely coincidental.

ISBN: 9798624634831

For my darling wife, Susan, with thanks for her help and patience.

Table of Contents

Chapter 1

Heather kissed her Mom, clicked the door shut and ran down the garden path. She was on her way to meet her friend Lucy in their local pub on the outskirts of Birmingham. She couldn't know that the course of her life would change forever in the next few minutes.

Heather, a bright, twenty-one-year-old with long blond hair and a cheeky grin, had recently qualified as a midwife. Most of her practical training had been carried out at Good Hope Hospital, where she was due to start her first shift the following week.

She glanced at her Seiko watch: eight o'clock. There was plenty of time. She'd decided to leave her car at home and walk. It would take about twenty minutes and the exercise might help with the few pounds she wanted to shed from her five-three frame. She'd been sitting in a lecture hall for most of Saturday morning listening to a dull but essential talk about confidentiality; she needed to get her body moving.

It was a mild evening early in May 1995. She put on her headphones, pressed play on her Sony Discman, then walked briskly, her short, red jacket swinging along in time to Bon Jovi. She didn't see the white van pull up just ahead of her, nor was she aware of the two men who jumped out until they grabbed her and swiftly manhandled her inside. Heather fought as hard as she could, but she was no match for the men. She didn't have time to wonder what was happening as she kicked and screamed. They threw her ignominiously onto the floor then climbed in beside her, pulling the doors shut with a clang. The van took off with its tyres squealing.

'Let me go you bastard! Fucking well let me ...' Heather's shouts were cut short as a filthy rag was stuffed hard into her mouth. Her earphones, which had been ripped from her head, were dangling freely by her knees. A tinny rendition of the music could still be heard as she felt her hot urine soaking into her jeans.

Heather glared at the dark-skinned man who was gripping her hands. He shoved her back against the wheel arch.

'You'll keep quiet if you know what's good for you,' he said. Heather stared at him contemptuously. 'If I take the rag out, you keep shtum, understand? No one can hear you anyway, you ugly, fat bitch.'

Heather clenched her teeth and nodded as he squeezed both of her hands into one of his rough-skinned ones then pulled the rag from her mouth. He sneered as he threw it behind the driver's seat but within easy reach. Heather gagged and gulped greedily at a lungful of air. 'I've warned you. Now keep quiet, or else it goes back in along with my fist.'

Evil fucking bastard, Heather thought. She bit her lip to prevent words from breaking out and jerked her head away to survey a light-skinned man sitting with his back pressed against the other side of the van. He was staring intently at her. Despite her fear, she thought how ugly he was. His face was pockmarked, and his nose appeared to have been broken, perhaps more than once. She clutched her small, red shoulder bag in front of her chest. 'You’re n ... not g ... going to k ... kill me, are you?’ she said.

'We might if you don't do as you're told.' His gravelly voice grated harshly on her ears. He reached across and pulled at the handbag. Heather held on. His face took on an expression that frightened her further: she relinquished it. He tipped its contents onto the floor, poked through them dismissively then returned them. He examined her driving licence then pocketed it. He switched the Discman off, pulled the earphones away from Heather and thrust everything under the front seat of the van.

'Where are you taking me?' Heather looked back to the tattooed man. 'Is this a prank?' She grasped at the possibility but she already knew the answer. She started to whimper, 'Please, please, I don't want to die.'

The driver glanced over his shoulder. 'Shut the fuck up! Nobody's going to kill anybody. We're just having a bit of fun, so pipe down and you'll be okay.'

Heather thought she heard sympathy in his voice and spoke directly to him. 'Please, please, just let me go. I won't tell anyone. I just want to go home.'

The tattooed man smacked her hard across her face. 'I told you to shut it, didn't I? Do you want the gag back in your stupid mouth?'

Heather shook her head vigorously. If I get out of this alive, she thought, I'll make sure you suffer. Although her mind held on to trivialities to allay her fear, she couldn't stop the angry bees that buzzed in her stomach making her feel like vomiting.

What were they going to do with her if not kill her? Hold her for ransom? Her family wasn't rich but they would do everything possible to get her back. Heather knew she was clutching at straws but refused to think of any other motives they could have.

The man with the tattoo turned to speak to the driver. As he did so, Heather saw his face full-on. Her eyes widened; she recognised him. She didn't know him, but she'd seen him before in an Asian Supermarket. She sometimes went shopping along Stratford Road with Lucy or her sister Susan. She enjoyed the bustling atmosphere and was always impressed with the display of fruit and vegetables on sale. It was while she and Lucy were inside one of the shops, paying for some apples that Heather felt a nudge from her friend's elbow. Lucy nodded her head and rolled her eyes to indicate a good-looking man talking animatedly to another man at the back of the store. Heather also thought he was attractive. He had dark skin and jet black, wavy hair he constantly flicked away from his tawny coloured eyes. His eyes never met hers but she remembered them and the serpent tattoo that wound around his forearm with its green and red striped head resting on the back of his hand.

She tore her eyes away thinking I'll never forget you, and the police will know where to find you if I get out of this alive. Giving no indication that she'd seen him before and trying to keep herself calm, she spoke in a small voice: 'Where are you taking me?' She hoped she might be able to escape once the doors opened.

'You'll soon see. We're nearly there,' the ugly man said, 'and don't think you'll get a chance to run. Will she, lads?'

It was as if he could read her thoughts. His voice was deep and liquid as he laughed. The other two men joined in; their voices pitched higher but no less frightening. Heather knew that she was going to die. No, please God, I'm too young to die, she begged silently. The van hit a bump in the road causing her head to smack sharply above the wheel arch. Heather scrunched herself into a tight ball as it came to an abrupt halt.

The driver jumped out then dragged open a five-bar gate. Heather heard metal clang and something being scraped along the ground. He climbed back behind the wheel and drove through the gateway, then jumped out again to shut the gate. The hinges screeched – needing oil. Heather's thoughts whirled around and around, one minute thinking she'd be able to escape, and sights and sounds were important, the next believing that she was already dead.

They drove along a rough track with the van throwing her uncomfortably from side to side as it hit hummocks of grass and potholes; Heather's stomach ached. She knew she wasn't going to get away from whatever they were going to do to her. She silently vowed that she wouldn't cry or plead with them and felt determined that she wouldn't lose control. She had no idea of the torture that they would inflict on her.

The movement ceased; the stillness terrified her. The back doors were thrown open and Heather was ordered to get out. She refused and was immediately grabbed by her ankles and pulled onto the ground. She hit the grass with a thud knocking all the air from her lungs.

Heather opened her eyes, and panic seemed to heighten her senses. There was a full moon that shone with an eerie light over a clearing on the edge of some woodland. The trees cast gloomy shadows on nearby water which trickled pleasantly over what sounded like a stony bed. She thought she could smell bluebells and caught a faint whiff of garlic. The sharp toe of the ugly man's boot kicked her in the backside, blotting out her other senses.

'Okay, don't mess about! Get your clothes off!' He barked the order and then said something quietly to the other two. They all burst into a fit of girlish giggles. Heather thought they sounded nervous or high on something.

'No!' Her nails dug into damp softness releasing a pungent earthy smell as she scrambled to get up. She ran towards the trees, but one of the men easily kept up with her vain attempt to get away. He laughed as he caught her by the ponytail and dragged her to where the van was parked.

'Okay,' the ugly man, who seemed to be the ringleader, said, 'take 'em off, or we'll cut 'em off, won't we, lads?'

Heather pulled away and started to scream like a wounded animal. She was knocked senseless by a blow to the back of her head with a log. When she came to, she was naked. She shivered violently but lay still with her arms clasped around her body. She continued to scream but only in her head. She sniffed the perfumed air and tried to concentrate on her surroundings; her eyes skirted over the men's boots.

'You're not very clever, are you?' the driver said. 'You can scream as much as you like – no one will hear you – but you'll be sorry if you do. And just in case you feel like fighting ...' He grabbed her wrists, wound gaffer tape around them, then trapped them at the top of her head while the ugly man held her legs down. Heather struggled in vain as she pleaded with them to let her go.

'Don't kill me, don't kill me,' she begged. Tears mixed with snot ran down her face.

'If you stay quiet, we won't. I told you we just want some f –'

'If you don't shut the fuck up, we'll do just that, so shut your trap.' The ugly man interrupted his friend and then forced his hand between her tightly clenched thighs. He thrust as far as he could towards her vagina. Heather screamed and was smacked hard across her face. She quieted to a whimper. He withdrew his hand and began to undo his belt.

'Hey, taking turns is what we agreed. I won the toss, remember?' The man with the tattoo shoved the ugly man out of his way.

Heather shut her eyes and desperately tried to divorce her mind from what was happening to her. 'I'll kill you, I'll kill you, and I'll kill you': she chanted the words to herself over and over again as the man pressed her legs apart and thrust into her dryness while the other two men held her still. He fucked her hard, repeatedly pushing into her now slick vagina. He finished with his mouth agape and withdrew. As he did so, he discovered that his penis and legs were smeared in blood.

'You dirty fucking whore,' he yelled, spraying spittle into the air.

Heather shrank away from him and drew her knees up towards her chest. Hurt as she was, she was glad that he felt fouled. His friends laughed as he stormed off to wash himself in the nearby stream. Heather lay still and cried quietly – afraid that if she started to scream again, she would die.

Suddenly, the man who had driven the van grabbed her arms and pulled her onto her side: 'Open your mouth! I don't want your dirty blood on me.'

Heather unclenched her teeth and spat hard into his face. His penis deflated, and he looked dismayed as he wiped away the drool and then punched the side of her head. He eased himself onto the grass, lit a cigarette, and gazed at his feet. No longer interested in his fantasy, which had somehow gone sour.

Seeing the driver walk away, the ugly guy could wait no longer. 'My turn,' he said and twisted Heather's lower half over so he could enter her anally. The pain was so intense and shocking that Heather started to choke and bit down onto her tongue. She screamed, and her cry of pain further excited him.

He reached around her and viciously squeezed her breasts. He pinched her nipples so hard that her scream became one long drawn out ululation until her voice died. He climaxed with a grunting noise and let go of her. Heather cried out, repeatedly thanking God as his penis became flaccid and left her agonised body.

The driver felt ashamed and sick inside as he walked back to the group, where he stood looking down at their victim. He hadn't expected her to be fucked anally or treated so brutally. He didn't know what he had hoped would happen. He knew all the fight had gone out of her, and he desperately wanted her ordeal to end. He took a Swiss army knife from his pocket, cut her hands free, then moved out of sight. Heather heard a match scraping against sandpaper and then smelled smoke as he lit another cigarette. He wasn't brave enough to tell the other two how he felt, but he couldn't bear to watch anymore.

Heather dismissed him from her mind as she brought her hands forward, causing the tape to pull out long strands of hair. She didn't feel the roots tear from her scalp; she was already in too much pain.

She wasn't aware that the tattooed man had returned until he said, 'Come on, you pair, let's leave the slut here and go. We've had our fun – I've got work on tomorrow.' He spat in her general direction and wiped his mouth on his sleeve.

Relief flooded through Heather – it was over – they weren't going to kill her.

The ugly man kicked the toe of his boot into a tuft of grass. 'Don't be stupid, Javid. We'll never be able to use this place to fish again. Sling her in the van; we'll kick her out somewhere quiet nearer Birmingham.'

He opened the van doors. Heather cringed as they picked her up and threw her roughly inside. She shrank into the side of the cold wheel arch as though it was her protector. She tried in vain to cover her nakedness with bloodied hands and arms. Her head was sore from where the tape had been. She sat sobbing and rocking gently to and fro.

'I told you to shut the fuck up, didn't I?' the tattooed man said.

The driver started the engine and began to pull away. Heather couldn't stop whimpering, and the tattooed man kicked her in her side. He kicked her repeatedly until he was flung against the bottom of the van as it hit a pothole. The violence had again excited the ugly man. He grabbed Heather by her feet and dragged her across the cold, ridged floor while managing to turn her onto her side. He again entered her torn and bleeding anus. Heather thought she would die; the pain was so intense. Her screams ceased as his foul-smelling hand covered her mouth.

I will kill you, and I will kill you, and I will kill you, she repeated silently, allowing her mind to slide away from the pain. It had become the mantra that she clung onto throughout the repeated rapes and brutality, which at times made her think death would be welcome. But Heather was mentally resilient; her character had a strong streak of self-preservation. She was determined to survive to exact vengeance on the animals that were raping her: prison was too easy an option. Deep in her mind, Heather knew that she would kill all three men if she had the opportunity: she'd make the opportunity. This steeliness kept her from going insane as she fought for her life. The van came to a shuddering halt, and the driver climbed over the seat into the back. 'Come on, that's a- fucking nuff.'

As the ugly man had moved away from Heather, the tattooed man, who she now knew as Javid, sat astride her and began fucking her breasts. The driver shoved him sideways off her. His grunting sounded pig-like as he finished himself off while on the floor. Heather moaned quietly – she was exhausted and bleeding profusely.

The Asian driver told them again that they'd have to go and climbed back into the driving seat where he revved the engine. The ugly man began to pull up his trousers and shuffled past Heather on his knees. As he did so, Heather reached out and punched him as hard as she could in his balls. She hadn't planned it – it just happened. She didn't think of any consequences that her action might bring. He cried out in a fury rather than pain and struggled to his feet. He kicked her in her side. Heather screamed, and this seemed to trigger violence within him. His face contorted; he carried on kicking out at her. He held onto the roof of the van with one of his hands pressed flat and dragged her up by her hair.

'Okay. That's enough,' the driver shouted. 'Just pack it in now – we've had our fun.'

He revved the engine again and began to move slowly forward, hoping that would make his friends stop the assault. The other two ignored him, and the ugly man carried on beating her. He punched her hard in the face and chest. The tattooed man joined in hitting her until she fell slowly to the floor. The ugly man reached under the passenger seat of the van and drew out a length of some heavy copper pipe, which he proceeded to use to beat her about her body and head. Heather scrabbled to get away from him and managed to get up onto her knees. She could smell her blood: it was intense and almost covered the stink of the men. The tattooed man kicked her forward, and she felt the sharpness of a metal stud from his boot as she sprawled on the unfeeling floor with her bleeding, violated backside in the air. The ugly guy threw aside the length of pipe and pulled a shorter one from under the seat.

He brutally thrust it into her anus and kicked it. Mercifully, Heather didn't hear her scream: she neither heard nor felt anything more.

The driver concentrated on what he was doing and barely spoke. He felt only disgust for himself and the men that had been his friends for so many years: he knew that he would never see them again when this was all over. The other two left their victim, where she lay unconscious. They callously passed a bottle of beer between themselves as they joked about achieving their fantasy. The driver wondered if he would ever forgive himself for being a part of the wickedness that had been carried out: he didn't think so. When they had decided to indulge their fantasy, he hadn't thought any further than having some fun. He'd never considered the feelings that the girl would have and had not envisaged her pain, other than being forced to have sex. He'd been wrong about what would happen and knew that he'd been evil to have been so dangerously naive.

The three men had been friends since their school days when they'd initially shared their fantasies. They had continued to explore and refine the possibility of turning their dreams into reality for several years after their school days were over. They had also agreed before they carried out their plan that the adventure would be a one-off, never to be repeated experience. They had no intention of going to prison and thought that they had left no trace. Their victim was random, and there would be no connection. It was as far as their imagination had taken them. None of them had noticed that Javid's name had been used or knew that Heather had heard it.

Karl drove steadily, hoping to cause the girl no further injury as they headed down the M42 leaving the motorway at the Solihull exit. When they reached a quiet, deserted stretch of road, the men in the back quickly pushed Heather out into the gutter and pulled the doors shut without a second glance. No one saw them arrive or heard the squeal of the tyres as the van sped away.

Chapter 2

Heather opened her eyes, moaned softly, and snapped them shut; brilliant light from the large picture window in the single room assaulted her. She sucked in a gasp of warm air, held it for a couple of seconds in lungs that hurt, and then exhaled a piercing scream. Within moments the blue door, weighted by an unpolished metal strip across its centre, burst open. Soft hands caught and held on firmly to her flailing left arm preventing her from jerking the cannula from her bruised hand. Heather's eyes remained tightly shut, and her body stiff as she continued to cry out with each gasp.

Moving with calm efficiency, Julie gave Heather an injection to return her to oblivion as rapidly as possible. The shrieks stuttered into mewling noises relatively quickly. The nurse's brown eyes- almost obscured by long, thick lashes- gazed with compassion on Heather's battered face. She stroked her patient's soft hand gently with her own until the sobs subsided.

Heather's eyes briefly flicked open and then closed as she relaxed and sank back into the mattress: she drifted into a comfortable sleep. In the ICU, after her operation, sedation had been substantial. Later she was transferred to the side room and was now under the lightest sedation. Julie straightened her back and shook her head, causing the tendrils of ash blond hair, which she wore in a neat bun at the start of every shift to loosen from their anchoring pins. She sighed and blew the escaping curls back from her attractive face. She'd been a Sister at Solihull hospital for two years, but she'd never felt as sorry for anyone as she did for the young girl who lay in the side ward.

Julie had been on an extra shift on the night that Heather Barn's ravaged and tortured body silently screamed that she had been the victim of a vicious attack. She now unwillingly re-lived the night that Heather was brought into the accident and emergency department. As the ambulance man had wheeled the stretcher into the hospital, Julie had taken one look and called out to her colleague.

'Nurse Eden, page Mr Sperry and arrange for the emergency X-ray department to be on standby.'

It was clear that the young girl's face and body had been savagely beaten, and her long, blond hair - matted with seeping blood- was missing clumps torn out at the roots. The casualty had been so physically traumatized that it had been impossible to hazard a guess at her healthy appearance: she was hurriedly admitted and taken to theatre.

The police had arrived shortly afterwards but, as Heather was unconscious, they left almost immediately.

Julie had logged a report from the crew that had brought her into the hospital. Heather was lying near a grass verge that bordered an ordinarily quiet stretch of road on the outskirts of Birmingham. The officers in the Lima Zulu 1 rapid response car thought that she had been knocked down by a vehicle; there had been accidents involving pedestrians before on that stretch of road. There was no pavement, and the grass verge was very uneven; risking a broken ankle seemed to be the lesser of two evils for many locals who chose to walk in the road.

Heather had been found by a couple who were taking their Labrador puppy for a last walk before turning in. They'd been laughing and sharing some light-hearted intimacy when they caught sight of the almost unrecognizable figure that was Heather. At the time, the woman had done all that she could to make the broken and bleeding stranger comfortable. The man had run as though night trolls were after him to the nearest house, where he proceeded to knock up the occupants.

'Phone 999! There's been an accident!' he said.

Then he ran back to where his wife cradled the victim's head in her lap. It was taking all her strength to prevent the puppy from exploring Heather's injuries. It wasn't until after the ambulance had driven off that they'd both overawed by the horror of their ordeal.

The on-call CID duty officer drove to the scene and thoroughly searched the surrounding area for discarded clothing or evidence of blood on the road. He concluded that Heather had been assaulted elsewhere and dumped there.

Although Heather had nothing to identify her, it was only hours before her parents, who were frantic when she didn't arrive home as expected, contacted the hospital. They soon recognized the mystery patient as their daughter.

Julie checked that Heather's vital signs were stable, and the saline drip that hung from a two-bag stand was functioning as it should be and then hurried away to attend to other duties. The heavy door closed quietly behind her on its pneumatic hinge.

Her thoughts lingered with Heather for some time as she went about her routine tasks. She couldn't believe that her patient would be able to return to normal even when the gruesome injuries, which her body had sustained, had healed.

Every so often, she gave a quiet sigh and slowly shook her head.

'Cup of tea, Julie?' one of her colleagues asked as she passed the nurse's station.

'I could murder one,' Julie replied. She pretended to pant like a dog. They grinned affectionately at each other; they'd been friends -both on and off duty- since their student days.

After about an hour of writing detailed patient reports, Julie lifted her head and began to rub her cramped hand. She nodded and raised her eyebrows to her colleague, indicating Heather's mother's tall, spare form entering the bathroom that adjoined the patient's day room. They were aware that Yvonne had again been trying to doze, with little success, in an overstuffed armchair in the comfortable but airless day room. One or other of them had glanced in occasionally to offer a drink if she was awake. Yvonne had refused, but Julie knew she was grateful for their concern. The nursing staff had become familiar with Heather's family. Her parents and her older sister Susan had been taking turns to remain at the hospital in the hope that one of them would be able to give some comfort and support when she woke. At times, during the long nights, the family's thoughts, fears, and tears had been shared. However, Julie saw no reason to let Yvonne know that, for a few minutes, Heather had been conscious and probably reliving the evil that had befallen her. Not that anyone knew what had happened to her.

Sufficient unto the day, Julie thought and tried to shut all unpleasantness from her mind as she bent her head to concentrate on report writing again. Mr Sperry, the surgeon who had spent several hours and all his considerable skill operating on Heather, wished to be informed of any periods of lucidity that occurred.

Unbidden, an image of Mr Ben Sperry's small, dapper figure came into Julie's head. Increasingly of late, she had found herself picturing his craggy face and the way his wispy, grey hair bobbed about cheerfully as he walked. She wondered if she was becoming a little too eager to see him appear in her ward. He'd been a senior consultant for several years at Solihull General and was known as an excellent surgeon and a kind and thoughtful person by patients and colleagues alike. He was single, and Julie had spent a little time wondering why he hadn't married. Oh, Lord help me if I'm falling for him, she thought. Her eyes twinkled at her flight of fancy. More like I need a man after midnight – she started to grin and quietly hum the famous tune.

She'd seen a lot of Mr Sperry recently as he'd made more visits than was usual to check on Heather. When she'd accompanied him on his rounds, he had said to his team that it would probably take more than a lifetime to repair her mental trauma. He'd spoken to Heather's parents and, with their consent, made tentative arrangements for a consultant psychiatrist, with whom he was friendly, to see her when she was able to talk to him.

Chapter 3

Dabbing at her eyes with a soft, cotton wool pad soaked in Witch Hazel, Yvonne made a vain attempt to repair some of the damage showing in her face. She felt old, helpless, and, at this moment in her life, ugly. The sleepless nights and horrific days were conspiring to turn her into a zombie. She peered with little interest in the small mirror above the wash hand basin and noted the streaks of grey in her chestnut hair and the tiny, newly formed lines around her mouth. Shrugging her shoulders, she turned away from the unwelcome image and returned to sit in the winged chair by her daughter's bedside.

She gazed intently at Heather's face trying to judge if there was any change in the lack of expression that she was becoming used to seeing: there was none. Heather looked blank; her once pretty, expressive features remained impassive. Yvonne felt the familiar sickening lurch in her stomach as she again registered the extensive bruising and cuts that marred her daughter's face, hands, and arms. She fleetingly speculated on the force used to inflict the injuries. Her hand flew to her mouth to prevent the bile, which had risen into her throat, from spilling out while her mind refused to shut out the picture of Heather's unseen trauma. God! Where were you? How could you let this happen to someone who had never harmed anyone in her short life? She ranted inwardly. She relived for the umpteenth time the meeting with Mr Sperry after he'd carried out an emergency operation on Heather.

It was evident that he was exhausted, but he had patiently taken time to assure them that Heather had responded well to the operation to remove a length of copper pipe from her anus and repair the internal damage.

'There will be some rectal scarring, but the team have repaired the deep cuts that she sustained. I am so sorry for all she has suffered, but she will recover.'

Yvonne and Susan began to cry as they listened to the extent of Heather's injuries. Mr Sperry gave them time to recover before saying that he thought it might have been a longer piece of pipe that caused Heather's broken ribs and inflicted bruising and lacerations to her face, scalp, and soft tissue. They discussed his decision to keep her sedated to allow some of the invasive injuries to begin to heal while she was in the ICU. He didn't share with them his fear that, if allowed to become conscious immediately, Heather might not be able to cope with the mental trauma or the pain.

Deliberately dragging her thoughts away from the horror her daughter had suffered, Yvonne sighed and settled back in the chair. Her nagging thoughts would allow no respite, so after a few minutes, she wandered off to the staff kitchen to make some tea. All the staff had been very kind. She poured milk from a bottle in the fridge into a chipped mug. A sad-eyed cartoon cat decoration reminded her of one that Heather had been attached to when she was a child. The staff allowed her to use all their facilities, including their supplies, and they refused all offers of payment. How is it, she found herself thinking in an almost detached way, that some people can be so caring and others so darkly evil?

She shrugged the stiffness from her shoulders and strolled back to her daughter's room. She smiled and said, 'Good morning,' as she passed the plump nurse sitting at a desk in the corridor. The nurse returned her greeting, but Yvonne didn't linger; she knew their hand over period left no time for unnecessary talk. She wondered how she could repay them for all their kindness.

Heather opened her eyes and checked the room. She knew that she was in hospital after an operation – she'd heard one of the nurses talking to her mother. She barely moved her head, but she could see Yvonne sitting in the chair by her bed, reading a paperback with her glasses at half-mast on her aquiline nose. The sight was so familiar that Heather felt an overwhelming love for her mother. She had always put her family first and had devoted her life to caring for them. Yvonne would be horrified at the plans that her daughter was making. She shut her eyes and feigned sleep. She didn't want to talk to anyone until she'd formulated the story that she wished everyone to believe.

Heather knew what had befallen her. The rapes and the assaults that she'd suffered – including every detail of the men's faces. She had no intention of allowing the police to trace her assailants and for them to receive a prison sentence of a few years. Heather wanted them dead: prison would be too easy an option for what they did to her. I don't know how, but I will kill them, she thought, repeating it over and over, as she had during the time she'd been held captive and abused. Everyone would think that the trauma had unhinged her mind, but she was sane. The only thing that had kept her mind whole was the certainty that she would kill all three of them. Although she knew that the tattooed man's name was Javid, she couldn't even think of him as anything other than Snake man. To her, he wasn't a human being. As for the other inhuman bastards, she could only identify them in her mind as the Ugly one and the Driver.

The scrape of chair legs on the blue speckled, composite flooring as her mother stood to greet her sister brought Heather from her reverie. She wanted to feel their comforting hands and hear their soothing voices. Tears forced themselves from under her lids as she opened her eyes.

'Mom,' she said. Her voice sounded faint and scratchy to her ears.

Yvonne moved quickly to her side and gathered her daughter gently into her arms. Heather flinched at the physical contact but then sank willingly into their shelter. They were the natural sanctuary that she so desperately needed. They held onto each other for many minutes until Susan took over and began to cry as she gingerly held her sister to her.

Heather lay back into her pillows – exhausted. She was grateful that they didn't ask her any questions, and she didn't volunteer any conversation other than to ask how her father was. Then, for a time, Yvonne and Susan sat either side of her bed, stroking her hands until she drifted off into a natural sleep.

The next time Heather woke, it could have been a day or a week that had passed. The light from the large picture window informed her that it was evening. She felt both hungry and thirsty and more than a little uncomfortable down below. All was eerily quiet as she searched around until she located the nurse call button and pressed it.

'Hello there, love – you awake? What can I do for you? To be sure, you should be asleep; it's the middle of the night,' the nurse said.

'It's still light outside – what time is it?'

'There's a full moon which makes it seem earlier than it is – it's two in the morning.'

'Oh, dear, I'm thirsty, and I'm hungry.' Heather gave a small smile, and the nurse chuckled.

'Good. You must be feeling better.'

While she was talking, the nurse was using the automatic adjuster to raise her patient. Heather cried out and asked for it to be lowered a little as the pressure on her backside became too painful.

'Are you in much pain, love? We've oral pain medication prescribed for you now. Shall I fetch you some?'

'Erm – yes, please. I'm very sore, and I'm thirsty,' Heather said.

'Okay,' the nurse bustled away while saying over her shoulder: 'back in a mo.'

After some pain medication, Heather managed to eat half a slice of buttered toast; it was soggy but tasted fantastic. The nurse helped her to have a drink of water before Heather shut her eyes and drifted off, only to be woken at five a.m. to have her catheter removed.

Free of tubes and a cannula, she was allowed out of bed and taken to the bathroom by an auxiliary nurse called June, who helped her to shower. June allowed her to stay for some time under the soothing hot water but eventually said, 'Okay, enough! I'd let you stay there all day, but I've other patients to see to.'

Heather smiled, but her good humour disappeared when she tried to use the commode. It hurt so badly that she started to cry.

'Why am I so sore?' she asked.

June patted her hand and smiled. 'Mr Sperry will explain everything later this morning when he does his rounds.'

A little later, when Heather was back in a freshly made bed, she tentatively ran her hands over her face and asked if she might borrow a mirror.

'Well, I don't think that we keep one on the ward, but I'll have a look for you, my love. Now be a good girl and try to rest until breakfast.' The nurse hurried away.

Heather had a strong feeling that she wouldn't bring her a mirror. She ran her hands over her face again, feeling the rough ridges of her healing cuts. It wouldn't upset me to see my face, Heather thought. I can imagine how I must look. I know what the bastards did to me. But she had no memory of the last act of wickedness that had caused her to lose consciousness.

The mirror never arrived. Heather lay still in her bed listening as the buzz of the early morning hospital routine went on around her. She enjoyed the clanking of the breakfast trolley and the crash of plates and dishes as hungry patients were satisfied. She knew from her own nursing experience that many people who were quite ill seemed cheered by their early morning cup of tea and looked forward to their breakfast. Although Heather had trained at a different hospital, it came as no surprise that the protocol was so similar.

As the morning routine went into a lull before doctor's rounds, Heather occupied her hands, picking at a loose thread in the blue cotton blanket that covered her legs. She knew the police would want to question her and wondered what would happen next. She had decided that she'd tell them there had been two men as far as she could remember.

Heather wasn't sure if there had been samples taken for a forensic department to work on but, if there had and they pointed to three different rapists, she would say that she'd been too traumatized to recall who was there. She hoped that none of the three had a criminal record as she thought it would make it too easy to identify them. The police were misinformed about the van to make it untraceable. The thought that it would be so much easier to give all the information that she had to the police was very tempting, but Heather only considered it for a second. Determined that they must die, not only die but suffer as they had made her suffer. She felt a wave of nausea overcome her as she opened her mind to the memories that would haunt her until the three of them no longer trod the same soil that she did. Her call for a nurse came too late – she vomited over the comforting blanket.

Heather was surprised by the strength of her determination to kill the rapists with her own hands. She wouldn't even kill a spider- and she loathed them. She'd become a midwife to help people, not take lives. But this was different, and they deserved to die. She tried to envisage how she would carry out her intention, but the clamour of the hospital intruded. I can wait, she thought – one step at a time.

Chapter 4

Yvonne tucked clean clothing into the locker and then seated herself on the bedside chair. 'It's beginning to know my contours,' she laughed. 'I'll help you to have another shower and get changed after you've seen the doctor, love.'

Heather smiled weakly. 'Thanks, Mom, he should be here soon. I heard the doctor talking in the corridor. Do you think he'll say I can come home?'

'I've no idea but don't get your hopes up, love. You've been very poorly, and he'll want to make sure that you're really on the mend.'

Heather pulled a rueful face and winced as the stitches in her cheek tugged at her healing skin. 'I just want to be at home, Mom.'

'I know you do, and it won't hurt to ask him when you can leave. Don't be in too much of a hurry, though, my darling.'

As Yvonne finished speaking, Mr Sperry and his entourage purposefully entered the room and stood at the bottom of Heather's bed.

'Now then, young lady, I'm glad to see you're awake. How are you feeling?' Mr Sperry asked. To his surprise, Heather answered in a controlled manner. He thought she sounded like someone in a business meeting.

‘I’m okay, thank you. I’m just very uncomfortable and grateful for the painkillers. I know you operated on me, so can you tell me what that involved?’

Mr Sperry’s face became serious. ‘You had several broken ribs, many wounds, and lacerations to your face and body and a hairline fracture to one of the bones in your left arm. All of which we treated, and they’re healing nicely.’ He paused and cleared his throat noisily. ‘And we had to remove a piece of copper pipe from your rectum and repair the damage it had caused. There will be some scarring, but I think it will all heal.’ Heather's solemn expression didn’t alter, and he hurried on, ‘I’m sure you will make a complete recovery.’ He paused again, obviously expecting a reaction from her, but she remained silent. He cleared his throat again. ‘The police will be coming in to see you later on today. I don’t have much to tell them, but I hope you can give them some information. But don’t worry about that now,’ he smiled.

Heather turned to face her mother, and her eyes filled with tears. Mr Sperry coughed and spoke briskly. ‘Now, if you’ll lean forward, I’ll just listen to your chest.’ Heather gingerly held aside her pyjama top as he used his stethoscope on her upper body. ‘Take a deep breath for me, please.’ Heather obeyed, and Mr Sperry said, ‘I believe you’re newly qualified as a midwife. Have you found employment yet? You could do worse than apply here. It’s a good hospital.’

He succeeded in distracting her as she answered him steadily. ‘I should have already worked my first shift at Good Hope, but they understand, and they’re going to hold the position open for me. I think here would have been good too. I’ve been impressed with what I’ve seen so far.’

‘Take a deep breath and hold it – again – again, okay.’ He straightened up and tucked the stethoscope back into the pocket of his white coat. Heather smiled weakly at him and pulled the front of her pyjamas together.

'Well, nothing wrong there. I think you're well on the road to recovery.' He perched on the side of her bed. 'You're a very courageous person, Heather, but you have been through a terrible ordeal, and we all need someone to talk to at times. I've arranged for a consultant psychiatrist, who will see you when, and if, you are ready to talk to him.'

Heather flushed and shook her head. 'Thank you, but I don't need to see anyone. I'm fine.'

He stood and began to walk away. Yvonne placed her arm protectively around her daughter. 'I think it's probably too soon for Heather to share what happened to her, but thank you, and we'll be in touch if she wants to talk in the future.' Heather sighed and lay back on her pillows, feeling wary at the thought of having to talk about the rape. Everyone was very kind to her, but she'd no intention of telling the truth.

'I'll see you again tomorrow, and maybe we can think of discharging you quite soon. Keep your chin up, brave girl.' He smiled as he left Heather's bedside with his silent gaggle of geese following close behind.

Later that day, two policewomen arrived and introduced themselves as Detective Sergeant Janet Leech and Detective Sergeant Margaret Brogan. They asked Heather to call them by their first names.

After gaining permission to ask her a few questions, Janet said, 'What can you remember about that night, Heather?'

Heather took a deep breath and held onto Yvonne's hand as she said, 'I really can't tell you very much. All I remember is a black van and two men and being in a lonely spot where I could hear water. I remember trees, and I felt cold as I fell from the van onto soft grass.' Heather trembled as she spoke to the blond-haired policewoman who was gazing intently at her. She thought that both the policewomen looked kind and they wanted to help her, but she shook her head vehemently. 'I don't want to think about it anymore,' she said and began to cry.

Yvonne comforted her daughter, and after a few minutes, Janet said, 'I'm so sorry. I completely understand. It must be very upsetting to talk about what you've been through, but any little detail that you remember might assist us. I'm afraid forensics isn't going to be able to help in this case,' Heather sighed deeply, 'do you remember how they got you into the van?'

'I just remember listening to Bon Jovi on my earphones; I didn't hear anything until they threw me into the back of the van. I know the floor was cold, and I ended up against a wheel arch. I've no idea where they took me to. I don't even know in what direction.' Heather wrapped her arms defensively around her slender body and began to cry silent tears that dribbled into the corners of her mouth. Janet stretched out a comforting hand towards her but quickly withdrew it as Heather flinched and moved her arm.

'I'm sorry to have to ask you, but can you give me a description of the two men?' DS Brogan asked. Her pen was poised, ready to write in her notebook.

Heather's fingers made ruches in the hem of the blanket that covered her legs. 'Erm, w-well, I didn't see them very clearly. It was dark. They were both white and had Birmingham accents, I think, and they both had dark hair.' She felt ashamed; prevarication wasn't usually part of her makeup. She was generally quite forthright, but she knew she couldn't safely tell them anything more.

‘Do you know what happened to your Discman? Was it left in the van? Or in the spot where you were.?’ DS Brogan asked.

Heather shook her head. ‘I don’t know, sorry, I can’t help more.’ She sniffed and looked to her Mom for support: Yvonne took Heather’s hand in hers and stroked it gently.

After a few more questions that Heather wouldn’t, or couldn’t, answer truthfully, DS Leech pushed her hair back from her forehead and started to replace her notebook.

‘I have to tell you, Heather, that we’ll do our best to find these scumbags, but we’ve very little to go on, I’m afraid. Would it be alright if we brought some photographs in to show you and see if you recognise anyone?’ Heather nodded, and the two policewomen stood up. ‘If you think of anything else,’ DS Brogan handed her a printed card, ‘please get in touch with me.’

Heather was relieved that their visit was over, but she wasn’t sure if they believed her story.

As they left the hospital, Janet said to her colleague, ‘Poor sod, she seems self-possessed considering the trauma she’s been through, and with what we’ve got to go on, we haven’t a cat in hell’s chance of finding the bastards.’

‘Ah, well! It’s amazing how some women cope. Hopefully, she’ll get over it given time. I wonder why they didn’t kill her,’ Margaret said, looking thoughtful. ‘The evil gits have done this once, so I can’t see them stopping there, can you? Maybe next time we’ll have more information to go on.’

‘I hope there won’t be a next time – fucking monsters. Come on, let’s get back to the station and start trawling through the files to see if we can find anything similar happening recently.’

‘I’m wondering about the copper pipe,’ Janet said. ‘Why would it have been there in the first place? We need to check to see if any plumbing companies use a black van that's been stolen recently or used with or without permission.'

'I'll get straight on it,' Margaret said as they got into their car, 'I'll not hold my breath though; most plumbers use white vans that have logos on the sides. Heather said that there weren't any as far as she knew.'

It was a week later Heather was discharged from the hospital amidst fond farewells. Many of the staff had grown to admire her resilience and sense of humour. Nevertheless, while she seemed to be in good spirits, she persisted in her refusal to talk to a psychiatrist or share what had taken place. When at home, she was unusually quiet, but that was all the difference that her family could detect in her demeanour. She behaved as though nothing dreadful had happened to her. At breakfast the following week after her sister and father had left for work, Heather took a bite of buttered crumpet and chewed slowly.

'I know you think I should stay at home, Mom, but I need to get on with my life. When the stitches have disappeared, I'm going to start work. I know I'd frighten the patients now,' she laughed, 'and I don't suppose my ribs would thank me either.'

Yvonne frowned at her, took a sip of her Earl Grey tea, and then said, 'You know, my love, I'm anxious about you. We all are.' Heather shook her head as her Mom took a breath. 'I don't believe anyone could go through the trauma you've been through and come out of it still whole.' She held up her hand as Heather started to speak. 'I know you're strong, you always have been, as a little girl, you didn't cry even when you skinned your knees. There was one time … but I'm getting off the point. What I want to say is, are you sure you don't need to talk to anyone about what happened? You haven't even told me, or your sister, what they did to you in those terrible hours.

I know I'd be a wreck.' She walked around the counter and perched herself on a tall bar stool opposite her daughter. 'I don't know how I could have given birth to such a resilient child, and I'm proud of you but so frightened for you.'

Heather took her Mom's cold hand gently in her warm one. She could smell her mother's favourite Lily of the Valley perfume as she stroked her wrist with her thumb.

'Well, don't be. I'm okay, really, and I don't want or need to talk about it. It's over, and I'm alive, thank God. I just want to get my life back on track.' She smiled at her mother's disbelieving look, then said, 'So at the risk of being rude, will you just shut up about it? I'm not a child anymore – I do know how I feel and what I want – okay?'

'Okay, love, but will you please tell me if you change your mind?' Yvonne got up and took her cup to the sink so that Heather wouldn't have to see the tears in her eyes.

'Of course, I will, you must know that I'm grateful for all your care. I love you and Dad and Susan so much.' She walked around the counter and hugged her mother fiercely.

Yvonne laughed. 'Okay, okay, I'll shut up now, and please mind your ribs. You're breaking mine.' She laughed again and extricated herself from Heather's embrace.

Chapter 5

When Heather's injuries had wholly healed, she began work at the hospital and, after a few weeks, persuaded Susan to go shopping for sensible shoes. Having completed their purchases, they headed back towards the Bull Ring car park. As they passed a stall selling copper bracelets purported to ward off arthritis – Heather bought three and slipped them onto her wrist.

Susan frowned. 'Why do you want those? Haven't got arthritis, have you?'

Heather shrugged aside the question, gave a broad smile, and then asked one of her own. 'What do you think, Sis? Will you come with me?' Heather lifted her arms as though she was lifting weights, causing the plain, shiny bracelets to reflect the lights of the arcade. 'Please, pretty please, I'd like you to come too.' It was the second time that Heather had asked her – the first time Susan hadn't taken her seriously.

Susan put her head to one side and pretended to be considering her sister's request, but she already knew she'd do almost anything Heather asked of her. 'Okay, I'll come with you, but if we start, then you're not allowed to leave me on my own if I enjoy it, and you don't.' Susan grinned happily and tucked her arm through Heather's.

It was now the end of August, and Susan remained very worried that Heather might suddenly start to show signs of post-traumatic stress disorder. She was behaving as though the rape had never taken place. She slept well and continued to show no sign of needing to share, even though as sisters go – they'd always been close. Susan hadn't pressed her for confidences – preferring not knowing the details. Heather had quickly settled into the job that she loved, but she hadn't wanted to go out alone or do anything else once she finished her shift on the ward. Now to hear her seriously suggest that they join a local gym allayed some of Susan's fears for her sister's well-being.

Susan wanted to shed a few pounds herself. She was a self-employed photographer, and taking wedding photos needed stamina, plus she wanted to do everything she could to help Heather. Going to the local gym with her wasn't much, but it was all that she would allow her to do.

The next week during their free introductory session, when the fitness trainer was showing them around, Heather made an excuse and fled to the Ladies. She returned after ten minutes, apologised briefly, then said she wasn't feeling too well and needed to go home.

When they were outside, Heather hurried Susan to her blue Mini Cooper through the pouring rain and then climbed in and fastened her seat belt. She did not attempt to start the engine, just sat staring through the windscreen, and then leaned her head onto the steering wheel.

'What the bloody hell's the matter with you? I felt foolish leaving like that,' Susan said. She reached across and felt her sister's forehead, it was neither hot nor cold, but Heather didn't move or speak.

'What's the matter, Heather? Tell me. You're scaring the shit out of me. Are you feeling ill?'

Heather raised her head and gazed in anguish at Susan's worry-contorted face: 'I'm pregnant.'

Susan flinched. 'No. You can't be. How would you know?'

'I am,' Heather repeated slowly, 'I know I am. I found out that I'd been spotting when I went to the toilet. I've not had a period since April. I just thought it was stress related– but I know the signs. It wasn't just the spots of blood – I threw up a load of bile while I was in there too. I know I can't be sure, but I am. Neither my uterus nor vagina was damaged, even though the odds are against it ...' she gazed out through the window at the leaden sky. 'I had a lot of tests taken for various things while I was in the hospital, and none of them showed as positive, thank God.' She shuddered as she thought of all the infections that she might have contracted. 'I was supposed to have another set of tests six weeks later, including a further pregnancy test, but, like a fool, I didn't think it was necessary.' She gulped in a sob and started to hiccup. 'I'm so stupid.'

Susan stroked her sister's arm. 'Enough. You're not stupid, but you may be mistaken, so we're going to the pharmacy right now to buy a test kit – okay?'

Heather nodded, blew her nose noisily, and then started the car.

It was a couple of hours later when the sisters sat on Heather's bed and stared in stunned silence as a distinct blue band appeared on the test strip. 'Oh, my God! You are pregnant,' Susan said. A few heavy minutes passed before she asked slowly, 'What are we going to do now?'

Heather considered her sister's face with a wry smile. 'We aren't going to do anything: I'm going to become a mother.'

Susan gasped. 'You could –'

'I know what you're going to say- but it won't happen. I don't believe in abortion other than for serious medical conditions.' She stroked her abdomen. 'It isn't the baby's fault no matter what, and I couldn't kill it,' her face contorted into a look of intense hatred, 'but I could kill its father.'

Susan burst into tears and moved into her sister's embrace. Heather held her sibling close and rocked with the force of her sobs, but her face remained emotionless, and her eyes were dry. She felt more determined than ever that all three of the rapists should die. Her baby would be hers alone. She silently vowed that it would be loved and treasured as much as Susan and she had been. It would never know about its father.

Gently disengaging the hug, then mopping at Susan's eyes with a tissue from her sleeve, Heather said firmly, 'Come on, no more upset. I want this baby loved by you and all my family, so let's go and tell Mom and Dad, eh?'

Susan was wide-eyed, and she shook her head back and forth. She couldn't even begin to understand how her sister could have the strength to behave as she was. There was no doubt about support whatever Heather decided to do. She held her hand tightly as they entered the sitting room, and Heather told her astonished parents her news.

'What I don't understand is how you think you will be able to love this baby without thinking about its conception. If you keep it, the father and all the details, which I can only imagine, will stay with you for the remainder of your life. There will be no getting away from that memory.' Yvonne slumped back on the settee, and reaching for her husband's hand, gave it a desperate squeeze.

Bob returned the pressure. 'Have you thought it through, Heather? Your Mom's right. The baby will be a permanent reminder of all that you've suffered.' He ran his fingers distractedly through his silvery, grey hair. 'You are a very determined and capable woman, but your life will become infinitely more difficult, even with our help. Have you truly considered all the changes and sacrifices you will have to make?'

Heather thought how kind her parents were as she said, 'I know you and Mom are only concerned for my welfare, but I do know my mind. I will love my baby, no matter what.' She spoke with passion as she knelt on the carpet in front of them like a supplicant. 'This will be your grandchild – will you be able to love it – or am I going to have to leave home and find a place of my own?' Her voice trailed away to a whisper at the thought of going it alone.

Bob released his wife's hand and then drew Heather to him as Susan gave a loud sigh. 'Don't worry, Susan, or you, my love. You can stay here as long as you wish. It's tough for your mother and me to believe that your decision to have this baby is the best one for you. But, of course, you are right. It will be our grandchild, and we will love it. I've said it before, and now I'm repeating it. You, my darling, are a very courageous person, and no matter what happens, we are your parents. We love you very much and will help you in any way that we can.' He made a space between Yvonne and himself and patted the cushion.

Heather smiled and became all child again as she said, 'Thanks, Daddy,' and then snuggled herself in the middle of her parents, linking their arms as she had done on many occasions. A heavy weight lifted from her shoulders, but she still had every intention of committing murder as soon as she was able. Her thoughts were a jumble of contradictions, but one idea was like a length of steel running alongside every other consideration. I can wait, but they will die for what they did to me. Constantly repeated, it strengthened her resolve that whatever difficulties she encountered, she would carry out her intention to kill all three rapists.

Susan joined in the group hug then asked, ‘Would anyone like a cup of tea?’ Her transparent attempt to break the tension in the room made everyone, including Heather, laugh. It was a welcome relief, and Heather went to help her sister in the kitchen, leaving their parents discussing practical ways in which they could help.

‘Perhaps it will be a blessing in disguise to have a new baby in the house. We will love it, won’t we, Bob?’ Yvonne looked doubtful as she sought reassurance from her stalwart husband. He had been her rock since their marriage, and he didn’t fail her now.

‘We need to forget about its father and concentrate on the fact that it will be Heather’s baby and our grandchild. Of course, we’ll love it. How could we do otherwise?’ He smiled affectionately at her. ‘We’ve two incredible children, and we’ll have an incredible grandchild, you’ll see.’ He kissed her passionately on the lips; his love for her still as strong as when he married her.

Chapter 6

Heather had never considered changing her hairstyle or hair colour before. She'd always thought she was lucky to be blond like her sister – it suited them both with their fair skin tones – but she needed to change her appearance. Both her mother and sister raised many objections, but Heather made an appointment at the local hairdressing salon. She returned home with auburn hair cut in a short, almost boyish style and admired her image in the backlit, gold-framed mirror in her bathroom. Her reflection was considerably different, but her plan to become ultra-fit and robust would have to wait until after the baby's birth. She wasn't about to do anything to endanger its life.

When Susan saw her, she chuckled with pleasure. 'I'm amazed. It suits you; I didn't want you to do it, but it's great. Perhaps I'll have mine cut short too because it often gets in the way if I forget to tie it back when I'm working.'

'No! Don't have it cut! It's beautiful. I felt that I just had to change mine, but you don't. So don't do it,' Heather said.

'Okay. Just a thought. But it does suit you, and so does your bump,' Susan patted her sister's abdomen where the tiniest swelling had started to show that she was pregnant. 'Has it started to move yet?'

'I think I felt a flutter the other day, but it could have been the wind. I'll let you know when it does. Exciting isn't it,' Heather said. She was delighted that her sister was showing an interest. Her one real fear was that her parents and sibling wouldn't be able to get past the circumstances of her baby's conception. She wondered how she could feel pleasure at the fact that she was going to become a mother while planning to destroy the baby's father. Am I insane? She wondered, but she was convinced that she was justified in carrying out her plans for vengeance. She marvelled at her ability to play the part of someone who was able to cope with such trauma on her own without going crazy, but that was the impression she knew she was giving her family. She was either able to blame her mood swings on her hormones or ensure that she coped with her feelings of desperation in private. She thought that she was succeeding in allaying their fears as it wasn't too long before Susan and her parents stopped treating her as though she would suddenly shatter into pieces and become a gibbering wreck. They gradually got on with their lives. Yvonne returned to her charity work. Susan started retaking photographic bookings. Her father, who had continued to attend his office throughout the whole nightmare, began to treat everyone, including herself, in his usual kind and humorous way.

'Well, someone has to keep the flag flying,' he often said in a humorous voice. It raised his family's spirits, and Heather loved him for it. As youngsters, both she and Susan would throw cushions at him to shut him up, but now Heather was pleased when he teased them.

She was grateful as the weeks passed that her colleagues stopped commenting on her changed appearance and began to talk about her pregnancy positively. She'd decided to work until she was thirty-six weeks if possible, but she knew that her family would like her to take maternity leave much earlier. She had to work hard to convince them that she wasn't ill, when in fact, she'd never felt so fit and well.

As she entered her second trimester, Heather often thought about going to see if Snake man still worked at the greengrocers where she'd first seen him. She felt sickened at the thought of seeing any of the rapists again, but she had to find him. He was the father of her child, but he was traceable. She wished she could talk to her sister about her intentions, but Susan would think that her fears had become a reality, and Heather had become insane.

Her parents continued to try to persuade her to seek professional help, but Heather reiterated her refusal. She was afraid that she would somehow tell the truth. The last time that her father had tried, Heather put her hand across his mouth and shook her head.

'I know it's because you are worried about me,' she said, 'but I wouldn't go to court and testify against the bastards. I couldn't bear to face them and have to relive what they did to me.' She shook her head. 'I mean it, Dad! I just want the whole thing to drop. I hate what the baby's father did to me, but I can't bear the thought of being asked to identify him or having to give evidence in court. I don't want my baby ever to know its conception. Can you imagine the horror of it? What do you think the damage could be to a young person to know the truth? No, Dad, it can't happen. I won't let it. Do you hear me?' Heather's voice broke on a sob, and she sank into a chair. She meant every word about her baby, but she was even more terrified that she would be unable to avenge herself.

'Alright, my love. Please don't upset yourself. So far, we've been able to keep any details of that night from the press, and I'm sure we can carry on doing that,' he said. He stroked her hair. 'I'll make an appointment to see DS. Leech tomorrow, and hopefully, we can make it all go away.'

'Thanks, Dad,' Heather said, between sobs, 'I know I should try to make sure they can't hurt anyone else, but I just can't. I have to think about my baby.'

Bob took his daughter in his arms and tried to reassure her that all would be well, but in his heart, he wondered if Heather would ever be able to come to terms with what she had suffered. He knew that she would be able to love her child initially but wondered if she was strong enough not to see the rapist's reflection in her offspring's eyes every time she looked at the child. The thought that his daughter would carry the aftermath of being raped for the remainder of her life appalled him.

Heather found it very interesting but also weird being on the receiving end of prenatal care. Either Susan or her mother usually accompanied her to each appointment, but she began to wish that she had more time to be on her own. She needed to locate Snake man and thought that the longer she left it, the less chance she had of finding him.

Taking advantage of every opportunity, she haunted the Stratford Road shopping area where she'd first seen him. She dressed in frumpy clothes and glasses, and with her new hairstyle, she hoped that Snake man wouldn't be able to recognize her. She knew she couldn't spend too much time in the greengrocers where he probably worked, so after buying fruit a couple of times and not seeing him there, she visited other nearby shops. Occasionally, to get out of the cold, Heather went into a cafe situated opposite the greengrocers and enjoyed drinking sweet, fragrant cups of coffee.

Sitting by the window, she had a good view of passers-by, but it wasn't until the third expedition that she saw him. Her heart gave a sickening leap in her chest, and fear made her shrink into herself as her eyes alighted on his hated face. She grabbed her woven bag, shoved her glasses onto her face, and hurried out of the shop, leaving her coffee to go cold. Careful to keep a distance between them, she followed him as he crossed the road, then turned the corner into Fent Road. It was the road where she'd parked her car. She stood confused, not knowing whether he would turn off into another road or whether she could get into her car and still see where he was going. Just as she decided to continue on foot, he turned into the entry to one of the houses halfway along the terrace. She quickly got into her car and waited. After about half an hour had passed with no sign of his return, she noted the number of the house, then drove home desperate to relieve the pressure in her bladder.

As she drove, her emotions were in turmoil. Snakeman looked so innocent as he walked past the cafe. But she knew, as her gut churned and her anger burnt like bubbling acid in her chest, that he wasn't innocent. He was an evil, vicious rapist that had fathered the child that she now felt moving quite frequently in her womb. She wanted to go back and kill him there and then but knew she had to plan carefully and that this would take time.

Before she could begin to plan, she had to ascertain if that was where he lived and find out his full name. She knew that he was called Javid, but that's all she knew. She also realised that she couldn't haunt the street where he probably lived – someone was bound to notice her blue car if it was parked there too frequently. Step by step, she thought as she put on her home face and demeanour. She couldn't allow her mother or her sister to suspect that she was anything other than happy and looking forward to bringing a new life into the world. She was delighted to be having her baby and fully intended to keep it, but she sometimes had a moment of panic. Was she wrong to want to keep it rather than putting it up for adoption and allowing it to have two parents? She always dismissed these thoughts as there was no way that she was going to give her baby away to anyone.

Chapter 7

Heather had kept in touch by phone and the occasional e-mail with Julie Freeman, the nurse who'd been so kind to her while she was recovering in hospital, but she was pleasantly surprised to receive an invitation to her wedding in October. She was even more amazed when she read that Julie was marrying Mr Ben Sperry, the surgeon who had operated on her.

Heather immediately rang Julie and said with a laugh, 'You dark horse! You kept this quiet. How long have you two been dating?'

'It began just after your stay in the hospital, so not very long really. But there's no reason to wait,' Julie said. 'I love him. He's kind, and he makes me laugh, and neither of us is getting any younger.'

Heather chuckled. 'Who is? I'm delighted that something good has come out of my stay. I can't wait until we see you again. Mom and Susan said to tell you that they will both be there.' They ended on an affectionate note and a promise to meet up before the wedding.

All the family routines were upset when Yvonne came down with a lingering chest infection that kept her in bed for a few days. It severely curtailed her strength for another month. It made them realize how much they all relied on her as they struggled to cope with work shifts and home chores. Heather did most of the work, assisted reluctantly and often awkwardly by her father and sometimes by her sister. Susan's business was doing well, and it frequently took her away from home, so Heather didn't get a chance to be with her friends before the wedding.

Bright sunshine ushered in the special day. Julie looked beautiful, as most brides do, and Ben was obviously in love with her – his eyes never left her.

Yvonne whispered to her daughters, 'He reminds me of a little boy opening his presents on Christmas morning.'

If Heather and her family were surprised to receive their invitation, it was nothing to the surprise that Julie and Ben had shown on their faces when they saw that Heather was well along in her pregnancy. After the ceremony, Julie extricated herself from the well-wishers, and before they sat down to the wedding breakfast caught Heather by her hand and hustled her off to the side of the hotel room where the tables shone by candlelight.

Heather didn't know whether to be amused or annoyed at being questioned when Julie said, 'Why didn't you tell me? It's not the sort of thing that you can keep secret, is it?'

Heather laughed. 'Why didn't you tell me sooner about you and Ben, eh? It's not the sort of thing you can keep secret, is it?' They both laughed. 'Look, Julie, it's your wedding day, and you've left your new husband wondering what on earth is going on. When you come back after your honeymoon, we'll get together and have a catch-up, eh? Go on!' she gave Julie a little push on her shoulder, 'go and stop him worrying! You look fantastic, by the way.'

Julie gave her friend a big grin. 'Are you okay, though? I must say you seem to be.'

Heather nodded and grinned back. 'Very much so. Now stop with the questions, and I'll satisfy your curiosity later.'

Julie pulled a wry face and crossed between the tables where some of the guests looked askance at her as she passed to join her husband and family at the top table. She didn't stop to answer the unspoken questions; she merely smiled and hurried to where Ben was making her mother laugh almost hysterically. She felt very curious and concerned about Heather but knew that she would have to wait until the time was right for an explanation.

Heather considered Julie's retreating back with affection, thinking that she could become her closest friend. But she could never know anything about her intentions regarding the men who had attacked her.

Heather was left alone by the police as D.S. Leech said that there was so little to go on that the case was now on the back burner. That suited her, but her parents were not too happy that there were two rapists still free to attack another girl. They also feared that their daughter would suddenly become overwhelmed by her trauma and that she wouldn't be able to cope, even though Heather told them repeatedly that she was okay and looking forward to giving birth. They eventually ceased to ask searching questions and allowed Heather to live her double life. She never gave them any reason to suspect that she intended to ensure her attackers would not be capable of carrying out more rapes.

Heather continued to go to work and felt well enough to complete her shifts until she was advised at twenty-nine weeks that her blood pressure was a little too high and that it was time for her to rest. In a way, she was ready to start her maternity leave, but she wasn't used to having so much time on her hands and soon became bored with television and reading.

Although she was sensible and took it easy, she tried to find out more information about Snake man. She spent many hours shopping on Stratford Road and, as often as she dared, sat in her car outside the house where she'd last seen him. She still wasn't sure if that was where he lived. On a couple of occasions, she'd seen an Asian man and a white woman as they left the house together and then slowly walked toward the main road. After a short time, they returned with bags of shopping. Since she'd seen Snake man initially, there hadn't been another sighting, and Heather began to think that she was perhaps wrong in her assumptions.

On one occasion, she saw the occupants leave the house to go shopping again; she was able to get a closer look at them as they passed her car. The woman was blond and very fair-skinned, probably aged fifty to fifty-five, Heather estimated. She gazed intently at her face and the yellow, highly embroidered top and loose trousers that she wore. The man appeared to be a little older. He had a neatly trimmed white beard and dressed in what she thought of as traditional Indian or Pakistani clothes. As she looked at them, she realized how ignorant of their culture, costumes, and traditions she was. She'd never considered herself to be racist, but she visibly shrugged her shoulders – she didn't want to learn anything about them unless it was specifically to do with Snake man. Her child would not be a part of his culture.

Just before Christmas, Heather had a stroke of luck. She'd been there when the door to the house that she was watching had opened. Snake man, accompanied by the Asian man and the white woman, came out into the street. The woman touched Snake man's hair and said something which made him sneer and then knock her arm sharply away from him.

She looked sad as they walked a little way up the road to where a white van was parked. They all climbed into the front seats, and then Snake man drove away. Heather ducked down – her heart was thudding uncomfortably in her chest as they passed. She didn't think that he would recognize her, but she didn't want to take the chance. Heather had never seen that white van in his road and suspected, with a sick feeling, that it might have been the one where the abuse had taken place. She couldn't be sure, as she had only the briefest recollection of the outside of the van while she was rolling around on the ground and trying to keep her sanity.

Heather knew she was jumping to conclusions, but she felt confident that they must be his parents and that he lived there. It would explain his light skin tone if he was the result of a mixed marriage, she thought. A cold feeling of deep satisfaction washed over her as she realized that when the time was right, she would almost certainly be able to find him. The strength of her hatred for him nagged away at her until she made a determined effort to control her feelings and thoughts. She knew from her training that stress, while she was carrying, wouldn't be good for her baby. She managed to direct her feelings toward decorating the nursery.

Susan was teaching her to paint with acrylics so that she could help create a Disney character mural on one of the walls. Yvonne and Ben had already bought a Moses basket and a pale-yellow cot with matching buffers; she knew that her baby would want for nothing even before it was born. Yvonne told her that they would wait until after the birth to buy a pram as it was bad luck to buy it before. 'Old wives' tales her husband had teased her, but no one denied its validity. Family can be amazing, Heather thought, knowing that she was extremely fortunate in hers.

As she continued to drive home, she became calmer and wondered if she would be able to find out Snake man's family name from the electoral roll. She decided to make a visit to the central library in the new year and look at the records she knew were available.

Chapter 8

Christmas was very close family time. They had their traditional breakfast of boiled eggs and toasted soldiers, and then, after they had exchanged gifts and the ‘oohing and aahing’ was over, they all joined in and prepared the vegetables. Their happy chatter drowned out the Carols playing on the radio.

Yvonne bustled round and set the table with a white cloth, red chargers, and white Limoges china. She always refused offers of help with this chore as it was her great joy to see what she could achieve each year. The smell of roasting turkey filled the house and added to their enjoyment – their home was almost everyone’s idea of a picture-perfect Christmas day. No one was allowed to suspect the thoughts that persisted in Heather’s mind, like maggots infesting a perfect looking apple, they made her day far from perfect.

When the family sat down to eat, the polished wine glasses picked up the glow from the centrepiece made from fir cones, ivy, and white candles. Everyone complimented the arrangement, and then, feeling not a little embarrassed, Yvonne put her hands together and gave thanks for the bounty that they had once again received.

Bob filled Heather’s glass with grape juice and poured sparkling wine generously for the others. He proposed a toast to absent friends as usual and then a welcome to their forthcoming grandchild. Overwhelmed by their love, Heather burst into tears, and the dinner was delayed for a few minutes while they comforted her.

Heather didn't realize that her tears brought back her parents' and Susan's fears that everything would suddenly become too much for her to bear. It took her a little while to explain why she was crying, she barely understood herself, and they all breathed a sigh of relief, deciding that it was hormones. Nevertheless, their fears remained, and her family never ceased to speculate on her state of mind when Heather wasn't around.

For the remainder of the day, they wrapped up in coats, new scarves, and hats to take one of their favourite walks in Brueton Park. Later, they sat companionably watching *It's a Wonderful Life* for the umpteenth time on television. Heather sat next to Susan and surveyed her family. She was surprised at how easily she was able to behave normally while her mind rarely left off scheming and planning for after her baby was born. She loved them all so very much and promised herself that she would keep her intentions secret and never let them know what she planned or tell them what she had done.

Julie and Ben invited Heather and her family to spend Boxing Day evening with them, but Susan and her parents had made other arrangements, and so she plucked up courage and went on her own. She hadn't seen them since their wedding and wasn't sure how she felt about being on her own in their company because she knew that Julie would be asking some searching questions.

During a delightful meal, Julie and Ben talked about their honeymoon in Bermuda, the highlight of which had been their weekly swim with the dolphins at Dolphin Quest. They sang the praises of a beautiful young trainer called Megan, who had looked after them, ensuring that their experience was the best it could be. They then showed Heather some of their photos that had her feeling more than a little envious of their evident love for one another and the pleasure that they took in each other's company. She thought how uncomplicated their relationship seemed to be, and her affection for them grew as the evening wore on.

'Enough about us. What about you, are you okay?' Julie asked Heather as she walked past her chair to hand Bob a balloon-shaped crystal glass that was a quarter full of golden liquid.

'No, not for me, thanks. I'm not drinking alcohol at all at the moment,' Heather replied with a smile.

'I know you aren't, you silly beggar.' Julie laughed. 'I meant, how are you coping now?'

'Oh, I knew what you meant really, but I don't know how to answer. I suppose you're surprised that I'm keeping my baby because you must know how I came to be pregnant. You're the only ones other than my family that know. We've told everyone else that I was going out with a man from Uni, and he ditched me after we'd shared a night. It makes me look a cheap fool, I know, but it's better than the truth. I don't mind you two knowing; you'll keep my secret safe.' She leaned back in her chair, her face glowing; her words had rushed out like a train seeking the light after being confined for miles in a dark tunnel.

'Of course, we will,' Ben spoke slowly, considering his words. 'I'm just surprised that you became pregnant; not many people do under such traumatic circumstances. It was just bad luck that it was the right time for you to conceive. I think you're courageous to go ahead and have the baby. Are you going to have it adopted?'

He shook his head in amazement as Heather stroked her finger across her copper bracelets and said quickly, 'No, I already love my child, and so do my family. It doesn't matter who its father was. It will only know that it has a mother who loves it and will protect it: adoption or abortion never entered my head.'

'Well, I think you're wonderful. I'm not sure I could have coped the way that you're doing – we're both with you all the way,' Julie said. Incipient tears made her eyes shine – she mopped them with a tissue and stood up. 'Let's not mention this again, eh. You'll tell us if we can help in any way, won't you? I can't wait until February; I could do with a baby to cuddle.' They all laughed and relaxed into the easy conversation until it was time for Heather to go home.

As the year drew to a close, Heather began to wish that the next month would go by quickly. Everything was ready for the baby, and she was becoming cumbersome and, at times, very breathless. Many hours passed just sitting, reading and watching her baby as it moved across her belly. She loved the sight and sensation as she tried to identify which parts of the baby's anatomy protruded and then slid back into another position. Talking and singing to the child was the norm. Heather tried hard to keep her thoughts positive and not allow adrenalin to taint her baby in any way. She didn't always succeed, though, as her hate for its father remained strong.

January was bitterly cold, and Heather was becoming scared to venture outdoors on her own. She was frightened that her waters would suddenly break, and she would go into labour in a shop or on the street, so she stayed home, becoming very bored and irritable. Everyone was glad when the contractions did start in earnest at the beginning of February, and Heather went into Good Hope, where she knew she was in good hands.

The birth was normal, other than Yvonne's hand becoming bruised. Heather was overwhelmed with emotion as her daughter lay against her sweat slickened chest. After examining her baby's tiny fingers and toes, she noted how pale her skin was against the mop of black hair, which she wore like a halo. No one would know that she was of a mixed-race she thought, and hoped that she wouldn't have to explain anything to anyone else about her daughter's lineage.

Heather hugged Lucy when she visited the next day and said, 'Oh, she's so beautiful! And she looks just like you! What are you going to call her?' She never mentioned the baby's father. And the two friends spent an hour discussing names.

Gradually Heather pushed her friends firmly into the background, spending the majority of her time in the company of the people who loved her; she needed time to be on her own to think.

Yvonne was in love with her granddaughter from the moment that she gave her first cry, and Bob followed suit shortly after. Susan became the type of aunt that every niece should have – a second mother in every way possible. The family never once mentioned the circumstances of the baby's conception. They joyfully vied with each other to see whose choice of favourite names Heather would pick.

The baby was three days old when Yvonne picked the child from her crib and said, 'For goodness sake, Heather, will you, please choose a name for her. We can't call her Baby forever.'

'Ahh, but I've already picked one for her. Meet Sienna.'

'Well, you are very naughty for keeping us waiting.' Yvonne peered at her granddaughter. 'Yes, it suits her. Hello, my beautiful little Sienna! You know she looks just like Susan when she was born.'

Heather smiled. 'Pass her over, Mom – I'll give her a feed.' Yvonne reluctantly did as Heather asked and left the room to make coffee.

Heather searched Sienna's tiny face again for any resemblance to Snake man and was glad that she could see no trace of anyone. Hopefully, I never will, she thought and hugged her daughter's sweet-smelling body to herself as tightly as she dared. She relished the comforting warmth that emanated from her child as she nursed her from milk-engorged breasts.

Chapter 9

Yvonne's tone was a little acerbic as she tried to reason with her daughter.

'Come on. You've scarcely been outside the house since her birth. Now, let me be a grandmother and do my share, will you?' She only received a frown and a negative shake of Heather's head. 'You're really daft, and I feel a little bit insulted that you think I can't care for her properly. I wonder how you and Susan managed to turn out so well if I was such a bad mother.'

'Oh, Mom! You know it's not that. I think you're the best Mom in the world – you know I do.' Heather then said in a quieter voice, 'I'm just so scared that something will happen to her to punish me for my wicked thoughts.'

'What wicked thoughts are you talking about, love?' Yvonne knelt in front of Heather and frowned. 'What do you mean? You aren't a wicked person. You're a kind one. Do you mean about Sienna's father?'

Heather's face blanched. 'No. I never think about him. Of course, you can look after her.' She sighed deeply and gently touched her mother's face. 'I've promised myself a trip into town to have a browse around the library, and perhaps have lunch on my own, have a bit of me-time. I suppose today's as good a time as any other. Are you sure you wouldn't like to come with me? Sienna's usually such a good baby when she's in her pushchair.'

'No, love. You go on and try to forget about responsibility for a while. I'll enjoy having her to myself, and you've expressed enough milk to last for today, haven't you?'

'Yes, it's on the second shelf of the freezer. Thanks, Mom. I know I'm an idiot, and I need to get out on my own sometimes. It'll be different when I return to work. I'll get used to not being with her then, won't I?'

Heather kissed her mother on her cheek. Then she went to change her jeans and check on Sienna. While getting ready, her mood lightened. She was looking forward to being able to think and search for the answer she needed.

A tranquil atmosphere greeted her as she entered the unattractive library that Harold Wilson had opened in 1974. It had replaced a beautiful old building, but Heather wasn't looking for aesthetics; she was only interested in searching the electoral register for the residents of number 34 Fent Road. The librarian explained that entries could only be in the public domain after ten years had elapsed. The earliest year available for Heather to peruse was nineteen eighty-five.

Heather pulled a face and changed her request. A somewhat austere man in a rumpled, grey suit found the records she needed.

After only a few minutes, Heather located the address and read quickly down the list of names. There were only three residents: Mr Ali Javid, David Javid, and Mrs Patricia Javid. She stared in disbelief to see that they all had the last name, Javid. The other two rapists must have been in the habit of calling Snake man by his last name. It also meant that he must be about twenty-eight years of age now to be on that electoral roll. As the penny dropped, Heather had a flashback to a time before she had known the sex of her baby. David was a name that she'd been considering had Sienna been a boy; now, she thanked God that she'd had a girl. It would have been dreadful. She could feel her neck becoming wet with sweat under her hair; she hated the very thought of her child bearing his name. She rubbed her hand through the dampness and told herself to get a grip: it hadn't happened.

Feeling unsettled, she strolled around the library occasionally, taking a book from the shelves, glancing at its title without seeing any of its content, and then replacing it. Her mind skipped about trying to make sense of the information that she'd just gleaned. She selected a book from the shelf nearest to her and sat at an empty table, opened the book, and read the flyleaf; the words didn't enter her brain. Many minutes passed while she stared at a bookcase situated opposite the table; she saw nothing. She shook her head, forcing herself to focus. She thought that it must be the same people, but on reflection, she supposed that it might have been a different family. She quickly dismissed the possibility. It was too much of a coincidence. The names of the males plus the first name of the female made her feel sure that she'd been right in her assumption; the man she thought of as Snake man did indeed live in the house that she'd spent many hours observing. Her stomach churned; it felt like molten lava boiling inside her.

Her train of thought strengthened her resolve to destroy the man who had fathered Sienna. He needed to tell her the other two names and where they lived before she killed him, but she had no idea how to carry out her intentions. She wished, not for the first time that she had someone in whom she could confide but knew that would be impossible. She didn't trust anyone enough to understand or condone what she planned to do. She had to work out the details by herself.

After a while, Heather left the slightly musty smelling library and walked through the crowded Bull Ring towards St. Martin's Church. She went inside the peaceful old building and sat for a short time in one of the pews. The light coloured wood was cold to the touch and its surface ultra-smooth, although no expert Heather thought it made from oak. She didn't say a prayer; she felt she'd lost the right to ask God for help while her thoughts dwelt on murder – no matter what the reason. Unsure of her motivation, she lit a candle and then put more than enough money into the collection box and quietly left the haven of tranquillity. She went into a nearby cafe and bought a cheese sandwich and a cup of tea which she ate and drank with relish – she hadn't realized she was so hungry until she began to eat. She decided to drive home via Stratford Road and check to see if she could catch sight of Snake man. She hadn't been there since Sienna's birth and felt a flash of apprehension in case the family had upped sticks and moved away. Why should they? They'd been there for at least ten years. Why would they move?

As she neared Fent Road, her mouth became dry. She turned in slowly and found a space to park a few yards from number thirty-four. It had started to rain a fine mist, the sort that quickly soaks through clothing and reduces visibility. She switched off the engine and peered across the road. Nothing seemed to have changed as far as she could see. The pale pink net curtains still stretched without gathers across the cream painted bay window. She contemplated the house while her heartbeat returned to an almost imperceptible rhythm. There was no sign of the white van or the people that she wanted to see. After about half an hour, Heather decided to return home to her daughter. She knew she could have lingered for a while longer, but she had started to miss her and had tired of her own company.

She put the car into gear and drove to the top of the road as a white van indicated to turn in. Her heart began beating a tattoo once again. She quickly grabbed her glasses and thrust them onto her now burning face. She turned the corner, making way for the van and caught a glimpse of Snake man's face as she did so; he was looking in the opposite direction. Her face continued to feel like a beacon as she drove home with her mantra playing over and over in her brain, I will kill you, I will kill you, I will kill you: it blocked out all other thought.

Chapter 10

Susan frowned at her sister, who was folding washing and placing it into the ironing basket.

'No! I haven't forgotten what happened the last time. I'm not too keen on returning to that gym,' she said.

'Oh, go on! You know it won't be the same. I'm not pregnant anymore, am I? So, there's no reason for me to feel ill and rush off, is there?' Heather grinned winningly at Susan's doubtful face.

'I know it wasn't your fault, but I felt so embarrassed. What if it's the same instructor?'

Susan moved to where Sienna lay on her play mat, gurgling happily as she reached for the brightly coloured toys that hung over her head. She hunkered down onto the floor and kissed her niece, then started to play with the toys. She squeezed a green, rubbery frog making it croak. Sienna broke out into noisy chuckles, vigorously waving her arms and legs. Heather joined Susan on the floor, where they spent ten minutes playing with the baby. They both looked forward to every tiny milestone that they saw in her development.

'Have you made up your mind, then? You definitely won't come with me?' Heather asked. She jumped up energetically and took a swig from a glass of water that she'd left on a nearby table.

Susan pursed her lips and put her head on one side, making her look like a puzzling cockatiel, as she gazed speculatively at Heather's downturned lips. 'I tell you what. If you let me have half an hour taking photos of you and Sienna, and allow me to use them in my portfolio, then I'll come with you.' She held her breath. The last time she'd asked the same question, Heather had refused point-blank.

Susan knew she hated having her photo taken, although she didn't object to pictures of Sienna. 'That's blackmail.' Heather smothered a laugh at her sister's manipulation. 'Can't you just use some photos of Sienna?'

'No. I want to show the emotion between mother and child – it's important to me. So, is it a bargain?' Susan grinned at the indignant look on her sister's face, but she knew she'd won when Heather shrugged her shoulders.

'Okay. But half an hour is about all I can bear. When do you want us to pose for you? You scheming wench, you.' They both laughed heartily.

'No time like the present. Just let me set my room up, and we'll go for it. Sienna seems to be in a good mood. Do you want to change your top? That one's too patterned for what I want to do – choose a plain one, will you?' Susan hastily left the room, anxious to get to her favourite occupation.

Heather picked Sienna up and went to her room, where she sorted out a suitable, pale green jumper and changed Sienna into a pretty, white Broderie Anglaise dress that emphasized the black sheen of her hair. Heather paused and considered how lucky she was to have her beautiful child. As always, the wonderment contained an element of wretchedness.

After half an hour, Heather called a halt as Sienna was becoming restless, and she'd had enough too. When Susan developed the photos and showed them off to her parents,

Heather was glad she'd agreed to pose with Sienna. Her sister was very talented. In a short time, she'd caught the indefinable depth of love between Sienna and herself.

Heather didn't mind them helping Susan in her work, and she knew that she was paranoid. The police or the rapists would never see them. As Susan handed her each print, she scrutinized it and saw with satisfaction that at nearly four months, and with her features starting to be more defined, Sienna still showed no resemblance to Snake man. If anything, Heather thought she caught glimpses of Yvonne. She told her mother what she thought, and to her amusement, Yvonne preened for a few days taking every opportunity to display the photographs of her grandchild and asking her friends and colleagues if they thought that Sienna resembled her.

The following week Heather and Susan both signed a twelve-month contract at a recently opened gym not far from their home. It wasn't cheap, and Heather offered to pay for Susan, who wouldn't hear of it. They'd heard that the contracts were hard to get out of and thought it would mean that they would go regularly. Heather made it very clear to the instructor, who introduced himself as Mr Roberts, that she not only wanted to lose weight but wished to become super fit and increase her strength.

Susan gasped in horror and said quickly, 'I just want to lose a little weight and become fitter, but I don't want bulging muscles.'

'That's okay. We tailor the programmes individually, and it's obvious that you and your sister's needs are very different. Come with me, and I'll show you around.'

They followed him through the grey, painted swing doors into a bright, airy room that was groaning with shiny new machines. He took them for a tour, told them the name of each piece of equipment and gave them a description of its use.

'Wow, they look like something I've seen in pictures of medieval torture,' Susan said.

Mr Roberts smiled politely. 'You won't need to use many of these, so don't worry. It's you, Heather, that will need to have a balanced training programme, and you'll have to be prepared to work hard to achieve your goals.'

'That's no more than I would expect,' said Heather.

He then showed them how to operate the treadmills and finished by taking them through a short warm-up routine. 'Okay then, over to you. Take your time, have a go, and get the feel of them. If you need me, I'll be at that desk over there, keeping an eye on you and working out a brief guide for your next session. I promise that I'll have a full programme drawn up for you by next week. I'll leave you to it then. Enjoy.'

After about an hour, they left the gym and bought a bottle of water each as they passed through a small cafeteria just off the foyer. Several men and women in tracksuit bottoms and vest tops or leotards stood talking. They didn't glance their way, and Heather got the impression that they were known to each other. I'm here to become fit, not socialise, Heather thought, but she felt a momentary pang that her life was no longer straightforward or carefree.

As they were leaving the reception area, the instructor called them over to an alcove. 'Just thought I'd let you know that If you are serious about becoming super fit,' he looked at Heather, 'I consider one of the best forms of exercise is hill sprints.'

Heather and Susan looked blank. 'What do you mean?' Heather asked.

'I mean – choose a hill by where you live, then after a brief, dynamic warm-up as I showed you earlier, run up the hill then walk back down – take time to recover then repeat it. You should both be able to manage about five times initially, but you'll be able to progress to around fifteen if you wish. It will strengthen your whole body and,' he looked at Susan, 'help you both to shed a few pounds. The sprinting, along with the regime that I set, will have you looking good, feeling good and becoming healthy and strong safely.' He turned to Heather. 'You sound very intense about becoming strong, and I'm sure you have your reasons, but I'd like you to remember that this should be an experience that enhances your life, not one that becomes your life.' He smiled.

Heather shrugged, 'It's okay, I do have my reasons. I've no intention of killing myself – but thanks for the warning.'

As they left the gym, Susan gave a little skip of sheer pleasure.' I enjoyed that, when are you planning to go again?'

'As often as I can, but don't worry, I don't need you to come with me every time unless you want to; I'm just grateful that you came with me this time. Mind you, we need to get our money's worth, don't we?'

'Yes, of course. I'll certainly come each time I can, but Sienna might need one of us if Mom can't mind her, and I get the impression that your need is greater than mine. I think I know why too,' she stroked Heather's arm. 'It wouldn't hurt me to be able to defend myself either.' As they reached Heather's car, Susan gave her sister a quick hug and said, 'I love you, you know?'

Heather returned the hug. 'I love you too.'

Chapter 11

Sienna held out her arms to her mother as she kissed her goodbye. Heather was on the way out for her Saturday afternoon run. At eighteen months, Sienna's only words were 'Momma,' 'Nana', 'anga' and 'Sues', but she understood everything that was said to her.

'See you in a little while, darling. Grandma's going to stay with you,' Heather said and immediately felt guilty as her daughter's eyes filled with tears. 'Do you want to come with me then?' Sienna nodded and smiled. 'Well, okay, let's get you into your harness.'

Heather fetched the seat that she sometimes took her daughter out in and strapped it in place with her mother's help. Sienna's legs dangled down Heather's lean back and bounced rhythmically as she paced to the door.

'Thanks, Mom. I'll only take her for a short run today. Do you want me to pick anything up from the shops?'

'No thanks, love. Enjoy yourself – but stay safe.' Yvonne didn't like Heather taking Sienna out strapped onto her back; she thought it was dangerous.

Yvonne watched her ultra-fit daughter as she jogged down the drive, Sienna's head bobbing along with each stride. She often took Sienna shopping and jogged home loaded up with both her daughter and full bags. Yvonne was amazed at the strength not only in Heather's body but also in her character. The family had waited in vain for Heather to talk to them about the horror of the night she was so severely injured, but they had stopped watching her closely. Yvonne understood why Heather had wanted to become fit and strong but hadn't expected her to go to such lengths. Her regime at the gym had developed her upper body muscles in a way that Yvonne thought tended to be a little unladylike, and she'd gone on to build her whole body. After a couple of months at the gym, Heather had joined a judo-style class aimed at teaching women self-defence. She would return home after each class full of beans as she showed her family the moves causing Susan to laugh and tell her to get a life, but after a while, they often practised together. It was fun for them, but Heather was deadly serious. She promised herself that not only would she be able to avenge herself, but she'd never be preyed upon and made to feel like a defenceless woman again.

When Susan had lost the few pounds that she wanted to and her contract came to an end, she'd not renewed it, but Heather had continued to work hard to the exclusion of any other activity outside of work and her daughter.

Yvonne admired Heather's tenacity but wondered if she wasn't becoming too obsessed with fitness as a means of subjugating her fears. She turned away from the window and walked into the kitchen while feeling lucky to have her girls and a granddaughter living at home. People expected their children to marry or be independent when they were working and in their twenties, but not her. She thought with deep affection of her husband, who felt as she did. He took just as much pleasure in his family and wouldn't appreciate significant changes, although they both knew change would happen eventually. Not yet, please God, she prayed as she went about her chores.

Later, noticing that it had started to rain quite heavily, she fired up the central heating for when they arrived home. Sodding rain, she thought as she remembered that Susan was taking outdoor wedding photos at a church in Evesham. Yvonne shook her fist at the sky then laughed as she made herself a cup of tea, knowing she could do nothing to help until they arrived home.

While she jogged, Heather was training her mind to shut out unpleasantness. She began to think about the job that she loved. The joy on her face when a mother heard her baby's first cry never became stale for her. She managed to maintain a friendly relationship with her colleagues while at work but kept them all at arm's length, refusing the many invitations that inevitably came her way. Although admired for her kindness, some of her colleagues thought that she was standoffish. When she refused to respond positively to their favourite doctor, who had asked her out on more than one occasion, she knew that there was gossip. Heather had always made an excuse, even though she was attracted to the handsome, young Dr Gordon. She felt it would be impossible to become emotionally entangled with anyone at this juncture of her life. She never lost sight for a moment of the revenge killings that she had every intention of carrying out – she was unable to forgive or forget how they had degraded and defiled her.

She couldn't explain her motives to anyone, so they didn't realise how much time she spent working out or remember that she had a daughter. There were only a few members of staff who still worked at Good Hope, who knew her circumstances. Heather knew that she different in many ways; she never joined in the hospital gossip and did her best to avoid controversy wherever possible. It was one of the reasons why she was happy to work nights while most of her colleagues preferred the day shifts.

After four hours of sleep following three consecutive night shifts, Heather meandered into the kitchen in her pyjamas. Yvonne was chatting to Sienna, who was dipping a biscuit into a cup of milk while she perched on the breakfast bar with her feet in her grandmother's lap.

'Morning, Mom. Do I smell coffee?' Heather asked with a yawn. Sienna chuckled and pointed at her mother's mouth as she hugged her and wished her a good morning too.

'I'll make some fresh, love. I didn't think you'd be up so soon.' Yvonne went to fill the kettle while Heather sat with her daughter.

'Are you busy today, Mom, or can you have Sienna for me? I'd like to go into town and start looking for some Christmas presents. It's only four weeks away, and I've not bought a thing yet. Just think, Sienna will be able to enjoy unwrapping her presents this year.' While she was talking, Heather threw her daughter up towards the ceiling and then caught her making her chuckle with glee.

'No, that's fine. I'll be here all day, and we'll have fun, won't we, darling?' Yvonne said. She took her granddaughter from her mother and rained kisses down on her face. Sienna giggled and landing some of her own all over her grandmother's face and neck.

'I'm going up to have a shower before breakfast if that's okay?' Heather said. She picked up her coffee, waved her hand and climbed the stairs.

It had been fourteen months since she'd last been to Stratford Road, and after her shower, Heather quickly departed, ostensibly to buy presents. After an hour with no sign of anyone that she recognised, she decided to take a walk and look in the shop windows, which were now primarily owned by the very close-knit Asian community that had settled there. It was November. Pulling on a loose fawn raincoat that had seen better days and some spectacles with plain glass, she muffled the lower part of her face with a brightly coloured scarf, left the haven of her car and began to walk steadily down the gentle slope towards Stratford Road.

There was such an array of various kinds of clothing worn on a multitude of different nationalities that she didn't feel she would stand out from the crowd who were intent on shopping. With her heart beating an uncomfortable tattoo in her chest, she gazed into a jewellery shop window and noticed a silver bracelet set with emeralds that she thought Susan would like. Plucking up the courage but fearing that she just might see Snake man inside the shop, she entered the brightly lit premises and quickly glanced around. There was only one softly spoken assistant who greeted her pleasantly. She paid for the bracelet and was thankful that she'd at least started on her Christmas list.

A few yards past the greengrocers where she'd first seen Snake man, there was a multicultural newsagent shop. Most of the signs and cards in the window were in both English, and what she suspected was Urdu or Punjabi. She stopped to look, and one of the advertisements immediately caught her eye. It was written on a plain postcard and advertised a local man with a van for hire. Her mouth dropped open with surprise when she saw the contact name: David Javid.

She groped in her handbag. Now she had a telephone number. Her spirits immediately dropped as she wondered, while she wrote the number into her diary, how that was going to help her. The card was dated two weeks previously, but she was no further forward with ideas on how to carry out her plan. Her mood swung again as she remembered how strong she was now; it gave her the confidence boost she needed. I must remember to get rid of that phone number after I've extracted the names of the accomplices, she warned herself. Twisting her bracelets around and around on her arm, she went back to where she'd parked her car. It had become a habit, but one she wasn't in any hurry to break. They were a constant reminder of her intentions.

She unlocked her car and wondered if she should use another road to park in future – her distinctive blue Mini just might catch someone's eye. Shut up. You're becoming paranoid, just like Clouseau expecting Cato to jump out on you every time you turn a corner. Nevertheless, she decided not to park there again.

Chapter 12

Heather questioned herself as she sat at a table with a sandwich and a cup of coffee in Marks and Spencer's café. Am I schizophrenic? Here I am searching for presents through gaily lit shops in the middle of the city when I've just been searching my brain for a way to kill three people. The two don't match up. Well, not to sane people anyway. But not many people have been driven to these depths of despair, she argued. She visibly shrugged her shoulders and told herself not to be so stupid. She wasn't mad; she was enraged and damaged enough to be determined to kill the men who had brought her to this state. Other people would think you are insane, though, a small voice said to her. Other people can get stuffed, she thought and told her conscience to back off. They deserved everything that they had coming.

She continued to sort through scarves, gloves and pretty nightwear for her mother, finally settling on a sensible pair of fleecy pyjamas. She bought her father a pullover in lilac, his favourite colour. Then she spent another hour enjoying searching in children's departments to buy various toys and clothes for her daughter. The vision of Sienna's joy on Christmas morning overrode every nasty image she had in her mind. Eventually, feeling fed up with having to wait in queues and loaded up with bags, Heather made her way back to her car in the Bull Ring shopping centre, then set off home. As she wended her way through the heavy traffic, myriad plans ran through her mind, but they were impractical

Where could she buy a gun or a Taser from without leaving a trail? How was she going to be able to put him out of action long enough to tie him up so she could interrogate him? As she neared home, she succeeded, with a struggle, in clearing her mind to greet her family. She sought and held on to the image of her daughter's beautiful face smiling as she entered a room.

She had been lucky enough to get Christmas and Boxing Day off. It meant that she would have to work New Year's Eve, but she didn't mind. So it was once again a real family Christmas consisting of their traditional breakfast followed by the joy of watching Sienna, who was walking and talking in baby sentences, tear wrapping paper from her presents. Several of her new toys caused her to give such squeals of delight that it brought tears to Heather's eyes. She thanked God that she had her, no matter how it had come about – she had brought so much love and pleasure into their lives.

Later, Susan's boyfriend, Leslie, joined them for dinner along with Ben and Julie, who seemed more like family rather than close friends. They had become honorary Aunt and Uncle to Sienna, and Heather loved them for the way they too took pleasure in the little things that her daughter did and practically every word that came out of her mouth.

As dinner progressed, with Sienna sitting between her grandmother and Heather, it became evident that Leslie wasn't enamoured with her. He told her to be quiet in an aggressive voice at one point when he was speaking to Susan. Sienna began to cry and had to be comforted by her mother. He seemed to dislike the child that everyone else loved. No one was surprised when Susan went to the local with him after dinner and returned after a half-hour, on her own. She had been going out with him for three months, but that was the last anyone saw of him. Susan didn't go into detail. Heather was pleased to see the back of him; he was handsome, but she felt he could be a bully. She'd overheard him one day cruelly talking to Susan. Susan had left the kitchen on that occasion in tears; she rarely cried, and Heather felt very protective of her. Her initial reaction had been to go into the kitchen and confront him. Deep down, she knew she wanted to hit him. She felt like striking quite a few men that she met these days but managed to curb her impulses, as she did on this occasion.

New Year's Eve proved to be a quiet night with no new patients admitted. Heather was able to take a break and nip up to ward five, where some unplanned festivities were going on. She had a mince pie, and a cup of coffee then returned to the staff room, where she was able to put her feet up for a few minutes. She shut her eyes, allowing her mind to wander. After several long minutes, her eyes shot open. The beginnings of a workable plan caused her feet to drop to the floor and her heart to race. She went over it in her mind and, barring accidents, she thought it was feasible. She returned to work with a spring in her step. If her plan worked, she would successfully end the life of one of her rapists without being caught. She felt no compunction about ending Snake man's life, even though it went against all her instincts.

The remainder of that night couldn't go quickly enough. Heather found she couldn't stop thinking about the plan that she'd begun to devise. An excellent start to a new year, she thought, as she left the hospital and braved the thickly falling snow. She hoped that it would start to bring about a conclusion, and she could begin to live one life instead of two.

For the umpteenth time, a picture of the faces of all three of the men assaulted her. She spoke aloud to their images: It's been three years since you killed a part of me, now it's your turn. She quickly looked around, hoping that no one had noticed her talking to herself. As she entered her car and turned the key, she called them all the swear words that she could think of and not for the first time.

It was two weeks before Heather was able to complete the shopping list that would have had her family asking searching questions if any one of them glimpsed its contents. She had been refining her idea and was trying to ensure that she had thought of everything by writing it down. Determined to carry out her plan but feeling sick at the thought of all the things that could go wrong. She knew Sienna would be well looked after if she went to prison, but the possibility made her stomach churn.

Heather was aware, from things that her father had said on occasions, that truncheons and other nightsticks would be difficult to obtain and illegal to own. Instead, she made a weapon using three heavy stones tied tightly into one of her father's socks. His socks often did the magical missing trick. A smile lit her face as she took one from the washing. She bought a black bra, that was three cup sizes larger than she usually wore, from a supermarket situated in the Black Country. The next week she went to B & Q in Halesowen and purchased a tin of lighter fuel and a large roll of silver coloured tape. She knew it would be strong enough to use on Snake man; it was the same type that they had used on her. Looking at the tape made her insides crawl as she relived the horror of being unable to call up any defence against their brutality. She purchased matches and some large black bags from her local supermarket, then went into the first charity shop that she came to and bought a couple of second-hand jumpers and skirts. She did the same in a few others, carefully avoiding the charity shop where her mother still did voluntary work one day a week. She went to another B&Q store in Walsall and purchased a second tin of lighter fuel. She paid cash for everything. She was unsure regarding how much petrol she would need to set fire to some clothing but decided that it would have to be enough.

After a couple of weeks choosing different shops, Heather had enough old clothes to fill two black bin bags. She kept all the items in the boot of her car until she was the only adult at home for the day. Then, after putting Sienna down for her nap. She tipped the contents onto black bags on the carpet and pulled on hospital gloves before going over each article to ensure there weren't any identifying labels. Once satisfied, she returned them to the car boot where all the other items, except for the bra, were stashed. Labels that she had removed were disposed of at the hospital – burnt with clinical waste. She knew that she was probably being extra careful but needed to do everything that she could to avoid detection. The following week she spent time perusing several estate agents' windows until she identified two houses that she thought might be fit for her purpose.

As soon as she could manage it, she drove to see the first house, feeling confident that one of them would be suitable. It was down a quiet lane where the houses were all set back in their drives, with bushes and trees sheltering the residence, giving the occupants a high degree of privacy. Heather noticed the discrete For Sale sign at the end of the drive as she slowly turned in and drove right up to the front door. The lovely, vacant property needed renovation, she thought admiringly, but she had no intention of using it pleasantly. She had no plans to go inside the house at all.

To the right of the porch, there was a double garage with two wooden doors that had seen better days. A fitted brass lock looked like an original. Heather looked back down the drive and shivered violently. The icy wind was making the trees and bushes sway eerily, like a scene from a horror movie, but she also imagined what she would soon be doing in this very spot if all went according to plan.

She turned her attention back to the garage. The wood surrounding the lock had rotted with time; Heather thought that she would have no trouble breaking in. The house wasn't alarmed. Well, she hoped it wasn't. There had been no mention of one, but even if the house was alarmed, then it was highly unlikely that the garage would be, she thought. She resisted the temptation to touch the doors without gloves, returned to the haven of her car and drove away.

Heather had no idea how long the house would remain empty, so she decided, with butterflies stirring her innards, that the time had come to set the wheels in motion to bring about an end to Snake man's life.

Chapter 13

Heather took her diary from her bag and checked her rota for the following month to ascertain what arrangements she needed to make with her mother and sister for the next week. There were only two days when she had no commitments; quite a small window. Nevertheless, the time was right – it had to be enough.

The day after Sienna's second birthday, the weather improved. It was still cold and windy, but the rain seemed to have decided they were all wet enough.

'Thank God it's given ovcr. I'm fed up of taking wedding photos indoors. It makes my job far harder, even though I do still make them beautiful,' Susan said. She pulled a demure face as she boasted.

'Well, you do not need to blow your own trumpet, you strumpet!' Heather laughed and left the house in her jogging gear. Sometimes it was all she could do to try and behave in a light-hearted fashion with her sister, but she managed it.

She thanked the gods that the deluge had ceased as she drove to a phone box, a few miles from her home, that was out of order. She tried to slam the door closed as she stepped out, but it shut slowly on noisy hinges. She drove to the next one in Olton and made the all-important call to Snake man. She felt nauseous as she heard the number ring out. After the sixth ring

Snake man answered. Heather recognised his voice. It made her hear the words, you dirty fucking whore, pound like a drum in her head. Her mouth became dry and tasting of blood when he repeated his telephone number and asked how he could help.

'Are you the man with a van?' Heather managed to say.

'Yes, what can I do for you? Is it a job?'

'Yes, but it's only a small job. Just a couple of black bags to take to a charity shop. Would that be okay?' She waited, chewing her lip as he gave a heavy sigh.

'When would you want it done? And how many miles away are you?' He asked in an offhand tone that made Heather panic. Was the job too small?

Heather's courage had returned by the time she replied firmly. 'The pickup is from ...' She gave him the address of the empty house, 'and the bags can be taken to a shop of your choice the next day.' Her voice speeded up as she continued. 'I'm selling up, and I have almost cleared it out, just these last few bags to go, but I need them done quickly. I'm only available on the seventh or the eighth at seven pm. Would you be able to pick them up then? The house needs to be empty by the ninth.'

'Hold on. I'll just see what day I can do ...' Heather could hear him turning pages in a book, 'the seventh's fine, and it'll cost you twenty-five quid,' he paused, and then asked sharply, 'do you still want me to do the job?' Heather understood that he didn't want the work and was setting the price high, but she wanted her job done and finished.

'Yes, but please be on time. I have to go out when I've finished clearing out the garage.'

'Paying cash?'

'Yes, no problem.'

‘Okay, seven on the seventh then.’ He put the phone down without a goodbye.

Heather felt utterly calm by the time the call ended. She didn’t understand why the longer she listened to his voice, the more coldly calculating she became. He had to die. She knew she was strong enough to deal with him, even if things didn’t go according to plan. She replaced the receiver, collected her change, then jogged to her car while trying to cover every eventuality in her mind. She couldn’t afford to make even one mistake, but she could only plan for what she could foresee. The jogging seemed to clear her mind, and by the time she returned home, she felt happier than she had for some time.

Although Yvonne had agreed to look after Sienna for the whole day, Heather found that being with her daughter helped her to keep herself steady. She handed over her responsibility for Sienna’s care to her mother at one o’clock and then took herself off to explore the area surrounding the chosen house. At the end of an evening run, her mother or sister usually picked her up. She ran whenever possible, and the family all thought she was marvellous for keeping up her regime and staying so fit. They were happy to help her out whenever they were needed.

But leaving the car in the driveway wasn’t an option, nor was parking it on the road nearby. There was no pavement, only a grass verge, and her car would raise questions, as it was sure to be noticed. All the big houses had large drives, and no one parked in the narrow lane. The house that she’d chosen only had one neighbour on the right-hand side. On the other, it adjoined a farmer’s field that had a short drive up to a five-bar gated entrance into a hayfield. She considered leaving her car in front of the gate, but she was worried that it would lead to possible curiosity and dismissed the idea. She knew that the field was somewhat hilly as she'd run through it before. She'd discovered that over its horizon was the main road that led indirectly into the outskirts of Solihull – not far from the pub that was her local. When she'd used this route previously, it had been early summer and the evenings were light. She didn't much fancy running it in the dark, but she had a heavy-duty torch that she supposed could be hidden in her backpack along with other things that she needed to keep out of sight.

Heather drove around the lanes until she located the parallel road and the parking lay-by that she knew was partially concealed by roadside grass and bushes. During the day, a van parked there. It dispensed tea and snacks; the counter faced away from the road and towards the hedgerow. She had never bought anything except bottled water from the van when she'd been jogging; she felt that the standards of hygiene might not be up to scratch. She had an idea that the owner packed everything up at six each evening and, in inclement weather, often didn't open at all. She drove into the lay-by and turned off the engine. Heather knew there was a Harvester pub about a half-mile along the road towards Olton, where she and her family had eaten out on a couple of occasions. She thought that she could leave her car there and jog back to the house if she left herself enough time to get there before Snake man arrived.

She wound down the driver's side window, leaned back against the headrest and shut her eyes. Unbidden images presented themselves to the inside of her lids: a trombone, a ballerina in a white dress, a ball bounced across a black and white crossing. She opened her eyes again. She couldn't think properly. Her senses were too frazzled with all the intense planning that she had been doing for the last few weeks.

Her nostrils were alerted to the aroma of bacon cooking in the tiny cafe van parked almost opposite to where she'd come to a halt. Saliva squirted into her mouth, and her stomach rumbled; she'd only had a piece of toast for her breakfast at eight o'clock when she'd fed Sienna. Oh, fuck the germs, she thought, and picking up her purse, strolled across to the van and ordered some bacon, egg and mushrooms in a bap and a cup of coffee.

'What time do you close up?' she asked the man. He turned her bacon with a spatula on the hot grill then cracked an egg that immediately started to bubble and turn brown around the edges.

'It's usually about five,' he told her with a smile, 'there's so little point after that – everyone's rushing to get home, the passing trade keeps right on going.'

He had long, brown hair tied back in a ponytail and an attractive grin she noticed as he answered her query. She looked at his hands, relieved to see that they looked clean, as did his neatly manicured nails. She thought she'd possibly misjudged the man out of hand. She probably wouldn't get food poisoning from his cooking. She walked back and sat in her car, where she opened the white serviette and took a large bite of the bap. The yolk of the egg broke and oozed gently onto her chin. She quickly licked it back into her mouth and smiled at her changed opinion. I suppose there's a first time for everything she thought – even murder. She shuddered.

Knowing that her mother had planned to take Sienna out to visit an old friend, Heather drove home to an empty house. She felt emotionally flat and moved as though in a trance as she collected everything that she would need and added them to the black bags in her car. Coiling her auburn hair that had grown long enough to make two bunches, one on either side of her head, into elastic bands, donned her black running fleece and jogging bottoms and checked that her spectacles with plain glass in them were in her bag. She then pushed disinfectant cloths, matches, lighter fuel, silver tape, a large, heavy handled screwdriver and a scalpel that she'd purloined from the hospital into her black backpack. Taking a change of clothes, she shoved them, along with a bottle of water, some paper and a pen, into her bag. Then she added a three-metre length of cord. At the last minute, she remembered that she had to change into her new, oversized bra. As she did so, it broke her out of her trance-like state. She looked in the mirror and laughed humourlessly at her reflection – it bore little resemblance to the innocent girl that had been Snake man's victim. She'd thought that, by now, she would be feeling apprehensive or even downright scared, but she felt calm. She had a job to do and was intent on doing it. As she drove away, she glanced back at her home and wondered if she would return.

Chapter 14

By the time Heather left her home, the night was already drawing in. As she drove to the chosen house, she went over and over the plan in her mind. She refused to think that in a short while, she was going to put an end to a person's life. He had never been a person to her mind; he was a monster. She just needed to put an end to him and ensure that she wouldn't get caught.

She drove up close to the garage after checking that she was alone. She put on surgical gloves, took the screwdriver from her pack and jemmied the garage doors open. The wood splintered, the lock fell apart, leaving the brass face intact. She would be able to push the doors together when she'd finished. She slipped inside the space that someone had done a decent job of clearing out. Other than an old Atco motor mower partially covered with a green tarpaulin, nothing remained.

She fetched the black bags from the car boot and put them just inside the right-hand door where it would be easy to prevent Snake man from seeing inside. He might wonder why she had on hospital gloves when any dirty work had already been completed. She didn't want him to think that there was anything even slightly amiss until the time was right.

She tucked her backpack with its precious contents behind the left-hand door and balanced her home-made cosh firmly on top of it. She felt a little light-headed as she pushed the doors back together. Had she thought of everything? Was it going to work? She chewed her lip as she questioned herself repeatedly – afraid that she might have forgotten something important.

After a few minutes, she ceased worrying and drove to the pub, where she intended to park her car. On the way, she drove through the lay-by. It was clear of any vehicles, and the cafe van was closed with the shutters securely padlocked. She continued to the pub, parked up, then retrieved her flashlight from the boot, locked the car and tucked the keys into one of her deep pockets. The car park was reasonably full; her car didn't stand out in any way, she thought as she jumped over a low wall and began to jog back to the house.

As she started to run up the incline in the field, her foot slid, and she went down hard onto her knees. She directed the beam of her torch downwards and discovered that she'd slipped in some dog mess and her trainers were filthy. Cursing, she wiped them over and over on the grass until she could see there was no trace of shit. She grimaced as she felt the damp dirt on the knees of her tracksuit. Telling herself not to panic and that she had plenty of time, she continued to jog but took more care over where she placed her feet. When she reached the gate, she peered into the deserted lane then walked unhurriedly along to the house. Her breathing and heart rate calmed.

Heather felt that she'd been lucky not to have been seen by anyone, as far as she knew. She pulled her sleeve over her hand to pry the garage door open and slipped inside. Everything was just as before. She delved into her pack and used a wet wipe on her knees, and then donned the hospital gloves and her glasses. She pushed the dirtied wipe deep into the bag to dispose of later. She felt in her top pocket where she'd shoved a twenty-pound note and a five-pound note folded neatly together – his payment which he would never be able to spend.

She glanced for the twentieth time at her watch; it was six-thirty, and she was ready for him. As the minutes ticked by slowly, she found that her last meal was threatening to leave her stomach. She knew that it was due to nerves and began to take deep breaths. After another ten minutes, she saw the van at the top of the drive. It began to reverse slowly towards her.

She quickly grabbed the cosh and stuffed it inside her bra. She knew that in broad daylight, she would look ridiculously lumpy, but the night was black with just a sliver of the moon showing through the high clouds that were scudding along, allowing occasional glimpses of light. As the van pulled up and the driver jumped out, Heather's heart began to pound so hard that she thought she could hear it. She pushed the garage doors open just wide enough to enable her to carry a bag in each hand as he opened the van doors.

He stepped towards her with his hand held out. Heather thought he was going to take the bags, but he said abruptly, 'Money?' and raised his bushy eyebrows.

Heather dropped the bags, fished inside her pocket and handed him the money which he stuffed into his pocket – he then reached for the bags, turned and started to sling them into the van.

Without hesitation, as he turned away and finished the throw, Heather brought the cosh from her hiding place and smashed it down on the side of his head. He slumped forward, bringing the top half of his body into the van. Heather's eyes became slits as she leaned in and hit him again before he could recover. Then again and again as her hate for him took over. He became unconscious, and as he sagged, she picked his legs up and shoved his dead weight into the partially empty van.

Without thinking, she grabbed her pack from the garage, pushed the wooden doors together and jumped into the van. She pulled the doors to and locked them.

He hadn't moved. Heather hoped she hadn't killed him – she needed some questions answered. Quickly, with hands that trembled slightly, disturbing the ice water that she could feel had replaced the warm blood running through her veins, she taped his hands and feet together. Already immobilised, Heather extended the tape to his elbows and knees. Not necessary, but she couldn't stop herself, then she felt in his pocket and removed her money, thrusting it into her pocket. Thanking God for her strength, Heather moved him towards the side of the van, grabbed the cord, wound it twice around his neck then tethered him as tightly to the metal struts that screwed onto the wall battens. She taped his forehead to a higher strut so that he couldn't accidentally strangle on the cord if his head fell forward. Heather covered his mouth before replacing the remainder of the tape, the scalpel and the cosh in her pack. She wondered as she climbed over the seats into the front of the van, what was in the other half dozen black bags piled just behind hers. Heather drove out into the lane. Her hands felt sweaty inside the gloves, but she didn't dare remove them – she couldn't risk leaving fingerprints anywhere.

As she drove towards the lay-by, she was relieved to hear grunts coming from Snake man as he became conscious. Not dead then, she thought coldly – so far so good. Her luck held as she pulled into the lay-by and parked opposite the closed cafe van. It partially hid her from the passing traffic she hoped would be light at this time of the night – it usually was.

She climbed into the back of the van and peered closely at him. He was coming round, but Heather thought that she had time to look in the other black bags before he regained consciousness. They, too, were full of old clothing and a couple of small pieces of china that clunked together as she moved the bags.

She hunkered down against the wheel arch that felt and smelled familiar. She was sure that this was the same van, but she was about to get her revenge, and the memory on this occasion didn't have the power to make her howl or whimper and cry silent tears, as it usually did. She pushed Snake man's foot hard with her own, and he groaned as his eyes opened.

He tried to move and began to cough as the cord tightened around his neck. He looked directly at Heather and made an unintelligible attempt to speak. Heather released the tape from his forehead, forcing him to hold his head upright.

Allowing her torch to light the inside of the van just enough to enable him to see her, she watched and waited a couple of minutes until his eyes seemed able to focus.

'Well, do you recognise me yet?' He moved his head. 'Well, you should. We've been here before, but that time I was the one abused. Fucking got it yet?' Heather said.

His eyes flashed angrily as he recognised her. He twitched his head and tried to shuffle his feet but found he could hardly move them. His anger changed to panic as the cord around his neck tightened and stopped him moving.

'Okay,' Heather said, 'I'm going to give you a choice – the same one you gave me. If I remove the tape, will you keep schtum?' He brought his head forward as far as he was able. Heather reached for her pack and took out the scalpel. Snake man's nostrils flared, and his eyes bulged. 'Calm down. I'm not interested in you,' Heather said. 'I want to know the names of the other bastards that were with you. It's the one that used the copper pipe on me – he's the one I intend to punish. It wasn't you was it?'

He shook his head slightly and tried to speak.

'Tell me their names and where they live. Otherwise, I'm going to have to force you to tell me, do you understand?' He gave a faint nod. Heather took the paper and pen from her pack and placed them by the side of the scalpel, which she deliberately moved – allowing the dim light in the van to reflect off its surface. Snake man couldn't seem to take his eyes from it and didn't look at Heather as she asked, 'Are you going to tell me what I want to know?' She made her voice low and threatening. He moved his head again. 'Okay. I'm going to remove the tape, but if you make one noise that I don't like, I will kill you. Do – you – understand?' she asked again. His nod was almost imperceptible as the cord bit into his neck.

Heather picked up the scalpel and then, reaching with her other hand, pulled the tape away from his mouth, leaving it flapping on one cheek. He gave an involuntary squeak as it came away, taking a few bits of stubble with it.

He spoke immediately, 'I 'aven't seen them since that night. So I don't know where they are. We were all sorry for what we did to you.'

Heather's lips twisted. 'Rubbish! You're a lying bastard. I've warned you, and I won't warn you again.' She knew he was always a nasty piece of work; she'd seen how he treated his mother. 'I'd be happy to use my scalpel to persuade you to tell me what I want to know. Try again. Who were they?' She moved the scalpel from one hand to the other; it glinted in the meagre light.

'Okay, okay. I can tell you, but I don't know if they still live there.' Snake man's voice shook as he spoke. He knew that she meant her threat. He enjoyed inflicting pain on others but was a coward when it came to himself.

Heather picked up the pen and paper. 'Don't bother lying. What I've done once I can do again. I would find you and make no mistake; I would kill you.' Snake man hurriedly gave her two names and addresses, which she wrote down. 'Where did you all meet?' she asked.

He glared at her. 'School. Now, will you undo this fucking thing round me neck and let me go?'

'Which school?'

His nostrils flared. 'Moseley.'

'How do I know you're telling me the truth?' she asked slowly. She leaned forward. 'Perhaps this will help you to think again.' She swiftly drew the scalpel across his cheek. He gasped, and his neck jerked forward, cutting off his air supply. He held his head away as blood began to run down his face and soak into the collar of his white t-shirt.

'No more, no more,' he whimpered, 'I've told you the truth – it's all I know – I 'aven't seen either of them for a couple of years. I'm sorry, please, please, let me go' Heather thought that he'd probably told her what she wanted to know, and she didn't see how she would know for sure that he told the truth until she tried to locate them. She watched a dark stain spread gradually around his crotch and smiled inwardly – he was as terrified as she had been.

'Yes, of course, I will.' The lie came quickly. She stood up and stepped forward with the scalpel in her right hand – the ice water in her veins became liquid nitrogen – 'Now, keep still while I cut the cord. I don't want to slip,' she said between gritted teeth. She stood to the side as far from him as she could while still maintaining her balance, and then she leaned towards him. Her heart thumped hard once but then resumed its steady beat.

Snake man held his head as far back as he could to allow access to the cord. He believed that Heather was going to let him go until she quickly replaced the tape across his mouth.

'I lied,' she sneered in triumph as she cut through his windpipe below the cord and leapt as far away as possible from the blood that spurted and then watched as he choked to death. When his feet had stopped drumming on the van floor, she moved quickly to where she'd laid her pack and pulled the contents of the black bags out. She wiped her hands and the scalpel before she pushed it into her backpack. She shoved the clothes towards the dying man and squirted lighter fuel onto them until the tins were empty. They soaked up the blood along with the petrol as she tossed her pack into the front passenger seat, then followed it over, sliding down behind the wheel. She cleaned her gloves and face with the wet wipes and checked to see if she had any blood on her clothing. She couldn't see any and hoped that she'd moved away quickly enough to ensure that she stayed as clean as possible. She threw the dirty wipes into the back of the van and glanced at Snake man.

She knew he was dead; his head hung forward, straining at the blood-soaked cord that still held him in place. She felt a rush of satisfaction that she'd carried out her plan to destroy him; he hadn't deserved to live. He hadn't been sorry for what he'd done to her and possibly other women too. He was a coward and a stupid one at that for thinking that she could let him go.

Just as she was congratulating herself for having disposed of Snake man, terror threatened to overwhelm her. A dark car pulled into the lay-by and parked directly in front of the van. Heather quickly ducked down; her heart threatened to burst from her chest as she fought to control her breathing. She heard the car door open and shut. A long minute passed before she plucked up enough courage to squint over the top of the dashboard. A portly, bald man in a dark suit stood with his back towards her while he relieved himself against the hedge. After zipping up, he walked to his car, perched himself on the bonnet, casually lit a cigarette, then flicked the spent match towards the hedgerow. He took a few puffs, then walked round to the car boot from where he extracted a large map book. As he closed the boot, he turned towards the van, he lifted his head and appeared to sniff the air.

Heather could feel sweat break out on her forehead. Had she remembered to lock the doors? Could he possibly smell petrol? Was he wondering what an empty van was doing there? Could she be seen? She almost wept with relief as he shrugged his broad shoulders, pinched the glowing end of his cigarette and checked it was out before tucking it behind his ear. Her heart sank as he began to walk towards the van. Heather was confident that she had locked the doors and slid into the well beneath the steering wheel. Footsteps sounded close to where she was scrunched down and walked to the back of the van. He tried the handle. When he came back, he tried the handle on the driver's door. Heather held her breath. If he had been taller, he would have been able to look in the window and see her. She breathed again as she heard his footsteps continue past and his car door click shut. After five minutes, Heather peeped out to see him examining the map book. Another minute and he slung the maps onto the passenger seat then drove away without another glance at the van.

Heather waited a couple more minutes then, with hands still shaking, forced herself to get on with her plan. She pulled some newsprint from her pack, screwed it into a tight strip and then lit it with a match. As it took hold, she mentally crossed her fingers then threw it into the back of the van onto the petrol-soaked rags; they burst into flames. Heather grabbed her pack, looked over her shoulder once, pulled the keys from the ignition, opened the driver's door and jumped out. She locked the door and looked around the deserted area before unscrewing the cap on the petrol tank and pushing one end of a strip of rag well inside. Heather glanced around again and then set fire to the other end. She didn't know if it would burn long enough to explode, but she didn't hang around.

She pulled off her gloves and tucked them into a pocket. She intended to dispose of them and the scalpel at the hospital. She looked around again, then sprinted away to the field where she vaulted over the gate and flung herself down behind the hedge – trembling from head to foot. She pulled a clean top and bottoms from her pack, donned them and stuffed the other ones in their place. She rose and started to jog with care until she was just over the brow of the hill. She knew she could be spotted outlined against the sky, so sat and tried to get herself to think clearly and recover from the violent act she'd just committed. She breathed deeply until the rhythm of her heart slowed into a steady thrum, then checked that the van keys were in her pocket. She removed one of the copper bracelets, wiped it carefully, almost lovingly, then put it into her pocket along with the keys to dispose of later. She felt good, and her blood sang in her veins as she allowed herself time to breathe and not think too deeply about anything.

A minute later, she heard a loud bang and thought that it had to be the van exploding, as she'd hoped it would. She realised that she urgently needed to get as far away from the scene as possible. She got to her feet, and, taking care not to twist an ankle, she continued to jog back to the lane where the house stood. She desperately wanted to get to the pub now and get a lift to her car. She summoned up her strength and ran as fast as she was able to work up a sweat. Her sister looked up and beckoned to her to come in, but Heather shook her head and gestured for Susan to come out.

Heather waited by Susan's Volkswagen Beetle until she arrived and opened the passenger door. 'Why didn't you come in? I was going to buy you a drink so you could cool down,' she sniffed deeply. 'Phew! Perhaps it's as well you didn't! You stink!' Heather grinned and waved her hands as she continued to pretend to be out of breath rather than explain anything

Chapter 15

On the way to Heather's car, Susan exclaimed, 'Cripes, just look at that! I wonder what's going on over there.' Susan drove on the wrong side of the road for about fifty metres as the lay-by was blocked off.

Heather had intentionally averted her eyes as they reached that stretch of road. But now she looked up and saw several vehicles belonging to the emergency services, including two fire engines. Again, a strong feeling of satisfaction washed over her. One down, two to go, she thought as her sister slowed down and opened the window to rubberneck. She rapidly closed it again when an obnoxious smell of burning assaulted their nostrils.

'Looks like a van or something on fire. Hope no one's hurt,' she said. Heather shut her eyes as though she was falling asleep and said nothing.

As soon as they had passed the scene, Susan dismissed it from her mind. But Heather never forgot the image of her handiwork; she had no regrets.

When they arrived at the pub, Heather said, 'Thanks, Susie, see you at home.' She felt only relief as she tossed her backpack safely into the boot of her car and then slid into the driving seat. It felt like her place of sanctuary as she settled comfortably into its familiar contours.

When she reached home, Heather's strength seemed to desert her momentarily. She stumbled as she got out of her car. All the stress, she thought as she quickly recovered and walked steadily into the house. She kicked her trainers off in the porch but, as the light hit them, she felt a jolt of panic as she spotted two red marks.

She grabbed them up and then, calling a swift, 'Thanks again,' to Susan and a greeting to her parents; she ran upstairs. She flung her backpack and trainers into her bathroom and lowered herself onto the floor of her bedroom.

Sienna was fast asleep in her cot with her thumb in her mouth. She's too big now to sleep there. Heather thought as she rolled onto her side and drew her knees up into the foetal position. She closed her eyes and allowed her body to relax, but her mind refused to be still. The words I've just killed your father, Sienna, played in her mind. The events of the night and the elation and fear that went with them were now taking their toll. She could feel bile rising from her stomach and rapidly crawled her way into her en-suite, where she vomited into the toilet and voided her bladder at the same time.

What if someone had seen her as she jogged away from the scene. Stop it, stop tormenting yourself, she thought. What ifs don't count – they hadn't happened.

Time passed unnoticed until she realised that her family would be wondering where she was. She jumped up, stripped her wet clothes off and dumped them in the claw-footed bath to be dealt with later. She scrubbed the blood from her trainers and promised herself that she'd dispose of them. Deciding to see to her backpack, later on, she showered with the water as hot as she could stand it until her skin became an ugly shade of red. The needles of spray brought her back into the present, and she began to recover her composure. Dressed in pyjamas and a warm dressing gown, she joined her parents and Susan in the sitting room.

When she thought about it a few weeks later, she realised how bizarre her behaviour had been to enable her to sit and converse with her family as though nothing untoward had happened. While planning to rid the world of a rabid beast, she'd thought that she would feel some regret and perhaps not even be able to go through with it, but she felt nothing other than relief. Now her life could go on as usual, for a while at least. Heather couldn't be sure that connections might not be made if she killed the next one on her list for at least a year. She didn't think that she'd made any mistakes that would allow her to be a suspect of killing Snake man, but she couldn't be certain.

Next day a brief report telling of a burnt man in a van made the local papers, but there had been nothing that had caused her family to comment. She hoped that she wouldn't need to react every time she saw a police car or an unexpected knock came at the door.

Later that week, as she passed the sitting room, she heard her Dad say something to her Mom ending with '… they think it was drug-related.' That was all she heard, as she didn't stop to listen. He may not have been talking about the van fire, but Heather hoped that he was.

When Heather returned to work a day shift the following Monday, she had a spring in her step. She was relaxed and unusually chatty and Bridget, the midwife, again asked her to join her and a couple of others for a drink after work. To both Bridget and Heather's surprise, she accepted, and they spent an enjoyable hour socialising in the nearby pub.

Bridget, who was about the same age as herself, an older midwife called Kay, and a male midwife called John, who she already knew slightly, as she'd worked a few night shifts with him, made her feel welcome into their group. John was gay and came across as very camp with his exaggerated hand gestures and way of speaking, but he was the sort of person that everyone liked. He was very kind, and now Heather realised that he was very amusing. She let their good-natured banter wash over her as she listened and joined in occasionally.

After downing a Jack Daniels and coke and refusing to have another drink, Heather said, 'Thanks for inviting me, Bridget,' she grinned at Kay and John. 'I've enjoyed your company and the drink.' She laughed at the look of surprise that showed on all three faces. 'I don't want to break up the party, but it's time for me to leave,' she smiled again. 'See you all tomorrow.' She picked up her bag and slid off the barstool.

'Hey, what's the hurry?' Bridget said with a smile. 'The night is young.' She hummed a few notes of a tune that Heather didn't recognise.

'Sorry, but I do have to go. I've my daughter to put to bed. Mom will want a break now, and I like to read her a story when I can,' Heather said.

'Oh, I didn't know you were married,' Bridget said.

'I'm not, but I have a beautiful two-year-old daughter called Sienna. I thought you all knew. I forget how the staff team has changed.' She began to walk toward the pub entrance and waved her hand.

'Lovely name.' Bridget called after her, 'See you in the morning!'

As she left the group, Heather thought that they would soon spread her status around the hospital. She found she didn't mind and wondered why she had reminded them about her daughter after all this time. Were more friends wanted or needed? Perhaps not, but she'd enjoyed being part of a group.

She wondered how quickly they'd reject her if they knew what she'd done. Would anyone be able to understand and empathise with her feelings? She didn't think it would be possible. She hadn't killed Snake man in a fit of passionate rage – she'd been calculating and cold as she planned his murder. Heather knew that she would be a monster to everyone, including her family. But perhaps her family and Julie and Ben might be able to forgive her. They, at least, knew what she'd suffered. This thought gave her mind a comforting crumb.

By the following week, Heather knew, if she hadn't already experienced it, how hospital gossip flared, spread like a small Australian bushfire and then just as quickly subsided. The midwives that she worked with had asked her to bring in photos of her daughter, and she had delighted in showing Sienna off to them. She was grateful that they hadn't asked any awkward questions. Bridget, however, was not so reticent. During their next break when she was looking at the most recent picture of Sienna dressed in jeans and a t-shirt with cute little teddies on the front, she asked quietly, almost casually, 'What happened to her father Heather, do you still see him?'

Heather had been expecting to have to face this one at some point and had her answer ready.

'No. No, I don't. I was young and stupid. We met while I was at Uni, and I believed it when he said that he loved me. We slept together one night, and the next day he wouldn't even look at me or talk to me. He started going out with another girl almost immediately. I found out later from a friend that he'd been seeing her at the same time as he was dating me.'

'How could he? the bastard!' Bridget shook her head.

Heather continued to embroider the story. 'It was just after I'd qualified and completed my degree that I found out I'd become pregnant. I never contemplated sharing the news with him; I didn't want him in my life or my child's.' She drew in a deep breath and could feel the tears start in her eyes as though her story was true.

Bridget put her hand on Heather's arm. 'Poor you. I'm sorry that I asked.'

'It's okay. I don't mind people knowing – I love my daughter, and I'll never be sorry that I have her – she is a joy.'

Their break was over, and they returned to the ward. Heather was hoping that Bridget would pass on the story to her other colleagues; then, she wouldn't need to explain again. She liked Bridget and trusted her not to put a negative slant on her retelling as she hadn't asked her to keep it secret. It didn't come back to her on the grapevine. Few sympathetic looks from some colleagues came to her. I'm getting used to planning and scheming to achieve my ends she thought wryly.

She pushed open the door to the delivery room and greeted the young girl whose face contorted with the pain of another contraction.

While she donned blue plastic gloves to examine the tired patient, she was trying to decide if she was indeed a wicked person. Can an evil person be good and kind too, she puzzled? She had no one to ask about anything, but she knew that her personality was decent and kind except where the rapists were concerned. Talking in her head had become her norm. She recognised the reasons for this and knew that it didn't mean she was insane. She told herself to stop worrying about things and motives so much. They all deserved to die for the evil they lived by, and perhaps when they were gone, so would the persistent chatter that went on in her head.

Another contraction hit the mother to be, and she pressed the face mask firmly in place as she groaned. Heather ceased to worry about her character and motives and concentrated as she examined her patient to see how far dilated she was. A short time later, she supported a new life into the world and then set about checking that the baby was healthy. I am a decent person, she thought.

Chapter 16

As the days turned into months with no sign of her being implicated in Snake man's death, Heather began to feel that she should be able to enjoy her life. She had a career that she loved, a cherished daughter and a family that loved her. Heather felt blessed. After killing Snake man, a heavy weight seemed to have lifted from her shoulders, but she still found it challenging to join wholeheartedly in the day to day pleasures that everyone else in her circle took for granted.

Susan had no shortage of boyfriends and sometimes brought friends home, hoping to match-make, but Heather never took a shine to anyone. They all seemed to be boring, full of themselves and often downright self-centred, in her opinion. Lack of empathy and trust were a result of her tainted past.

Heather had booked annual leave in June, and she decided to take Sienna to stay at the family caravan kept on a small site by the River Severn at Stourport. Susan had offered to accompany them and drive back to Birmingham for her appointments when necessary, but Heather had declined as she was looking forward to spending time on her own with her daughter. Susan was concerned that Heather would have too much time to dwell on the past. She told herself not to be like a mother hen, and as she waved her sister and niece off, she pushed her fears into the background where she hoped they would stay put.

However, as they were leaving, Yvonne held Heather tightly to her and said, ‘I don’t care whether you want us to or not, my love, your Dad and I are coming down to visit and perhaps stay overnight in the middle of the week. Is that okay?’

‘Of course, it is.’ Heather hugged her mother back. They finished the walk to the car with their arms around each other. Yvonne opened the rear door and leaned in to plant yet another kiss on her granddaughter’s soft cheek.

‘You come with us,’ Sienna said clearly, grinning broadly with excitement, ‘we are going to the caraban.’

‘I would love to come, darling, but you’ll have a good time with Mommy, and we’ll see you later in the week. Okay?’ Sienna nodded, and Yvonne blew more kisses as Heather drove away.

Hardly a day had passed when Sienna hadn’t seen her grandparents at some point, and she loved them every bit as much as they loved her. Yvonne knew that Sienna would miss her and wondered how she would feel if, and perhaps when, Heather chose to make a life away from her family. She shrugged and went into the house. It hasn’t happened yet, so stop worrying about something that Heather has shown no sign of doing.

Heather was well aware that her parents and her sister still worried about her mental health, and she knew that they found it very hard to believe that she could be undamaged by her trauma. She hoped that she’d never let them see just how damaged she was.

As they travelled south, Sienna nodded off in her car seat, allowing Heather a rare moment of peace. Her mind started freewheeling, meandering along its usual pathways. She pictured the look of surprise and horror on Snake man's face as the blade slid across his throat. She felt glad that he knew he was going to die. She continued to feel no remorse for her deed and remained astounded that it had been so easy to carry out. She had expected to have nightmares and some regrets, but there had been almost no adverse reaction. Night after night, she slept soundly in her bed, only waking to tend to Sienna's needs or when the alarm clock prodded her into starting her day.

She shook her head and concentrated on the busy road. She'd always loved going to the site when she was a little girl and was pleased that her parents still owned a caravan. It was more luxurious than the one they'd had when she was a child; it had a bathroom, not just a porta-potty in a cupboard by the door. She smiled at the memory of herself refusing to sit on the seat in case she fell into the yawning depths.

When they arrived, Heather unbuckled Sienna from her seat and put her gently down on the ground with the firm instruction not to move away. She nodded and began to make a daisy chain while Heather settled in, then made a pot of tea and buttered toast, which they ate while sitting on the wooden deck. She gazed at the familiar view across the fence and the pathway that bordered the site.

'Look, Sienna,' she said, pointing out the wide river and the way the water flowed lazily, creating swirling green eddies caused by detritus caught underwater. Crosscurrents were throwing up occasional waves that shone where the sunlight tickled them into bright ripples. The image invoked peace, but it shattered as the clamour that usually went on in her head started up.

She shook her head vigorously; I am not going to think about you bastards, she told the images of her rapists and allowed her eyes to take in the greenery and the clean air to penetrate her soul. This is my holiday with my daughter, and I am going to enjoy it.

For the first time in many months, Heather felt utterly calm. She enjoyed taking Sienna on long walks into Stourport and sometimes further up the river as far as Lincomb lock. They usually lingered by a small, white bridge and quietly watched shoals of chub and dace swimming through the crystal-clear water. On one of their walks, Heather had thrown the keys to the van where she had killed Snake man, as far out into the river as she could. Her first copper bracelet later joined them. It felt like a confirmation of his death. Her eyes followed its arc as it twisted with the sunshine reflecting off its polish until it barely broke the surface of the calm river.

She wasn't lonely; Sienna was a bright child, and Heather enjoyed teaching her the names of the wildflowers and insects that they discovered. They ate many of their meals outdoors and went strawberry picking at a farm on the other side of Hartlebury Common. They filled a punnet with the berries, giggling as some went into their mouths rather than the basket. Heather noticed other pickers wiping smears from their mouths before their strawberries got weighed. There aren't many things in life that are free, Heather thought with a grin as she wiped Sienna's mouth, then her own on a paper handkerchief.

On Wednesday, Yvonne and Bob arrived early in the afternoon to find Heather happier than they'd seen her in a long time. Sienna was playing in a small paddling pool just outside the van, and as she saw them, she screamed with excitement, then flung herself into her grandparents' arms – ignoring the fact that she was wet. Her adventures spilt out of her mouth and had them entranced with her stories and her appearance.

She'd spent each day running about in a sunsuit, and her skin had become a lovely golden brown.

'How beautiful she is,' Yvonne whispered to her husband after they all turned in early because Sienna hadn't yet learned that grown-ups needed to sleep later than she did.

Back home again, facing the reality of her life, Heather once more found that she frequently questioned herself: was she wicked, or was she insane? How could she carry on as though nothing dreadful had happened in the last three years? There were no answers. She still didn't think she was either wicked or insane but didn't know how she could judge herself. Perhaps the torture that they'd put her through had unhinged her mind, she sometimes thought. She tried to keep such unsettling notions from tormenting her, but it was impossible. She was finding it difficult to come to terms with the fact that Ugly still lived whatever life he had carved out for himself. She was determined to wait a full twelve months before she took his life. She knew that it was the only sensible thing to do, but to her mind, he was the one that deserved to die the most, and she wanted it to happen now. She comforted herself by remembering that while she couldn't carry out her plan right away, there were things that she could do.

She had resisted looking at the rapists' names and addresses since she'd stuffed the paper into her backpack and later hidden it under the lining in her fitted wardrobe. She'd carefully returned the scalpel, then disposed of the tape and gloves in a bin designed to take clinical waste at the hospital, but she still hadn't glanced at the paper. She wanted to avoid any knowledge that might encourage her to act hastily – she had too much to lose. She didn't even know if Snake man had told her the truth before she cut his throat. She thought that he had, but there was only one way to find out for sure. She would have to locate the addresses and try to identify the evil bastards. She was confident that she'd recognise them, even allowing for the passage of time.

Heather left the house and jogged round to the gym where she was now a well- known figure. Her run wasn't pleasant; a chilly wind blew directly into her face as she trod carefully to avoid piles of wet leaves that covered some of the pavement making it hazardous to put her feet down hard. Heather felt glad that the gym wasn't very far from her home. She was tired after working three days in a row and not getting very much sleep because Sienna didn't seem to want to settle through the night at the moment. But withdrawal symptoms plagued her under four times a week – her Mom called it her second home. She still hadn't become socially engaged with the other users, but at least she now knew some of the regulars by name and was greeted in a friendly enough fashion.

Heather's body ached as she contemplated the dreadful possibility that some other girl had suffered while she was taking so long to kill the rapists. There had been nothing reported, but perhaps it just hadn't reached the papers; her attack was kept quiet. It didn't mean that Ugly and Driver and even Snake man before she'd killed him hadn't continued to rape and abuse other girls. It sickened her to contemplate that it would be her fault.

As Heather lay on her back, with her shoulders raised using the bench press to improve her upper body strength, she decided that on her next day off, she would visit the address that she had for Ugly. It was eight months since she'd assisted Snake man on his way to hell, and now she needed to look at the second rapist's name even though she shuddered at the thought. All her feelings of hatred and desire for revenge burned like acid eating into her soul.

Chapter 17

Heather's hands shook as she unearthed the crumpled piece of paper that she'd hidden. She held it in her hand and then replaced the lining of the wardrobe. She sat on the floor; her knees pulled up to her chest. Allowing the pounding of her heart to steady, she looked at the names and addresses written there. It was her writing, but it was an unfamiliar scrawl. She read Paul Graham and the address of a house very near to Trittiford Mill. She knew the park well. She had jogged there with Lucy when they were young and several times recently.

Lucy lived with her parents just on the other side of the River Cole. While they were at University, Heather had sometimes stayed overnight with them. They'd always woken up early to jog around the peaceful lake, enjoying the sight of the moorhens as their red beaks broke the surface of the water and listening to their raucous calls, which disturbed the silence. Thank God that I haven't accidentally bumped into him, she thought with a frisson of fear. It would be one thing to see him on her terms, but to see the ugly bastard unexpectedly would have been another matter.

The paper fell from her hand and lay ignored by her side. She continued to sit against the wardrobe while the picture and bodily smell, as Ugly raped her repeatedly, assaulted her mind. Hot tears gushed from her eyes as they looked inwards at images that she tried so hard to suppress. She sobbed more than she had for many months. She grabbed her pyjama sleeve from the end of her bed and stuffed it into her mouth. Gradually, the outpouring of grief, for her shattered innocence that Ugly and the others had destroyed so cruelly ceased.

'Heather, are you okay? Shall I come up?' Her mother called anxiously from the bottom of the stairs.

Heather pulled the gag from her mouth. 'No. It's okay, Mom. I'll be alright in a minute. Just let me wash my face, and I'll be down.'

'Alright, love. Tea'll be ready in a few minutes. I love you, my daughter,' she finished quietly.

Heather heard her mother walk across the parquet floor and enter the kitchen. She held onto her toes, stood upright and walked into the bathroom then washed her face. She patted her face dry then quickly applied some cover stick to the dark patches under her red-rimmed eyes. She hadn't intended to cry like that and let everyone in the house know how distraught she was. Her mother was bound to ask her questions that she wouldn't wish to answer. She wanted to kick herself for being so stupid as to allow his ugly image to bring all the dreadful memories back to attack her once more. She shrugged her shoulders as she returned to her room and picked up the paper from the deep pink carpet. Nothing I can do about it, she thought but hoped that Sienna hadn't heard her making such a noise. She glanced at the other name on the paper and stuffed it into her pocket. Then, feeling as though she could sense it pressing hotly against her skin, she pulled it out again, flung it into a dressing table drawer then hurried down to face the music.

Yvonne took a tray of scones from the eye level oven as Heather went over to her and planted a kiss on her cheek.

‘It’s okay, Mom; I just had a silly turn. Take no notice. I’m alright now. Where’s Sienna?’

Yvonne gazed without comment at her daughter’s swollen eyes, then pointed into the garden where Sienna sat giggling in the swing while being propelled forward by her aunt. They were both bundled up in fleece jackets and wore funny hats. Susan looked up and waved, indicating the Mickey Mouse ears on her hat. She pulled a funny face and spoke to Sienna, then pointed to Heather, who was looking through a window in the conservatory doors.

Sienna let go of the sidebars and waved her arms excitedly.

‘Mommy, come here.’ Heather mimed shivering, and shook her head. She could see that Sienna was asking Susan to bring her indoors and her indulgent aunt happily complied with her request.

Heather shivered in earnest as the two of them brought the cold air in with them. Sienna ran into her mother’s arms, talking animatedly about a spider that had spun a web from one of the bushes across to her swing.

Heather felt annoyed for not listening attentively to her child as she enthused about the spider and her aunt’s bravery in transferring it further down the garden. She was still finding it difficult to clear her head of the images and smells that were plaguing her mind. The sooner the other two are disposed of, the sooner I will be able to begin to live my life. Sienna deserves a mother whose mind isn’t somewhere else when she needs her attention, she thought.

While they were having a hot drink a little while later, Yvonne said, ‘I thought that if you had no plans for today, I’d take Sienna with me to visit your Aunt Marge. I haven’t been to see her for ages, and you know she loves to see how Sienna is coming along. Would you like some time on your own? Or would you rather we stayed and kept you company?'

Heather was touched that her Mom was giving her the chance to repair her hurt – in whatever way that she felt able – without asking her any intrusive questions.

'Please take her with you. I know she'd like that.' She turned to Susan. 'Do you want to come into town with me, or perhaps go into Redditch shopping?'

Susan shook her head. 'I have an appointment at three,' she grimaced but looked pleased at the same time, 'but maybe soon. We must start our Christmas shopping. I must be getting old; Christmas seems to be coming round with alarming speed.' They all nodded in agreement and then chuckled as Sienna began to behave like a nodding dog at their feet. Heather scooped her up and played drawing a snake on her back, a game that the little girl delighted in as she guessed which of her mother's fingers dotted it.

Heather felt a pang of guilt as she'd hoped that her sister wouldn't be able to accompany her. She shook the feeling off and thought that perhaps fate had decreed that she should go to where Ugly lived now that she had a free day. Hopefully, when on his territory, she could begin to make plans for his extermination.

Feeling a touch of déjà vu, Heather parked her new, red Peugeot close to the address in Chinn Brook Road that she'd written on the paper. It was a wide road, and some of the houses looked as though they had at one time belonged to the Council, then been bought by the tenants when the possibility arose. The house she was there to see was painted white and looked maintained. She wondered if Ugly was married and pitied his wife if he was. She found it difficult to picture him as a married man house owner. She hated the thought that he'd prospered in the intervening three and a half years. She felt sure that his type of evil must have shown in his behaviour enough to prevent any woman from joining her life to his.

The house looked empty, but so did the ones either side. Perhaps this isn't where he lives, and Snake man had lied, after all, she thought. She started the car and drove towards Trittiford Mill, where she parked and went for a stroll around the serene lake. Heather was disappointed; she didn't know what she had expected to see but knew she hadn't thought it through properly. Even if he did live there, he would almost certainly be at work. She came to a bench and sat down with her gloved hands tucked underneath the arms of her sheepskin coat. She hadn't a clue how she was going to find out whether Ugly lived at that address or not. She watched the ripples blowing across the lake as the wind teased the dark green water. A little later, she began to walk briskly back to her car and looked at her watch; it was five to three. She dismissed the thought of returning to Chinn Brook Road: she didn't much fancy the idea of sitting for any length of time in such a quiet, open space. Her stomach gave a loud rumble of annoyance, and she realised that she was both hungry and thirsty. Returning home had become an attractive proposition, and she hoped that her mother and daughter would be there – she felt in need of some warmth and family love. She'd waited this long to continue with her plan; surely, she could afford to wait a little longer. She needed to think and work out the details, just as she'd done with Snake man. She indicated and pulled out into the stream of traffic.

While she drove, she decided to check out Driver's address and took a detour along Warwick Road. Opposite an art deco building that she knew had once been a cinema was the house where he supposedly lived. Windolene smeared in white circles across the bay window. Heather's heart sank.

She got out of her car, crossed the road, walked up the path and peered in at the window. She could just about view the room through a small patch that had been missed by the cleaner. There was no furniture that she could see. Deciding to take a chance that Driver wouldn't be in, she knocked on the door. A hollow, empty sound echoed back at her.

She knocked on the house next door and waited. It was eventually answered by an elderly lady who wore a long, blue, flowery dress and a black nylon wig that placed with the fringe towards the back of her head. She had made her face up with bright green eye shadow and black mascara that had smudged around her eyes. Her lips were stained red in an exaggerated bow shape that almost touched her nose. Her overall appearance was very peculiar and somewhat scary, Heather thought.

'What do you want?' Her voice was husky. It sounded as though she'd spent a lifetime wrecking her vocal cords with cheap cigarettes. She glared at Heather and started to close the door.

'I'm sorry to bother you,' Heather said, 'I thought that my friend Albert Smith lived next door, but the house is empty. Can you tell me a forwarding address please?'

'Never heard of him. The family who lived there were Pakis. I never spoke to them, but they were called Patel, I think. Don't know where they went,' she curled her lips and frowned, making her look like a bottom-feeding fish. 'Now bloody well piss orf and let me get in out of the cold.'

Heather felt sorry for the old woman who was a bigoted product of her generation and what she politely thought of as being touched. She hated the possibility that her daughter could perhaps face such prejudice one day.

She crossed the road back to her car. God knows how I'm going to find Driver, she thought, feeling sure that God wouldn't help her. But I can leave Driver until I've got rid of Ugly, and I think I know where he is.

Chapter 18

Heather stood looking down at her daughter's tousled, dark hair and gave a rueful grin as she replaced the storybook on her bedside table. She always enjoyed their quiet ten minutes bedtime together, but tonight Sienna had fallen asleep as soon as her head hit the pillow.

Shutting the bedroom door as quietly as possible, Heather crept downstairs. She stopped by the front door, where she pulled out the phone book from the cupboard in the hall and searched for Ugly by name. She fumed inwardly as it immediately jumped out at her. It had taken her a month to remember that even though their telephone number was ex-directory, many people were within its pages. Now I know that Snake man didn't lie, I need to try and find out what his day to day movements are, she thought. She rolled her eyes as she figured the possible number of hours that she would have to spend watching his house. She knew nothing about him, but she wouldn't be able to plan her strategy until she knew some basic facts. Did he live alone? Did he go to work? And, more importantly, where did he spend his evenings? She was very reluctant to give her time to this, but she had no choice; the compulsion to rid this world of his ugliness burned stronger than ever.

On reflection, she decided that the Christmas and New Year celebrations had to take precedence over her hunt for information. Her family would find her frequent absences peculiar at this time, as someone always had to be available to mind Sienna. Both Susan and their mother were willing to take care of her but nearing Christmas, there were other demands on their time. It was the time of year when everyone seemed to feel the need to have parties or visit friends, and Heather was no exception. Julie and Ben had invited her for Boxing Day, and Bridget, John and Kay wanted her to go for a meal with them, too. The more she saw of them socially, the more she liked being with them. Many of her off duty hours spent laughing and relaxing in their company made her agree to the planned meal out at a local Indian restaurant. I must be patient; she thought as she replaced the phone book. Deep in thought, she went to join her family in the sitting room.

'Glass of Chardonnay, love?' Yvonne said as Heather settled next to her on the leather sofa.

'Mm, yes please, Mom. It seemed as though the clinic would never end today. There were far too many bookings, and Bridget was off sick. I hardly had time for a cup of tea, let alone a proper lunch break.'

'That's just not good enough; I hope you complained,' Yvonne said.

Heather snorted. 'Don't be daft. Where's Susan tonight?'

'She's round at Sean's, where she is most nights lately,' Yvonne said. She handed Heather a glass of wine and then curled up in the opposite corner.

Heather thought that her mother sounded a little gloomy when she mentioned Susan's absence. It made her wonder if Susan was out most nights. She'd been so wrapped up in her day to day living that she couldn't be sure.

'Sean's nice, isn't he, Mom? You like him, don't you? Have you met any of his family yet?' Heather peered intently at her mother's face.

Yvonne's mouth started to twitch at the corners. 'And which question would you like me to answer first?' she laughed. Heather rolled her eyes to the ceiling.

Bob rustled the pages of his broadsheet and surveyed his wife and daughter over the top of half-moon glasses.

'What are you two like? Of course, your mother likes Sean. He's a very presentable young man; she's just wary in case one of you leaves home. Not that it wouldn't be about time, I'm tired of supporting you three women,' He chuckled at his sense of humour and then continued. 'Seriously though, I think that Sean may well be the man that Susan has been hoping to find. They spend every possible moment together. I wouldn't be surprised to hear she is going to cost me a fortune shortly.' He chuckled again as he disappeared behind his newspaper.

'Who rattled your cage?' Yvonne asked, but her voice held no sting as she threw the words his way and then turned to her daughter. 'To answer your questions, Heather. Yes, I do like Sean, he seems to be a very kind and generous person,' she took a deep breath, 'I met his mother when I was in the supermarket with Susan the Saturday before last. She seemed to be very pleasant too and gets on well with Susan. Perhaps they will make a go of it. I wouldn't mind. I'd like some more grandchildren while I'm still fit enough to enjoy them. But he's right as usual.' She nodded in the direction of her husband, who gave another chuckle but carried on reading, 'I shall be sad when either of you leaves home.' She took a drink then refilled her glass, holding the bottle out towards Heather, who held her hand over the top of her glass and shook her head. 'I will be happy for Susan if that's what she wants to do and you too when your turn comes but don't be in too much of a hurry.' she sighed, 'Losing Sienna will break my heart.'

'Oh, Mom, you are daft! Even if we each had homes of our own, do you think that you wouldn't always be a big part of our lives?' Heather snuggled her feet towards her mother until their bare feet made contact.

'Susan feels just the same as I do, you know.' Yvonne smiled as Heather continued to speak. 'I think we should get off this topic now. There's no point in thinking about things that may never happen – and you taught me that.' She grinned cheekily at her Mom, and they went on to talk about the young woman who lived next door who was expecting a baby.

After another small top-up of wine, Heather yawned. She kissed her parents' goodnight and then went to her bedroom, where she took the piece of paper from the dresser drawer and forced herself to look at it again. After memorising the names and addresses, Heather cautiously lit the Yankee candle that often perfumed her room with apple and cinnamon. Then she held the corner of the paper to the yellow flame. It flared and burned quickly before she transferred it into her empty water glass, where it curled up as it blackened before the flames went out. Heather didn't think that the precaution was necessary, but she preferred not to have any evidence in her room, linking her to two men who she intended to kill. After looking in on Sienna, who was sleeping soundly with her thumb, still held firmly in her mouth, Heather climbed into bed and slept soundly.

Christmas day dawned bright and crisp, and by eight o'clock, the frost, which had decorated the shrubs and trees and lay like a white blanket covering the lawn, had dissipated. After breakfast, Heather and Susan took Sienna out to the nearby park, where she always enjoyed the slides and the brightly painted animals, in the shape of a rooster and a pig, which had strong springs beneath them. Sienna bounced about with a little extra encouragement from her aunt, who had loved the same playground toys when she'd been a little girl. Heather sat on a bench and watched as Susan lifted Sienna from the pig and chased her to the rooster, causing her to scream in mock terror. Once more, Heather realised how lucky she was to have a loving and supportive sister and to have been living with her ever since she could remember.

The talk that had taken place in the sitting room about a month ago returned to Heather; it wouldn't only be her parents who would be sad if Susan married and left home, she too would feel bereft. She supposed that, at twenty-six years of age and with her outgoing personality, it was probably going to happen sooner rather than later. I'd better get used to it. Hopefully, she won't be going off to live in America or Australia, she thought. Her peaceful ruminations ended as the two people who she loved unconditionally ran back to her and insisted that shc get off her bench and jog home with them. It amused Sienna to hold a hand of each of the adults as they lifted her boot-clad feet above the ground so she could pretend that she was jogging as well.

The family dinner was, as usual, a merry and sparkling affair. Yvonne had built the table centre higher than usual as there were only five of them sitting down. Sienna was becoming very well behaved when placed in her chair between Susan and her grandmother. They were all very proud of her, and she was only too happy to be the centre of attention.

They listened to the Queen's speech before Julie and Ben arrived, followed by Bridget and then Lucy a couple of minutes later. Susan had left after dinner was cleared away and gone to fetch Sean and another friend called Brian. They arrived a little after five o'clock, and the evening was off to a great start. Susan and Julie had volunteered to be the designated drivers and drank soft drinks, so the others were able to have a real drink, as Ben called it.

About eight o'clock, Susan picked up a glass from the buffet table and clinked a spoon against it, making a melodic, but demanding sound.

When they had everyone's attention, a pink-faced Sean said in a firm voice, 'Earlier this afternoon, I asked Susan to become my wife, and she has said yes. I hope you'll all be very happy for us.' His face had taken on deepening shades of pink while he spoke. He took a black velvet box from his pocket and slipped a diamond and sapphire engagement ring on Susan's finger. They kissed while everyone clapped, and congratulations resounded around the room. Susan held out her left hand and proudly showed off the ring.

'Erm,' Bob pretended to cough. 'Excuse me.' He made his way between their guests and shook Sean's hand, and then kissed his daughter. 'I'm not too surprised – it's about time someone took her off my hands.' Everyone laughed, including Yvonne, who poured herself another drink a few minutes later and then plonked down in an armchair.

It wasn't long before Susan found her and kissed her cheek. 'I know what you're thinking,' she whispered, 'but don't worry, I won't go far away.'

Yvonne smiled ruefully and said, 'Just ignore me being silly, I know you won't – I'm pleased for you, my darling – it'll just take time to sink in.'

Chapter 19

Heather parked her car next to her friend's grey BMW and gazed in admiration at the house that Ben and Julie had bought early that summer. Detached, it had large bay windows set either side of the closed-in porch. The mellow red brickwork gave the house a warm, welcoming appearance. When they had first bought it, there had been little in the way of structural repairs needed. Heather was now looking forward to seeing the improvements that her friends had made.

As she waited, after ringing the doorbell and hearing the chimes echo through the hallway, Heather glanced around the well-tended front garden that was Julie's baby. Shrubs and graceful trees surrounded it with a sculpted lawn at the side of the drive. Narrow borders were colourful with winter pansies. Heather knew little about gardening, but she thought how pretty the pale blue and yellow splashes of colour were against the green background of the grass.

The heavy oak door opened, and a ruddy-faced Julie stepped out and hugged her friend. 'Good, you're here.' She drew Heather into their brightly lit hall. 'We've another guest who should be here soon.'

Heather hung her coat in the closet and then followed Julie into the kitchen. She perched on a breakfast bar stool while

Julie put the finishing touches to a batch of mince pies by dredging them with icing sugar.

'Mm! They look good, and something smells wonderful.'

Julie grinned. 'I hope you're hungry. I've cooked far too much for the four of us. Ben had to go and look in at the hospital, but he'll be back soon, and then we can sit down.'

Heather nodded. 'I'm famished ...' Chimes sounded.

'Will you get that?' Julie asked.

Heather opened the door and raised her eyebrows when she saw who stood on the step. 'Hello, what are you doing here?'

'Same as you, I expect. It's nice to see you too.' Dr Gordon replied with a wide grin that emphasised his smile lines. He stepped into the hall and hung his coat in the closet. Heather thought that the doctor was just as much at home as she was. 'Where is everyone?' he asked.

Heather shut the door and stood with her mouth open, gazing at him as though she'd seen a ghost; then she remembered her manners. 'It is nice to see you; it was just a surprise, that's all. I didn't know that you knew Ben and Julie.'

'I've known Ben for many years. Shall we go in and find them?' he said and turned away.

Heather moved quickly; she felt foolish as she went back into the warm kitchen. She thought that perhaps he wasn't such a nice guy; after all, he was undoubtedly sarcastic. She half wished that she hadn't agreed to spend the day with her friends.

Julie clapped her hands together to remove traces of icing sugar.

'Hello, Stephen. Glad you could come. Ben will be here in a minute; he had to go to the hospital. And I think that you know Heather already, don't you?' She didn't wait for an answer and avoided Heather's eyes as she indicated both red and white wine and held out two glasses. 'What would you both like to drink?'

'White, please,' Stephen said and glanced at Heather.

'Yes, white for me too.'

Heather poured the drinks for them, and Julie carried on with her baking. Heather smiled as she called him Dr Gordon in a voice loaded with sarcasm. She felt hijacked by her friend who'd set them up.

'His name's Stephen,' Julie said. 'Why don't you take your drinks into the sitting room and let me concentrate on finishing up here?'

Obediently they both went into the other room and sat in silence until Ben let himself into the house a couple of minutes later wiping his feet noisily on the doormat. The sound brought his wife into the hall. She kissed his cheek, playfully patted his bum and told him that dinner would be about ten minutes. Then she hurriedly returned to the kitchen where the air was laden with tantalising cooking smells.

Ben greeted Stephen and Heather, poured himself a whisky, then sank with a tired sigh onto the sofa. The two men began to discuss the reasons why Ben had had to go into work, so Heather excused herself and went to see if Julie needed a hand.

She didn't. But Heather perched herself on the barstool. 'And what do you think you are doing, eh?'

'What does it look like? I'm making your dinner.' Julie tried to keep a straight face, but she couldn't stop grinning as she caught her friend's eye and tried to feign innocence.

Heather snorted derisively then laughed. Aware that Julie was only trying to bring some more happiness into her friend's life because she had been so happy since her marriage. Heather could never share her reasons for not wanting to become entangled with anyone. If she married, or even if she became deeply involved with someone, they would almost certainly want to know her movements, and they would be entitled to have a say in her life. So far today, Dr Gordon or Stephen, as she now had to call him, wasn't someone that she would like to get to know any better. She wondered if he'd known that she would also be a guest when he'd agreed to be here.

Sipping her wine, as Julie moved purposefully around her kitchen, Heather said, 'Did Stephen know that I would be here today?'

'Yes, of course, he did. Why do you suppose he came? Now shut up and take the veg through to the dining room, please,' Julie said with a grin.

Heather picked up a dish of julienne carrots, another piled high with broccoli florets and made her way into the dining room. Julie followed, carrying a leg of pork that would have fed a family of four for a week. The table setting would compete with Moms, Heather thought and complimented Julie as they all sat down and tucked in with enthusiasm.

The conversation was somewhat stilted at first. Heather and Stephen concentrated on putting forkfuls of food into their mouths and avoided looking at each other. They both refused another glass of wine as they were driving but changed their minds when Julie pressed them.

'Just a small one won't put you over the limit by the time you have to leave,' she said. Then proceeded to half fill their wine glasses without waiting for permission.

'Bully,' Heather said, immediately reaching for her glass and taking a sip. Stephen followed suit shortly afterwards. As the alcohol worked its magic, the atmosphere lightened, and conversation flowed smoothly between the four.

When the meal finished, Ben and Stephen volunteered to clear up and load the dishwasher, and Julie gratefully sank back into a comfortable chintzy chair in the conservatory. Heather joined her friend, and they talked desultorily about the garden and Sienna's progress until suddenly, Julie jumped up and went to sit beside Heather on the sofa. She grasped her friend's hands, and Heather was amazed at the change in her expression. She looked excited, her face radiant with happiness as she said, 'I was going to wait until Ben was here too, but I can't, I'll have to tell you, or I'll burst ... I'm pregnant.'

'Whoo, whoo.' Heather became as excited as Julie looked. 'Oh, congratulations! I know how much you wanted to start a family. I bet Ben is over the moon.' She leaned over and kissed her friend on her flushed cheek. 'I would never have guessed. Mind you, your top is loose. How many weeks are you?'

Julie lifted her blouse and showed Heather her bump. 'I'm fourteen weeks,' Julie smirked proudly. 'Ben can't wait to be a dad. He's hoping it's going to be a boy so he can take him to see Aston Villa play. I've told him not to be sexist as girls follow football clubs too.' She laughed. 'We've opted not to know what sex the baby is – we want a surprise.'

'I'm so pleased for y ...'

'What's all the noise?' Ben asked as they returned to join the women. Heather and Julie became silent as the men entered the room.

Ben grinned boyishly at his wife, whose cheeks were still glowing. 'You've already told her, haven't you, and without me too.' He put on a sad expression but spoilt the effect as he laughed and said to Heather, 'What do you think, eh, aren't we clever?'

'Very clever. It's wonderful news. Congratulations.' Heather jumped up and kissed his cheek.

'What am I missing here?' Stephen sounded bemused as he sat opposite Ben and crossed his long legs. He shuffled back in the armchair and ran his fingers through his spiked, fair hair.

'My turn,' Ben said with a grin at Julie, 'we are pregnant.' He gave Stephen an even bigger smile.

'Congratulations and about time too!' He stood, hugged Julie and shook Ben's hand, then sat down again as he said, 'I thought you'd never give me a Godchild.'

'We'd love it if you'd both be Godparents,' Julie said, looking from Stephen to Heather. They both chorused their willingness, but as she spoke, Heather doubted if she should, or could, inflict their child with a murderess for a Godmother.

Stephen broke into her dour thoughts by asking if anyone fancied a walk. 'Yes, I need to walk some of that lovely dinner off,' Heather said. She stood up, expecting them all to follow suit.

Stephen stood, but Julie and Ben made excuses not to accompany them. To Heather's annoyance, she was soon outside, walking briskly with Stephen. She found herself watching his breath leave his mouth in white puffs, like smoke that quickly dissipated in the cold air.

They walked in silence for a short time, then Stephen said, 'C'mon, I'll race you to the main road and back here again.' He had no idea how fit she was and thought he would easily match, if not beat her.

Heather stopped walking and looked thoughtful, then she said, 'Okay, ready, steady go!' She then took off like a bullet out of a gun, leaving Stephen completely wrong-footed. He sprinted as fast as he could after her, and as Heather passed him on her way back before he'd reached the end of the road, she grinned in triumph at him.

By the time he arrived back at their starting point, Heather was waiting for him just inside the driveway. Stephen didn't know whether he was mad at her or if he admired her more than he had before.

Heather watched him patiently as he recovered his breath. Then, to his surprise, she linked her arm in his, and without speaking, they entered their friend's house together.

Chapter 20

It was ten o'clock. Heather had been twiddling her thumbs and pretending to read a map book for the last half hour while sitting in her car almost opposite Ugly's house. She'd figured that Saturday was possibly a day when he didn't work and had hoped to begin tracking his movements while she was supposed to be in town shopping. Yvonne was minding Sienna, so there was no hurry to get back, but Heather was feeling anxious and impatient. She'd wondered if she still felt the same intense hatred as the months wore on, but no speculation was needed. Hatred for him again boiled in her brain. She felt desperate to kill the piece of filth who had abused her more than either of the two others.

An hour passed, she felt stifled by the confines of her car – she needed exercise. Missing her early morning session at the gym always made her tense and irritable. She decided to drive to Trittiford Mill and go for a jog around the lake.

As she turned her car around and drove back past Ugly's house, she glimpsed the outline of a figure through his window. Startled, she braked. The car skidded on a patch of ice. Her heart thudded wildly. Even though she controlled the skid by steering into it, her bumper touched gently against the bumper of an oncoming car. It was fortunate that the driver of the other car had slowed almost to a standstill as he saw her car skid.

He pulled into the kerb, extricated himself from his car and went to see if she was alright. Heather, too, pulled her car into the side of the road, allowing the traffic that was building up behind them to continue their journeys. She got out and assured him that she was merely shaken up. She thanked him for his concern as they walked around both cars.

He shook his head. 'No real damage to either car, love. I don't think we need to exchange details, do you?'

Heather barely heard him; she was so upset. Then, as she turned her head, she saw that Ugly was standing in his gateway, looking curiously in their direction. Heather's pulse raced – what if he recognised her? She told herself not to be so stupid.

'Oh, that's great, thank you.' She couldn't wait to get away from there.

'That's okay, love. This icy weather's a nightmare to drive in – I've had a couple of near-misses in my life. You did well not to panic. We might both have been in trouble. Are you sure you're okay?'

Heather thanked him again and ducked down into her car. She drove cautiously homeward. Nearing the gym and needing to calm down, she went in. An hour later, she felt serene enough to return to her daughter and behave as though nothing untoward had occurred.

Seeing Ugly again had scared her far more than she liked to admit, even to herself. It strengthened her determination. He was evil. She didn't yet know how she would murder him but was positive that she would. And it would be as soon as she could devise a plan. She hated the thought of seeing him even once more, but at least she now knew for sure where he lived.

'Hello, love.' Yvonne looked up from the yellow blanket that she was crocheting and surveyed her daughter's unkempt appearance. 'You don't look as though you've been shopping.'

Her mother's raised eyebrows made Heather laugh. 'I needed the exercise more than shopping and stayed there much longer than I intended. Has Sienna been okay?'

'She's always good. I don't think she knows how the terrible twos are supposed to behave.' she laughed. 'Mind you; she's always had enough of us to love and be with her, hasn't she? So I don't suppose she's had much chance to be naughty. She has a nice nature anyway. Both you and Susan did too – you had your moments – but you were usually amenable and well behaved. I see some other children out and about who are dreadful – I don't know how their mothers cope.' Yvonne put her work down and walked past her daughter into the kitchen. 'Do you want a cuppa now? Or are you going to have a shower first? Susan will be back with Sienna soon. They've only gone to the village.'

'I need to shower, and then I'll make us some lunch if you like?'

'Mm, please.'

Heather ran upstairs where she stood for some time under the hot water before beginning to wash her hair. She thought how adept she'd become at lying to her mother and others, something she'd never have done before being raped. Shame left her, knowing that the lies would continue until the other two monsters were dead. She prayed that her family would never find out what she'd done. She didn't know how they could forgive her – but she excused herself. Only she knew what she had suffered.

Heather sang quietly to herself and tried to clear her mind of all the evil that had accumulated there. She studied her short hair in the mirror as she wielded her brush. It was her natural colour again, and she idly wondered if Stephen found it attractive. Thoughts of him began to replace the sickening ones she'd been harbouring. A tingling flush spread over her body as sensual images formed in her mind.

Heather had begun to like Stephen very much towards the end of the evening at Ben and Julie's. Then when she'd been on duty with him on New Year's Eve, as the clock struck twelve, he had kissed her and whispered Happy New Year. Heather had returned his kiss, and more than a touch of desire had flooded through her body. She was looking forward to their next encounter, even though she couldn't allow herself to become involved with him. It struck her again that closeness was impossible for her; it would always mean a need to lie. She should never allow herself to be close to anyone. It wouldn't be fair either now – or in the future. How could anyone be expected to love someone who had killed and intended to keep on doing so? Determinedly, she dismissed her train of thought, pulled on a fresh tracksuit and went downstairs to greet her daughter.

Heather picked Sienna up and swung her round and round, making her giggle as her long ponytail brushed back and forth across her Mom's face. 'Hello, my little one. Have you had a nice time shopping?'

'Yes, Mommy. And Auntie Susan bought me ice cream – she said it was too cold to eat one.'

'And was it too cold?'

'Yes, so I didn't eat all of it. Auntie Susan finished it off for me.' Sienna blew a kiss to her aunt, then snuggled into Heather's neck. 'I missed you. You should have been with us. You could have had a too cold ice cream as well.'

‘I’m sorry, darling, but I had to be somewhere else, and you love Auntie Susan, don’t you?’

‘Yes, I do – up to the moon and back,’ Sienna said. She squirmed to be put down and ran into the kitchen, where she asked her grandmother for a drink.

‘Thanks for taking her,’ Heather said to her sister. ‘You have a wedding this afternoon, haven’t you?’

‘Mm, yes, but I wish I hadn’t. It’s so bloody cold everyone will be shivering and wanting to be indoors.’ Susan pulled a face and tossed her head as she boasted. ‘But I’ll still take the best pictures anyone could.’

‘You’re getting a big head,’ Heather said but watched with an indulgent smile as her sister stuck out her tongue and went up to her room.

She joined Sienna and her mother in the kitchen, which was scented by bunches of dried thyme and sage tied with raffia and hung near a framed picture of herbs. She felt grateful to be at home.

‘You’ll need to make arrangements with Susan and the baby-minder in two weeks love,’ Yvonne told Heather while they were eating a cheese salad lunch together. ‘I’m going to Inverness to visit your grandmother. She’s becoming too frail to travel now, so I’ve promised to spend the week there with her. Your granddad asked if you and Susan could visit too, but I told him that you couldn’t just take holidays at the drop of a hat. I know that Susan has quite a few family portrait bookings, so she won’t be able to come with me either.’ She delicately scratched at her hair and patted it into place. Heather nodded and slipped a piece of bright red tomato into her mouth. ‘I think I’ll go up on the train, I’ll enjoy the journey, but I shall probably fly back with your father. He’s flying up to join me on Friday, and then we’ll return on Sunday. Will you be able to manage without us love?' Yvonne's long fingers played with the blue crystal that hung around her neck on its gold chain.

'Oh, of course, I will, Mom. Sienna loves going to Shelly's, and she'll be glad of some extra cash. I'll just go and ring her now to make sure she's available.' Heather put down her fork and left the room. Yvonne could hear her talking to Shelly. She returned a few minutes later. 'That's all sorted, Mom. Shelly said she'll take her whenever we wish. Have you told Susan yet?' She began to eat again.

'Not yet, but she knows about the visit. I just hope that Mom isn't becoming too much for Dad to manage. She has fallen backwards recently, and the consultant has had to adjust her tablets. Seems to have helped, but Dad always has to be with her just in case. Her arthritis is terrible – I hope Lupus doesn't run in our family.' Yvonne poured herself another cup of tea and took it with her into the sitting room. Heather followed her, and they laughed at Sienna's antics as she played with her tea set and poured drinks for them both.

'I certainly hope not.' Heather's eyes narrowed as she watched her daughter. She wondered what awful diseases might be in Snake man's genetic make-up but realised that she would never know.

Chapter 21

After being away for four days, Yvonne rang to say that she would be staying in Inverness a little while longer to help her father. Susan had a few words with her, then had to dash off for an appointment. She passed the phone to Heather.

'I'm sorry, darling, I feel so torn, but your granddad needs to have a break. He's so good with your grandma, but he looks drained. Are you managing with the arrangements for Sienna alright? I know Susan's helping, but she has Sean to consider.' The line went dead for a few seconds, and Heather wasn't sure if they were disconnected until her mother's said, 'I do feel that I need to stay love, at least until the change in her medication has settled into her system and helped with the pain. She has problems sleeping too and often keeps your granddad awake.'

'Don't worry about it, Mom. We miss you, but you should stay as long as you need to. Poor Grandma and Granddad too. Please give them big hugs from us and tell them we'll visit as soon as we can.'

'Okay, love.'

'Now stop your fretting. We're all fine here. Sienna has been asking for you, and I've explained to her, but I don't think she can understand where you've gone. She's sleeping at the moment, but I'll phone you later this afternoon, and you can speak to her yourself.'

'Alright, love, I'll pass your message on. I've phoned your father at work, so he's coming up as we arranged, but he'll fly back alone. Okay then, love, I'll go now and hear from you later. Kiss Sienna from me when she wakes. Bye love ... bye.'

'Bye Mom, take care.' Heather replaced the receiver and burst into tears. She missed her mother's common-sense approach to everything and her way of solving any problems. Heather felt as though she had received a blow.

She brushed her tears away and decided that she must be mad. She could kill one man and be planning to kill another two without shedding a tear, but she was now crying because her mother wasn't coming home when she had expected her to. She gave a sardonic laugh and made her way into the kitchen to make a cup of tea. As she plugged the kettle in, she thought, ah, tea, the British panacea. She smiled, and her mood lightened.

She took her magic potion into the sitting room and began to relax as she drank. Her thoughts turned to Stephen, as they frequently did these days. She'd only worked one shift with him since New Year, and they'd been too busy to spend much time talking. But Heather thought if he asked her out on a date again, she would probably say yes even though she believed that she shouldn't. Her thoughts were pleasant by the time her daughter woke from her nap. Sienna talked to her Grandma on the phone and seemed to understand why she couldn't return home.

'I miss you, Grandma,' she said. After a couple of minutes, she handed the phone back to Heather.

Heather was glad that the sun shone next morning, and she was able to take Sienna out to the local park and play for a while before she took her to her childminder and prepared herself for a night shift.

Later that night, Heather handed a mug of coffee to John. 'Where are your family from originally?'

It was two in the morning, and for the last four hours, they'd been assisting a patient while she gave birth to twin boys. They were feeling the strain and glad that there were enough midwives on duty for once to enable them to have the break that they were entitled to but were often unable to take.

'Guess.' John raised his eyebrows and grinned at her curiosity. They'd been friends and colleagues for over twelve months and occasionally had a drink after their shift finished, but it was the first time that Heather had shown any interest in his personal life.

'Oh, I can't,' she put her head to one side and surveyed him intently, 'Jamaica?'

'Nearly right. But I was born in Brixton,' he smiled. 'Not a bad guess though really. My parents emigrated from Jamaica in nineteen fifty-four and settled in London where they were needed. They later moved to Birmingham to be by other families who had come here to work on the railways. I was brought up in Handsworth and still live there with my partner Sam. He's a great bloke, you'll have to meet him.'

'I'd like that,' Heather said. She sipped her coffee. 'Have you been together long?'

'About three years. Sam would like to meet you, too. I've told him that we occasionally have a drink together. What about this Saturday? Come to dinner if you aren't on duty. And bring Sienna too – we'll have a little early celebration for her birthday. She's going to be three now, isn't she? I remember you told me a couple of weeks ago that you'd bought her a card matching game. Can't say I know what you mean, but I'm no technological genius or baby toy expert. What d'you say, you up for it?'

'Mm, I'd like to meet your Sam, and Sienna behaves most of the time, so thank you, kind sir,' they both grinned, 'we'd love to accept your invitation. What time?'

'How about coming around three? We'll have dinner at six o'clock – we'll eat early, so Sienna doesn't become too tired. Is that okay?'

Heather smiled and nodded. John wrote his address on a page from his scribble pad which she tucked into her pocket as they returned to the ward.

Although Heather was beginning to feel that she had things to look forward to in her life, she continued to fret that she'd no time to try and understand Ugly's daily movements. Susan was kind enough to mind Sienna whenever she was free, but her reputation had spread, and she worked long hours even though she had cancelled her delivery service. Sean was happy to babysit with her sometimes, but Heather thought she shouldn't ask too often.

To use time wisely, she curtailed her visits to the gym and used the time to go to Chinn Brook Road. She'd managed on two frustrating occasions to park her car around midday just a few houses away from where Ugly lived, but there had been no sign of him. She concluded that she needed to be there in the evening – perhaps then she might spot him either when he returned from work or going out at night. She had to be patient, as she knew it would be impossible to be there at that time for at least another two weeks. The time would go by quickly enough, so she resolved to enjoy her work, her daughter and her friends for the present.

On Saturday, when Heather and Sienna had arrived at John and Sam's home, they found that both men had gone out of their way to ensure that they enjoyed themselves. Heather had been encouraged to put her feet up, literally onto the couch, while Sam and John sat on the floor playing games with Sienna. Later, John had refused Heather's help preparing dinner while Sam put on some music and began teaching Sienna some dance steps that she quickly picked up. Heather could feel her eyes starting to shut as she relaxed in the warm atmosphere.

'C'mon, lazy bones! It's dinner time.' shook Heather's shoulder gently. She opened her eyes, sat up quickly and stared around, unsure where she was for a minute.

'C'mon, Mommy. I'm hungry, and I've been having fun while you've been fast asleep.' Sienna tugged at her mother's arm.

Heather got to her feet with a look of chagrin on her flushed face. 'I'm so sorry. I don't know how I could have been so rude.' She bit her lip as the two men laughed until she saw the funny side too. 'I need the bathroom. Do you want to come with me, Sienna?'

'No, I've been, Mommy. John gave me a little stool to stand on just like we have at home. And I've washed my hands too.' She held out her hands for inspection.

'She's been a perfect girl, haven't you?' Sam said.

Sienna nodded vigorously. 'Yes, but I want some dinner now. So hurry up please, Mommy.'

John was already carving a roast chicken when Heather returned. She gazed around their dining room while she ate and admired the tasteful decor. Pastel shades of mauve complimented a picture of sweet peas which adorned the chimney breast. The meal was delicious, and afterwards, John showed her around the rest of the house. It was obviously their pride and joy – everywhere was bright and looked loved.

Sam worked for a company that designed computer software. Heather knew little about technology. He offered to set a computer up in her home.

'That's very kind of you, but I don't think that I'd have any use for one.'

After talking to Sam for a while about its use, she changed her mind and gratefully accepted for Sienna's sake. Sam said firmly that every home would eventually find that they needed one. Heather shook her head in disbelief but wondered if he could be right.

As Heather strapped Sienna into her car seat, the two men brought a big teddy bear with golden fur from the house and put it into her arms. 'Now please look after Fred,' John said, 'he told us that he wanted to come home with you.'

Sienna squealed with delight and hugged the bear tightly as she kissed its nose. Heather thanked her two friends for their kindness, saying it was her turn next.

She couldn't remember when she'd had a more enjoyable afternoon and evening. As she drove away, Heather pondered why they were so lovely and other men so evil. Not all men are vile; she reminded herself thinking of Stephen and her father. Thoughts of Stephen continued to impinge on her consciousness even when she tucked Sienna up in bed with Mr Fred.

Just before her eyes closed, Sienna said, 'I love Uncle John and Uncle Sam, Mommy. Can we go to their house again?'

'I'm sure we can, and they will stay our friends and visit here too, my darling.' She shut the door and walked along the landing to her room. Stephen disappeared from her mind as she began to scheme once more.

Chapter 22

Heather continued to retch after vomiting onto the grass verge surrounding the lake in Trittiford Mill. Lucy put her arm around her friend's shoulders and held her. 'Whatever's the matter with you, love?' Sienna began to sob as she watched her mother's strange behaviour. Lucy quickly released Heather and lifted Sienna out of the pushchair. They walked a little way along the lake to where mallards were diving for morsels of food. Entertained briefly by the ducks, Sienna stopped crying, but she soon looked back at her mother. Heather was now wiping her mouth on a tissue she'd taken from the bag attached to the pushchair.

Sienna tugged at Lucy's hand. 'I want to go to Mommy.'

'Come on then. I'm sure Mommy's better now.' Lucy ran after Sienna, who had managed to jerk her hand free and was running back to Heather as fast as her legs would take her.

Heather picked her up and Sienna gently stroked her mother's face. 'It's okay. I've just got a tummy upset, love. I feel better now. Let's get you into your pushchair, and we'll go back to Auntie Lucy's, eh?' Sienna nodded and began to climb back in.

'You okay?' Lucy asked.

'Sorry. I must have scared you both- it was so sudden. I don't know what came over me. Let's go back – I could do with a drink, my mouth feels awful.' Heather looked doleful as she wiped her tongue on a clean tissue. She dropped both tissues into a bin as they passed.

As they walked, Heather said, 'I'm sorry, Lucy, but I think that perhaps we shouldn't stay for lunch. I still feel a bit queasy. Are you okay to come with us to the Sea Life Centre for Sienna's birthday tomorrow? John and Sam are coming, and I'm sure you'll like them.' Heather ran her fingers across her forehead, 'They're fun and very kind.'

'I'm looking forward to it, but are you sure you'll be well enough?' Lucy's look of concern tweaked Heather's conscience as she swigged water from the bottle that she kept in her car. She knew what had caused her to vomit, but it wasn't something that she could tell Lucy about.

'I feel fine. It was probably the sausages that I had for breakfast. I'll give you a ring first thing in the morning just in case, but I want to see Sienna's face when she knows what her Birthday treat is. I'm glad that you can come with us. She'll be excited that you're all there to make her birthday special. Are you going to be able to join us afterwards for tea? Susan and Sean will be there too.' Heather said. They reached her car and stowed the pushchair in the boot.

After Heather dropped Lucy home, she forced herself not to think about anything. She listened to Sienna's chatter, and they sang her favourite song, "Follow the Yellow Brick Road." Heather knew her Mom wasn't due back from Scotland for another few days, but she wished that she was already home. Another urge to vomit gripped her as she let herself into the empty house. She took Sienna from her pushchair, went into the kitchen, grabbed a bottle of water from under the countertop, and then lifted Sienna onto the surface beside her while she gulped the water greedily.

'Mommy's tired, Sienna. Would you like to come and have a nap with me?' Sienna nodded. As soon as she had a drink of milk, they went and lay on Heather's bed, where she covered them with a blanket. Sienna quickly fell asleep, but as soon as her daughter became quiet, Heather allowed herself to relive the scene at the park that had caused her stomach to clench violently and relieve her of her breakfast. She had recognised his hateful face as he came towards them and sped past without a glance in their direction. He wore a dark tracksuit, very much like the one that Heather often wore when jogging while the weather was cold. He was even uglier than she recalled, but his face was etched deeply into her brain.

It had only been ten o'clock on Friday morning. She would never have imagined that he, of all people, should suddenly appear before her eyes. The shock had brought a rush of painful cramps into her belly. The vomiting had nothing to do with sausages, but she couldn't explain to anyone the feelings of revulsion and hatred that swept through her as she set eyes on him.

Snake man's appearance had caused her heart to race, but she didn't react so violently in response to seeing him, as she had done when she recognised, Ugly. Heather had been terrified when she caught sight of him. He hadn't seen her or heard her voice – he'd been engrossed in listening to whatever was playing through his headphones – but it had shaken Heather to the core. How was she ever to muster enough courage to kill him when one look could cause her body to respond so forcefully?

It took her a while to remember that she was no longer the same person that she'd been when the attack had taken place. She reassured herself, once again, that she was fit and strong and knew how to defend herself. She would be physically capable of overpowering him, if necessary. You will be able to do it, she told herself firmly as a glimmer of a plan entered her mind.

Firstly, she needed to find out when and where he jogged. Heather doubted it had been a one-off occasion when she saw him; once people took up jogging, they often became addicted. She could only hope that he was no exception. She told herself to make damn sure that the next time she saw him, it would be when she was mentally prepared. Did he go jogging before he went to work? Or in the evening? Or was it only at the weekend, she wondered? Without further thought, she drifted into a doze beside her daughter.

She woke to find Sienna kissing her face with gusto and laughing at her mother's wrinkled nose as she wiped away the wet with her sleeve.

'I'm thirsty, Mommy. Can we go down now?' Sienna said. She rolled off the bed and trotted to the door. She could open the door now, so Heather obligingly followed her example, and they went down into the kitchen.

'Do you remember what day it is tomorrow, love?'

'Mm. Yeah, it's my birthday, and we're going to see the fishes.' Sienna danced into the hall and back again, making Heather laugh proudly at her daughter. She was a gift from heaven that she'd treasured since her birth. Heather shuddered at the thought that one day Sienna would ask what had happened to her father. She didn't regret killing him. Sienna wasn't his child. Her daughter was surrounded by people who loved her, and Heather knew that she always would be no matter what the future held.

'Would you like to help me make some cakes and dips towards your birthday tea? We can put the cakes in the tin and the dips in the fridge.'

'Yes, and can we eat some for our tea tonight? I'm hungry now.' Sienna's bottom lip trembled, and she began to cry.

'Whatever …' Heather realised with dismay that when they arrived home, she hadn't given her daughter any lunch. 'Oh, my darling! I'm sorry. We forgot to have any lunch, didn't we? I'm a terrible Mommy, aren't I?' She rapidly shook cornflakes into a bowl, added milk and a sprinkle of sugar then pushed them across the counter to her daughter, who began to eat hungrily.

After a couple of mouthfuls, Sienna said, 'You're the best Mommy in the world. I love you up to the sky and back again.' She dipped her spoon back into her cereal as Heather came around the counter and gave her a resounding kiss.

'I love you too, my darling,' she said, reaching to steal one of Sienna's cornflakes, causing her to shout playfully.

Heather still felt a little nauseous and made some toast for herself before gathering the ingredients together to make fairy cakes. She was glad when she heard the front door open, and Susan, who looked half-frozen, greeted them both. Heather quickly flicked the switch on the kettle.

'Mommy was sick in the park,' Sienna told her Aunt as she drank her tea.

'Were you, Heather? What's wrong? Are you poorly?' Susan asked.

Heather told her the story of the dodgy sausages. Will the lies never end, she asked herself as her daughter skipped into the conservatory where she'd left Mr Fred.

Full of concern, Susan offered to mind Sienna while Heather went for a lie-down.

Heather reached up and took a bag of flour from a cupboard. 'Thanks, sis, but I'm okay now. I've had some toast, and we had a nap when we returned from Lucy's. I want to get on with making the cakes for tomorrow, but you can help if you like, you're a better cook than me. I'm sorry that you can't come with us tomorrow. Lucy. John and Sam will be meeting us there, then coming here afterwards. I invited Stephen and Bridget, but they are on duty.'

'Oh, you invited Stephen, did you?' Susan teased her sister. Heather ignored her, but her face glowed like a beacon.

Susan donned the apron that always lived behind the kitchen door, grinning as she said, 'Well, I can come. I rang both my appointments, and they were happy to rearrange their sittings. I can't miss your birthday, can I, lovely girl?' She kissed Mr Fred on his gold-coloured nose.

Heather and Sienna beamed at her as she began to put butter and sugar into the mixing bowl.

'That's great news. I'll do the dips in a minute. Come on, darling. Let's wash our hands before we handle the food.' Sienna chuckled and hopped her way into the bathroom.

Heather always remembered Sienna's third birthday. Sienna was enthralled with the fishes. She insisted on spending much of their visit, watching the giant turtle swim past as she pressed her face against the glass. John and Sam took turns carrying her around on their shoulders and never let her out of their sight, leaving the women to enjoy the exhibits in a leisurely fashion.

When they were home again, Shelly arrived with two other small children that she minded, and Sienna's day was complete. She showed her friends her new toys that she willingly shared, except for Fred. She took the bear to John and asked him to look after it. He smiled with some satisfaction as he tucked it down behind the sofa and promised to guard it with his life.

Sean arrived in time for tea, and Yvonne rang to wish Sienna a Happy Birthday and sang to her down the phone. After tea was over, their guests departed amidst kisses and hugs from both Sienna and Heather.

Sienna had been awake for an hour after her regular bedtime, and Heather was preparing to exercise all her persuasive skills to get her daughter to call it a night when Sienna cuddled up to her favourite blanket and asked to go to bed.

'Come on then; I'm almost ready myself. Has it been a good birthday, my love?' Heather said.

Sienna nodded sleepily and headed for the stairs. Heather followed, but again Sienna fell asleep before the end of the first page of her storybook.

By ten o'clock, Heather was able to say goodnight to Susan and Sean and go to her room. She usually brushed her teeth before bed, but she skipped her routine and slept soundly through the night. She didn't remember having one thought about murder as so frequently happened during the night.

Chapter 23

Heather smiled at her mom while they shared the inevitable pot of tea in the sitting room. 'It's so good to have you home. We've missed you.'

'I never thought I'd be able to come home; it's been such a stressful time. Your grandma's so poorly, and it's sapping all your granddad's strength just trying to cope with her. He's devoted and determined that she won't have to go into a care home.' Yvonne took a deep breath; her tired face looked troubled. 'When your father flew up last weekend, the four of us had a long talk. We agreed that they should sell their house and come to live with us, where we can continue to help them.' She sighed and stood up to look out of the window at the driving rain for a minute. Then she went to sit beside her silent daughter and said, 'I'm so sorry, my darling. It will mean that you'll have to share with Sienna again; they'll need her room.' A worried frown appeared on her drawn features as she waited for Heather's reaction.

'Mom!' Heather exclaimed. She clasped her mother's hands in hers to still their distressed fluttering. 'As if I would mind. I think that's the best thing that could happen – it will be lovely to have them here with us, and we'll be one big happy family. Sienna and I will be perfectly okay in my room;

it's certainly big enough.' Heather looked thoughtful. 'What about the stairs – will Grandma be able to manage them?'

'Well, she's managing at the moment, but we'll probably have to see about a stairlift and some other adaptations to their bathroom. But let's wait and see. There's no point in rushing into things. They've yet to sell their house, and I suppose they could always change their minds. They've lived all their lives in Scotland, and it will be a significant upheaval for them. I've promised to go back and help when the house sells. Dad was going to contact the estate agent this morning, and he said he would ring later and let me know the result. Yvonne relaxed back on the sofa and yawned. 'It's good to be home. I'm more than happy to look after Mom, but I do miss my own home when I'm away.' She yawned again.

'It'll all be okay. Why don't you go up and have a nap before Dad gets home from work? I'll cook the tea – I'm not on duty until tomorrow night, thank goodness. I can't wait to see Sienna's face when she finds that you're home.'

'Where is she? At Shelly's?'

'Erm, yes, but she'll be home shortly. Shelly will drop her off on her way to the shops.'

'I'll go and freshen up. I can't wait to see my granddaughter either – she sounded so grown up on the phone.'

Later, Heather lay on her bed, thinking about her need to discover Ugly's routine before her mother had to return to Scotland. She was working a day shift the next day and wondered if her Mom would be okay to mind Sienna if she went to Trittiford Mill. Heather felt compelled to find out if Ugly jogged in the evening or if he only ran in the park on Fridays. Yvonne made it easy for her. She was more than willing to mind Sienna that evening.

Yvonne had no suspicion about her daughter's plans when Heather changed into a black tracksuit and a warm, black hoodie. She knew that the temperature dropped quite low as soon as darkness fell, and she often went for a run at night.

It was six o'clock when Heather left the house and drove to Priory Road. She intended to exercise before parking outside Ugly's house. She could see a young couple who were strolling arm in arm as they left the park. When they passed her car, they were oblivious, interested only in talking to each other.

Heather got out and began to jog along the right-hand path, which skirted around the lake in an uneven circle ending back at her car. It was dusk, and the lake looked pitch black with scarcely a ripple on its surface. Most of the trees were still bare; their branches bent in weird, twisted shapes. She could see that the deciduous bushes bordering the path were overgrown, so much so that in the distance, their leaves almost concealed the entrance to a white footbridge that crossed the river. As she passed the small island in the middle of the lake, something disturbed the sleeping ducks. A cacophony of angry or frightened squawks assaulted her ears, disturbing the tranquillity of the setting. She ignored them and continued to jog until she arrived at the bridge and looked across to Scribers Lane – then she knew for sure that she was alone. She sat on the next bench she came to and thought what a long shot it was to suppose that he would be out jogging at the time she thought he might be. After a few minutes enjoying the earthy smell of the night and the silence that was broken only by the sound of the shallow river as it flowed slowly within its narrow banks, she continued to jog back to her car, completing the circle.

Disappointed but not despondent, Heather decided that she'd have to try to be there on different days and times to be sure that he didn't jog each evening. She sighed, and her shoulders slumped as she eased herself into the driving seat and prepared to drive away. Then as she put the car into first gear, her heart skipped a beat when she saw him. Although night had fallen, what little moonlight there was, coupled with the glow from the street lighting, allowed her to be sure that it was him. He was just entering the park and moving at a steady pace on the path furthest from where she sat. He must have jogged from his house because he hadn't parked a car. She looked at her watch and noted that the time was seven o'clock. Did he do this every evening, and at this time, she wondered. A frisson of fear and excitement caused her body to flush and her breath to come in rapid, shallow gasps. As he went from her sight, she began to calm down and decided to sit tight and wait for him to reappear. She hadn't timed him, but it didn't seem to be long before he jogged past her car and started the circuit for a second time. This time he appeared to take at least ten minutes longer before he reappeared, although he didn't seem to be out of breath or jogging at a slower pace. Heather wondered why it had taken him so much longer to complete the second lap. As he left the park, he continued to jog along the road, confirming her supposition that he jogged to and from his home. He appeared to be very fit. For the first time, Heather wondered if she would be able to take him on if necessary. She sat for a few more minutes, waiting until her fear and doubts dissipated, and then drove home, hoping that she would be able to return the following night.

'I'm sorry, love, I can't. I'm going to dinner with some important clients that your father needs to entertain. I've said I'll help. Perhaps Susan will be able to mind Sienna for you.' Yvonne bit her lip. She hated having to refuse Heather's request, especially as she knew her daughter hadn't been able to keep up her fitness regime while she'd been in Scotland.

'Don't worry, Mom. It's okay. I don't have to go. I'm selfish, wanting to run two nights on the trot.'

'You aren't selfish, love, I understand, but I'll be here all the rest of the week. Sienna will be well looked after on your two nights at work, and as many of the other nights that you want to go out, I promise.'

'Thanks, Mom. I'm going up to have a shower, and then how about a glass of wine, eh?' Heather said.

'Sounds like a plan,' Yvonne said.

As Heather left the kitchen, Yvonne went to open a bottle and fetch some glasses. She'd just taken them from the cupboard when Bob arrived home.

'Whisky for you, my love?' Yvonne called and laughed aloud as she continued, 'oh, and by the way, hello.'

'Hello, dear –yes please,' Bob said. He hung his coat in the hall closet, threw his briefcase in after it, then went into the kitchen, kissed Yvonne and took the glass of whisky from her hand.

'You look all in,' his wife said. 'come and sit down and I'll massage your neck.' Bob smiled gratefully and scrunched his shoulders with pleasure as her hands worked their magic.

'Have you heard from your Dad today?' he asked.

'He phoned this afternoon; the house is on the market, and he says he can't wait now for it to sell. I'm so worried about them both, and I feel as though I should go back as soon as I'm able and stay until they can move. I'm going to talk to Heather about helping me to get the rooms sorted out – perhaps this Saturday when she's finished her night shifts.'

'It's a shame that she has to move Sienna out of her room. She hasn't long settled into it, has she?' Bob kicked his shoes off, crossed his legs and relaxed with his drink in his hand.

'Do you think we need a bigger house?' Yvonne asked slowly. She was thinking of all the upheaval that it would entail.

'No, I bloody well don't.' Bob shook his head emphatically. 'I like this house, and we'll all manage okay, and don't forget that Susan may be getting married and have her own home shortly. I know you hate the thought of it, my love, but it's going to come sooner rather than later.'

'Oh, I know, she spends an awful lot of time at Sean's parents now. Our lives are changing, and I just have to get used to it. We all do.'

'What do we all have to do?' asked Heather. She came into the sitting room with her hair still damp from the shower.

'We all have to get used to change.' Yvonne handed her daughter a glass of wine. And cheers to that, thought Heather as she nodded.

Chapter 24

The following Tuesday, a week to the day when she'd last seen Ugly jogging in the dark, Heather parked in Scribers Lane, jogged across the footbridge, then sat on the nearest bench. She could see very little until her eyes became accustomed to the gloom, and she watched the reflection of the moon dancing slowly on the still water. It had rained earlier, and the bench was wet, but her tracksuit bottoms were thick enough for her not to mind. She continued to look at her watch every few minutes hoping that Ugly would appear. After about fifteen minutes, she saw him approaching with his head down as he loped along. Heather plunged stealthily into the cover of the laurel bushes that formed a thicket the other side of the narrow path behind the bench where she'd been sitting. She could just about hear the River Cole as it sluggishly trickled a few feet further down the bank from where she was hiding. The leaves flicked cold droplets of water across her face as she pushed into their protective darkness. She was sure that he'd been too far away to have seen her, but her legs trembled nevertheless. She remained still as he passed without a glance in her direction and carried on towards Priory Road. It wasn't long before she could no longer see him, but she didn't dare to move. If he followed his previous routine, he would jog twice around the lake then pass the bushes where she was hiding for a second time. She didn't have to wait very long before she saw his tall figure in the distance. He was jogging at his usual pace. Her pulse began to race as he neared her hiding place, and then, to her surprise, instead of jogging past, he settled himself onto the bench where she'd sat while waiting for him to appear. He peered out across the lake with his hand tapping at his side. Heather supposed that it was in time to music that was playing through his headphones. She felt a jolt of fear as she thought that he might have seen her on his first approach before she disappeared into the bushes and was playing with her. It struck her that this was more than likely his routine and hoped that it was. She shivered, frightened to breathe even though she knew that he wouldn't be able to hear her. Her thoughts were all over the place. After about ten minutes –she couldn't truly judge the time-lapse – she breathed a silent sigh of relief as he stood, grasped each ankle in turn and flexed his legs before jogging past her – back towards the other end of the park.

She waited for a few minutes until he was out of sight, then left her hiding place and ran back to her car. She tried to calm her mind as she drove home; it was impossible. She switched the radio on and turned the music up as high as she could bear it. An orchestra was playing "Ride of the Valkyries." She ceased to think and forced herself to become absorbed in the harmony of sounds as she drove automatically.

Sienna was already asleep when she reached home and, after a shower, Heather settled down with Susan and Sean to watch television. She had no idea what she was watching. Bob and Yvonne had gone to the cinema and were going for a meal in their favourite restaurant afterwards. They'd decided to celebrate their wedding anniversary early in case Yvonne had to go back to Inverness.

When the programme finished, Susan suggested switching the television off as she wanted to talk. They did talk about Sienna, Susan's business and Sean and Heather's jobs, but Heather had a feeling that Susan wanted to talk about something specific. She wasn't surprised when her sister stood up and began to pace around the room, picking up ornaments and immediately replacing them in the same spot.

'Okay. Spit it out. What's the matter?' Heather asked.

'Sean and I want to get married in June, and we're wondering how on earth we're going to break it to Mom because we want to do it without any fuss. We've put an offer in for a house not too far away, and they have accepted it. It needs a lot doing to it, but we want to move in as soon as possible.' She took a deep breath. 'I know Mom's going to go ballistic. You know how much she wants us both to have big weddings. I just don't know how to tell her.' Susan's hand gestures were erratic as she blurted everything that was troubling her into her sister's waiting ears.

'Is that all that's the matter? I thought you'd at least killed someone.' The words were out of Heather's mouth before she could think about what she was saying. She could feel her cheeks begin to colour and the sweat on the nape of her neck. Fortunately, neither Susan nor Sean noticed anything amiss, and Heather continued to speak, 'Do you want me to tell her?'

'Oh, would you? I know it'll be better coming from you – she'll be able to say what she wants and then think about it before she sees me.' Her hand went to her mouth. 'Oh, aren't I being devious? But I don't want her to be upset – and she will be if I spring it on her. If you tell her when I'm not about, she'll have time to get used to the idea, won't she?'

'Yes, she will. We both know she's not going to like it, but she also has Grandma and Granddad to worry about, so perhaps it won't upset her quite as much as you think. It's not as though you'll be far away, is it?'

While Heather was trying to reassure her sister, she was thanking God that Susan hadn't done anything so awful that she couldn't ever tell anyone how wicked she was. She was fortunate to have such a simple, easily fixed problem.

Heather sighed inwardly and was brought back into the room when Sean said, 'We'll still babysit for Sienna, won't we?' Susan leaned sideways and kissed his cheek.

'We love her, of course, we will.'

It was Sean's turn for his cheeks to become pink as he thought about having a family. He wasn't sure that he wanted children but knew that Susan did and that he would love them for her sake.

Heather laughed and thanked them, then offered to make coffee for them all.

Susan smiled. 'I need it to be made with milk or I won't sleep, 'oh, and I'll need a biscuit or two.' She giggled like a two-year-old and snuggled deeper into Sean's willing arms as Heather left the room.

When she returned with three mugs on a tray, Heather asked them what they meant by marrying with no fuss.

'Well, we're just not sure that we want to get married in church. We'd prefer the registry office, and a small family do afterwards – here at home. We thought that we'd get caterers to set it all up, and we'd like you and Stephen to be our witnesses,' Susan finished quickly.

'What about you, Sean? Is there no one that you'd like to be a witness from your family or friends? Why would you choose Stephen? You hardly know him.' Heather said.

Sean shook his head. 'There's no one, really.'

She knew that all her family liked Stephen and hoped that he and Heather would make a go of it, but it wasn't going to happen.

Heather's face fell. 'I'd love to be a witness for you, but I think you should choose someone other than Stephen. What about Julie? Or Ben? Or John? You like them all, don't you? Anyway, I'll leave you to think about it.' She finished drinking her nightcap, then put her empty mug down. Neither Susan nor Sean spoke before Heather continued. 'What date in June do you have in mind?' She glanced at Susan, whose face looked stricken with guilt. 'Have you already booked it? June's a busy month for weddings.'

'Well, yes, we have it's booked for Saturday the fifth at 11 o'clock, and we'd like to have our house ready to move into by then.' At that moment, Susan looked like a little girl instead of a twenty-seven-year-old woman. 'Do you think Mom will be upset? I just couldn't stand the thought of an argument that would spoil the day.' She looked at Sean, who grinned nervously. 'So we decided if it were a fait accompli, she would just accept it.'

'Perhaps, she will. Anyway, it's done now, so there's no point in worrying about it, is there? Leave it to me, big sister,' they all laughed, 'I'll talk to her.' She yawned, stretched her arms above her head, then got to her feet. 'Bed. Night-night.'

They chorused goodnight, and Heather waved her hand casually at them as she closed the door behind her and climbed the stairs.

Over the next week, the priority for them all was to ensure that Yvonne's parent's room was made ready and the bathroom adapted to make life as easy as possible for them. Bob contacted a company that specialised in fixtures and fittings for people with disabilities, and in three weeks there was a wet room built to their specifications. Their bedroom had been decorated in a soothing green and grey scheme, and a special king-size bed to be delivered shortly. Yvonne was satisfied that everything was ready. And Sienna and Heather were settled in their room. She began to relax.

After a couple of days, when they were on their own, Yvonne passed Heather some cutlery to set the table ready for when Bob and Susan arrived home. Heather seized the moment: 'Mom.' Yvonne looked up from the carrots she was scraping and smiled at her daughter, then lifted her eyebrows. 'I need to talk to you about Susan.' Yvonne stayed her hand. 'They want to get married – what I mean is they are going to marry in June.'

Yvonne wiped her hands on a tea towel and perched on a nearby bar stool. 'I'm not sure what you mean. Tell me properly.' Heather gave her mother all the details. Tears trickled down Yvonne's face. 'If that's what they want to do, then that's okay. You know I hoped to see you both walk down the aisle dressed in beautiful wedding dresses, but I understand that Susan sees enough of that sort of wedding in her work. I'm not surprised that they want a small wedding, and I don't really mind – I'll talk to her tonight after dinner.'

'You're the best, Mom,' Heather said. 'Susan will be so relieved. She was dreading telling you. Oh, and they've bought a house, too. But I'm sure she'll tell you about it herself.'

Yvonne's mouth dropped open.

Chapter 25

Heather had managed to make three more visits to the park, and each time Ugly had followed the same routine. The shock of seeing him had worn off; she no longer trembled as he approached. She was determined to carry out the next part of her plan before the evenings became pleasant and light enough for more people to be using the park.

It was the last Tuesday evening in March when Heather arranged for Sienna to be minded and decided to go ahead with her mission. She had watched and waited enough. Now she was confident that Ugly jogged in the park each evening and invariably took a break and sat on the same bench. It was time for her to rid the world of his revolting presence. The night was dark – the moon was hiding behind clouds that had obscured its unwelcome light.

She dressed carefully in her overlarge bra covered by a black tracksuit with its hooded top, donned her black trainers and loaded three heavy stones into another of her father's socks. She put a spare set of clothing, a lidded plastic bowl she'd half-filled with water, a flannel, a towel and a bottle of water into the boot of her car. Her hand shook as she placed the new scalpel that she'd taken from the hospital onto the passenger seat, but she then drove steadily to the park. She parked up at the back entrance – not too far from the white bridge. She told herself over and over to stay calm while she loaded the sock with its lethal contents into her bra, leaving the zip of her tracksuit top part of the way down to give her easy access. After looking around but seeing no one, she reached over for the scalpel and then tucked it carefully into the top pocket of her tracksuit. Her heart was pounding in her chest, but she gritted her teeth and jogged until she reached the bench where he always rested. What if he didn't still sit there she asked herself, but she didn't have time to think further. Heat flared in her chest as she caught sight of a distant figure jogging towards her. She disappeared into the bushes and waited. He was early – was it his first circuit of the lake or his second? Terror clouded her mind momentarily; she wasn't ready. She took several deep breaths and held them in, trying to calm herself as the figure approached. He jogged steadily past the bench. She exhaled. It wasn't him; this man was about the same height as Ugly, but he had a much heftier figure. Her heartbeat continued to thud uncomfortably as the man disappeared. She didn't dare to leave the sanctuary of the bushes and wondered pessimistically if this was going to be the night that he didn't show up. Or perhaps the other man would do a second lap just as Ugly did. She wondered if she should abort her plan and leave the park while she had the chance. What if the other man came by at the same time as Ugly? She hovered between going and staying – she had no idea of the passage of time – she couldn't see the dial on her watch as the clouds continued to obscure the moon. She felt as though she'd been hiding for at least an hour when she saw Ugly and watched with bated breath as he passed her on what must be his first lap around the lake. As he too, became a tiny figure then disappeared from her sight, Heather knew that she just had to pee. She was desperate and quickly relieved herself seeing with dismay steam rising from the wet patch on the ground. It would have dissipated by the time he returned, she thought, hopefully with his headphones in place. With hands still shaking, she took a pair of hospital gloves from her pocket and donned them.

She could see him and, as he approached the bench, she became coldly calm just as she had before killing Snake man. She pulled the sock from her bra and cautiously removed the scalpel from her top pocket, ensuring that she gripped the handle and not the blade. As Ugly sat down on the bench with, as she'd hoped, his earphones blocking his ears, Heather eased herself up the slight incline, stepped out of the bushes and glanced around. All was quiet as she silently approached him. At the last minute, some sixth sense must have warned him that he wasn't alone. He started to look round just as Heather brought the sock down full force onto his head, then dropped it onto the ground and smoothly transferred the scalpel to her right hand. As he slumped forward towards the path, Heather grabbed his hair, pulled his head back and swiftly drew the scalpel sharply across his exposed throat.

'What the fu …' were all the words he managed to get out as blood spurted from the deep wound and filled his throat. Heather looked around again to make sure that there were no witnesses. She felt nothing as she remained behind the bench while his body went limp and tilted further forward with blood spurting from between his fingers. Fingers that were desperately trying to hold the gaping wound together. He fell from the bench to his knees and then rolled onto his back. Heather watched as he tried to scream, but only bubbles of blood left his mouth.

'You'll never rape anyone else, you bastard,' Heather said vehemently as his life drained from his body. She pulled the bloodied gloves from her hands and tucked them into her sleeve where they felt unpleasantly wet. Then, stooping down, grabbed the sock and quickly entered her hiding place. She threw the stones into the river. She pushed the empty sock back into her bra and waited for some time in the bushes until Ugly lay still. Heather wanted to check to ensure that he was dead and took a step forward, but her courage failed her. She couldn't bear to see his face again, even if he was dead. No one was in sight as she left her hiding place and ran.

As she crossed the bridge, she felt neither remorse nor elation and automatically steadied her pace to a jogging rhythm until she reached her car. There were a couple of other unoccupied vehicles parked near to the closed shops, but no people. Thankfully, she drove away from the main road back down Scribers lane, where she pulled over by the field.

She opened the boot and quickly changed her top. She could smell Ugly's blood on her sleeve, and her stomach clenched as sickness tried to overwhelm her. She gulped deep breaths of air until nausea lessened. She then rolled the bloodied gloves and scalpel inside the dirty top and pushed them into a plastic bag. She flung it into the boot before washing her trembling hands and arms. Forcing herself to carry out the remainder of the precautions that she knew were necessary, she took a flashlight from the side pocket of the boot and shone it over her trousers and trainers and then the driver's seat. She couldn't see any blood but thought she could smell urine.

Nevertheless, too anxious to take the time to change, she emptied the bowl into the hedgerow, hesitated, then threw it into the boot. She needed to get away from the park and drove home, hoping that his body would be undiscovered until the next day. She thought that perhaps she should have kicked his body into the lake, but not only would she have been covered in blood, the lake also wasn't all that deep at the edge. And the pool of blood on the bank would have alerted whoever was unfortunate enough to find him.

Heather was exhausted both physically and mentally, but as she drove, she felt nothing other than relief that it was over. She was sure that she hadn't left anything that could, in any way, link her to the beast that she'd just killed.

Heather needed another year to pass and then go after the third rapist. She didn't know how she was going to be able to locate him, even though she knew his name. I'll figure it out, she thought, as her hatred for him coiled quietly in her brain.

Entering the house as silently as she could, Heather ran upstairs to her room and shut herself in the bathroom. She tore off her clothes and wrapped them together in a bundle with the towel and flannel from her car. Her top felt stiff with coppery smelling blood from where the sock had been thrust back inside her bra. She showered and thoroughly washed the second of her copper bracelets, leaving it on the sink to dispose of later. She left the bathroom wrapped in a white towel with a smaller one wound around her hair and sat on her bed. She gazed lovingly at her daughter's relaxed face. She is so beautiful, and I don't suppose that many people would say I deserved her if they knew what I'd done, she thought, then berated herself silently. She had to believe the rapists deserved to die, and she didn't deserve punishment. She had suffered enough punishment at their hands, and she was preventing them from putting anyone else through the agony that she had endured, she told herself.

She dried her hair, pulled on fresh pyjamas and her warm, pink, terry towelling dressing gown, and then picked up the bundle of clothes from the floor and carried it downstairs. In the laundry room, she set the washer on cold so that the blood wouldn't cook and remain in the material. At the last minute, she decided to wash the sock before she binned it. She breathed a sigh of relief as she left the machine to destroy any trace of her revenge. She had three consecutive day shifts starting in the morning; she couldn't wait to be at the hospital where she could dispose of the gloves and scalpel. She'd taken the time to wash both items before she threw the water into the hedgerow but didn't feel that it would have been sufficient to destroy every trace of blood. She rewashed them in the laundry room sink and then took them back up to her room and hid them in her workbag. She wanted to dispose of the bowl that she'd used and had left it in her car until she could decide what to do with it.

She opened the door to the sitting room and peeped in. Her mother and father were snuggled up together on the sofa.

'We didn't hear you come in. Were you all sweaty?' Yvonne asked, then holding her finger to her lips, said, 'Shh,' and turned her head back to the war film that they were watching. Heather took the hint and quietly closed the door.

She was grateful that she didn't have to talk and went to make herself a hot cup of cocoa which she took into the conservatory. Trying her utmost to drive Ugly's face from her mind and take on her home persona, she picked up the wool and hook that her mother had given her when she was trying to teach her how to crochet and began to chain. A little later, when the wash cycle had ended, she threw in the two towels that she'd just used and started it off again on a sixty-degree wash.

Yvonne called from the kitchen that their film had ended and asked if she was going to join them. Heather declined and remained in the conservatory until she was able to put the washing into the drier. As the clothes came out of the machine smelling sweet and with no trace of the murder that she had carried out that night, so Heather's mind became cleansed of the killing too. It was as though she had never been to Trittiford Mill, but she felt a deep sense of contentment that Ugly was gone.

Next day, Heather returned from work after disposing of the gloves and returning the scalpel, which she had steam autoclaved along with other instruments. She was sitting with Sienna and listening to her day with much amusement when the phone rang. Her stomach had had butterflies fluttering around all day, and she was feeling some anxiety that she couldn't explain. The phone's continuous noise exacerbated the bad feeling. She picked up the receiver and held it to her ear without speaking.

'Is that you, Heather?' Lucy sounded excited. Heather knew what she was going to tell her. 'I just had to phone. Something dreadful has happened.'

'Whatever's the matter?' Heather barely got the words out of her mouth before her friend spoke again.

'Well, you know the park by my house where we sometimes go?'

'Yes. What about it?'

'Well, there's been a murder. I don't know too much about it – but a man was killed there last night when he was jogging. It's frightened me to death – I'll never use the park again.' Heather remained quiet. 'Are you still there, Heather?'

'Yes, I was just waiting for you to tell me more. How did the man die?'

'I don't know, but the place was swarming with police when I went to work this morning. An ambulance was parked as I passed along Priory Road. It's bound to be in the papers. I'm just going to the newsagents to buy the *Daily Mail*. I'll let you know, but I don't think you should bring Sienna there until they've caught whoever did it.'

'Okay, of course, I won't. How awful for the family. Let me know if you hear any more. It'll be a shame if we can't use the park. Sienna loves to see the ducks when we visit you, doesn't she?'

'Yes, um, yes. Okay, I'll let you know what's in the *Mail*, but you'll probably see it yourself, won't you?'

'I don't think so, Dad doesn't usually buy it, and I don't suppose a murder will make him do so. Anyway, thanks for telling me. I hadn't planned to go there, but you never know what's going to happen, do you? Go on then, speak later.' Heather disconnected the call.

The butterflies did a mating dance in her belly as she wondered what would be in the papers. When Lucy rang back later, it was to tell Heather that the man lived locally and the police were investigating the murder. Heather didn't see how she could be involved – there should be no connection – and the more she went over the details in her mind, the less she thought that she'd left any evidence that could get back to her.

Chapter 26

Susan did a twirl and beamed. Then spritzed herself with her favourite perfume, Chanel N°5. Its distinctive aroma filled the room like a heady bouquet.

'You look so beautiful,' Heather said as she watched. 'I'm glad you chose to wear that dress. Mom hasn't seen it yet, has she? She'll cry – she's looked forward to seeing us dressed like this since we were little girls. I don't think that she'll mind now that the wedding is to be at the registry office.'

Susan's mouth drooped. 'Oh, I hope not. I don't want her to be upset.'

'It'll be fine, and the photos will be great even though you won't be taking them. Have you shown John how your camera works?'

'Do you know how many hours he and I have spent ensuring that the photos will be good? He was really patient and so pleased to have been asked to do the job – he is such a great guy,' Susan said, surveying herself in the cheval mirror.

She suddenly turned and took Heather's hand. 'I've just noticed in the mirror that you're only wearing one of your bracelets. You've always worn all three; what made you take them off?'

Heather laughed. 'What a thing for you to notice right now! Just keep looking at yourself. I got tired of them and threw two away, but I still like to wear this one.' She held up her arm and stroked the shiny copper. 'Right, I'm going to call Mom now so stand just as you are.' Heather returned with their mother, who burst into tears when she saw that Susan was wearing a traditional, white wedding dress as a surprise for her.

Yvonne was feeling elated as she left the girls to it and went to her room. She shut the door and then proudly dressed as Mother of the bride in a pale lilac dress and jacket. As she was trying on a matching hat, she looked up and caught her husband gazing intently at her.

'I just hope that Sean and Susan will be as happy together as you and I have been.' She kissed him. 'Come on, my handsome man.' She led him downstairs where both of their daughters were making last-minute adjustments to their hair.

Bob kissed Susan and said, 'I'm so very proud to be your father, you know.'

'Don't make me cry,' Susan said. 'You'll ruin my make up that Heather has applied so expertly.'

'I'm proud of you, too,' Bob said to Heather, making everyone laugh.

The wedding party trooped out to the waiting white Rolls Royce, leaving the caterers to put the final touches to the buffet that already looked enticing. Yvonne had excelled herself with a white and silver table decoration that she'd insisted on making, and an elegant white iced, three-tier wedding cake stood waiting on a side table.

Yvonne looked back as they left the house and felt a pang of regret that the wedding of her first daughter wasn't to be in church with an organ playing traditional music, but it only lasted for a second or two. She loved Sean as if he were her son and was more than happy that they were to be together in their own home.

She climbed into the waiting car while shading her eyes from the bright sunshine that made the ride into town a pleasure that had nothing to do with the wedding. Sean's parents and an Aunt met them at the Registry Office, and Yvonne breathed a sigh of relief to see that neither of the other women also wore lilac.

Heather glanced at Stephen's profile as they signed the register as witnesses. She smiled to herself as she thought how determined her sister had been that Stephen should be her partner. He was handsome, and there was no doubt fanciable with his clean-shaven, strong jaw and twinkly eyes. She already knew he was kind and conscientious from working with him. Husband material, but she still felt that it would be wrong to form a relationship that could have no basis in truth, and there was no way that she could be truthful with him. Sadly she couldn't be honest with anyone.

She turned her attention to her sister, who positively glowed with happiness as she leaned her head on her new husband's shoulder. 'Let me be the first to congratulate you in your new name Mrs Phillips.'

'Thank you, my favourite sister.' Susan's smile blossomed as Heather laughed.

'But I thought there were only two of you.' Stephen looked puzzled. Sean scratched his head as Heather and Susan grinned at each other.

'I'll explain later,' Heather told Stephen, but she never did. She thought it was the type of joke that only two close siblings would be able to appreciate.

Many of the photos were beautiful and had the Hall of Memory as a backdrop. Susan declared that she was satisfied and called a halt. Everyone was hungry. They headed back to the house where, as soon as they'd drunk a toast to the happy couple, they tucked into the excellent buffet.

'You cost me a fortune,' Bob said, 'I knew you would.'

'Oh, Dad!' Susan hugged him tightly, 'Thank you, I'll try not to cost you any more money.'

'You are worth every penny I have, my love.'

He clinked a spoon against his glass and, when everyone was quiet, made a short speech welcoming Sean and his family into Susan's family. He then behaved in his inimitable jokey fashion that had all their special friends and a couple of distant relatives laughing merrily. As soon as he was able, he hurried to keep Yvonne company; he knew that she was feeling a little lost.

Later, Susan went to change into her going away suit, and Heather watched her sister's face as she held onto Sean's hand as they ran upstairs. She was very happy for her but, as she walked through the conservatory into the garden, she too felt lost and more than a little sorry for herself but remained unable to share her feelings.

Everything felt a bit flat after the bride and groom departed until someone put some dance music on. The men helped to carry the dining tables to one side, and then some of the young ones began to dance. Some were tipsy, and a few were well past that stage. Sean's maiden aunt was having the time of her life as she swayed unsteadily on the spot with her arms raised above her head. Eventually, Sean's father and mother persuaded her to sit with them and, about an hour later, they made their excuses and left for home. They promised Yvonne that they would stay in touch while their children were away.

As the night wore on, guests departed or wandered into the sitting room to join Yvonne and Bob. Heather was dancing with Stephen when John called them into the conservatory.

'What's the problem?' Heather asked as she looked at their expressions of dismay.

'I'm so sorry,' Julie said. Her face twisted in pain.

'She's gone into labour,' Ben said with an apologetic smile, 'all over your carpet. We need to get her to the hospital, but I've been drinking. Well, we all have. Julie was designated driver tonight. We'll have to call an ambulance – I don't fancy risking it in a taxi at this hour on a Saturday night.'

'Even I've had a few,' Lucy said, 'So I can't drive either. I'm spending the night here. I never gave it a thought.'

'I've already contacted the emergency services, and they should be here shortly,' John said and held his hands out palm up. 'Mind you; there are enough of us here to deliver one small baby.' He frowned. 'I can't believe how quickly the contractions are coming. You're not due for two weeks, are you Julie?'

Julie groaned.

'I know,' Ben said, 'but I think the hospital is the best option.' He took Julie's hand in his while another contraction held her in its grip.

'Let's get you onto the couch, Julie, and then I'll find you a nightdress. It'll make you easier to examine if you don't mind,' Heather said and indicated to Ben and Sam to assist her.

Julie grimaced at her friend. 'Well, I did as much for you a few years ago, so I don't suppose I'll mind. I'll be more than grateful if these contractions don't slow down.'

Heather borrowed one of her mother's no-nonsense nightgowns and became very professional as she said, 'Sam and Lucy, would you mind joining Mom and Dad in the sitting room – I think that Stephen might be there too.'

When they'd left the conservatory, she helped Julie to change then made her comfortable on towels spread on the couch. Julie's contractions seemed to be coming at a rate of knots now. When Heather timed them, they were less than two minutes apart.

'No sign of the ambulance yet, John, would you go and see?' Heather asked. Ben didn't want to let go of his wife's desperate clasp. 'Would you mind if I see how far dilated you are, Julie?'

Julie shook her head as yet another contraction claimed her and caused her to groan. Heather went to the kitchen and carefully washed and disinfected her hands. She felt annoyed for not having gloves handy, and her mind slapped her as it reminded her where she'd used the ones that she'd had.

Stephen popped his head around the door and offered to help if necessary, but Heather said that she'd give him a shout if they needed him, so he returned to the sitting room. She felt that it was kind of him to stay, but he was the last thing on her mind as she went quickly to examine her friend and told her that she was almost fully dilated.

'We don't have time to wait for the ambulance; she's going to deliver here, I'm afraid,' Ben said. 'Come on, my love. Let's get this baby born, okay?'

Julie silently nodded an agreement, then followed Heather and John's instructions as she worked to push her daughter into the world.

Heather had felt affection for each one of the babies that she'd assisted with, but she was surprised when she felt such an intense rush of love as her goddaughter was born.

'Come to Auntie Heather,' she said as she separated the baby from her mother. The little girl cried instantly, much to everyone's relief, as they continued to help complete the birthing process. A few minutes after their daughter was born, the ambulance finally arrived, and Ben and Julie went to the hospital.

Heather and John set to and cleared up the mess and washed the carpet before they went into the sitting room where Sam, Lucy and Heather's parents were sat talking excitedly. Stephen had already left for home, but they wanted a blow by blow account and pestered Heather for details. She slumped down in her chair and said, 'Over to you, John. I'm pooped. It's all been too much excitement for me.'

'Hmm – you – lightweight,' he teased.

Although Heather was very tired the next morning after being woken by Sienna at 7 o'clock, she went with Yvonne to visit Julie. She was sitting up in bed, looking rested and was delighted to see them. When the greetings and the hugs and unwrapping of presents for the baby completed, Julie turned to Heather and said, 'I'm only here because they want to keep an eye on my baby for twenty-four hours. Well, she was born in such a rush. They said it was mine and Ben's choice, as we didn't need to come into the hospital at all, strictly speaking. Ben said that we should go home, but I wanted to stay the full twenty-four hours. I know I'm a fusspot, but I never thought I'd be a Mom. So ...' She held up her hands and looked very proud of her achievement.

Heather shouted with laughter. 'Well, you've done something to be proud of.'

Julie clasped her friend's hand in between both of hers, but Heather withdrew them.

'Sorry, Julie, I can't stand being held – let me hold your hands instead.' They swapped.

Emotion made the timbre of Julie's voice lower than usual as she said, 'You know I believe there's a reason why people become friends, and I mean real friends, ones that last a lifetime. You and I have that bond, and I want to thank you for being there when I needed you so much,' Heather smiled warmly, and Julie continued to speak, 'Thank you for delivering our beautiful daughter and calling yourself Auntie Heather. I shall never forget it, and neither will Ben. We both wondered whether you'd mind if we named our little girl after you and John.' Tears came as she finished speaking. Heather sat on the side of the bed and held her until she stopped crying. Yvonne excused herself and took Sienna to buy a drink for them all.

'Come on, you. Your hormones are all over the place at the moment. I'd be proud to share my name. But … John? I'm not sure that she would thank you for that one,' Heather said.

Julie smiled. 'We want to call her Heather Jo – do you think that would be okay?' She managed to stop crying long enough to ask.

'Of course, it's lovely, and I'm sure John will be delighted too.' Heather hugged her friend again as she said, 'I feel the same way, Julie. We've been there for each other, and seeing you both well and so happy is enough, thanks. Now, where's your beautiful daughter?'

As they drove away from the hospital, Heather looked in the mirror and asked Sienna, 'What did you think of Julie's baby?'

'I'd like a sister just like that one,' Sienna said.

Heather's heart sank as she thought how unlikely it was that Sienna would get her wish. While they'd been dancing, Stephen had asked her to go on a date with him the following Thursday when they had a night off. She'd agreed to go for a meal with him, but all the while she was saying yes, her conscience had been saying no.

‘Where would you like to have lunch?’ Yvonne asked. She fortuitously wrenched Heather’s thoughts away from troubled waters.

‘What about that little cafe that we went to last week? You know – the one just off the high street?’

Heather carried Sienna in her arms from the car park because they hadn’t brought her pushchair, and she was too sleepy to walk. ‘It’s a good job you’re so fit,’ Yvonne said as they neared the cafe with its cheerful red check curtains.

Chapter 27

Bob laughed uproariously and shook the pages of his newspaper. 'Now I've read everything. There's a real concern that the Trekkies are going to be as big a threat to society as the Millennium bug. Even the prime minister is warning about what may happen to businesses as the clock strikes midnight. It's a good job we don't all scare so easily. Mind you, look at the ease with which he lied about – '

'Okay dear, get off your soapbox! You know I hate anything to do with politics or wars. Please go back to talking about the bug.'

Bob blew his wife a kiss and disappeared behind his paper again.

'There's a lot of concern at the hospital; no one knows what's going to happen when the clocks on the computers reach midnight. Perhaps the programmes will return the date to the beginning of the last century. If that happens, it'll create all sorts of problems, and I know it isn't my problem, but I am worried,' Heather said.

'Well, don't worry about things that you can't do anything about, love. Hadn't you better get ready? Stephen will be here soon. Where are you going for this meal?' Yvonne asked and smiled knowingly.

'Mom!' Heather protested. 'This is only one date, and I don't suppose there will be another one – so don't be getting your hopes up. We're going to the Indian, so I don't think I'll be late home. I'll just go up and get changed. I hope he's not early. He's booked the table for seven-thirty; can't say I'm looking forward to being alone with him, I bet we run out of things to say.'

'Oh, go on with you, you'll be fine. He's a very nice person. Look how happy Susan is now that she's married to Sean and living in her own house,' Yvonne said.

Heather stood up and, on her way into the hall, said, 'She was happy before she married – and so am I.'

Contrary to her expectations, Heather enjoyed the evening. Stephen was excellent company, and he ensured that the conversation flowed smoothly. They both ordered chicken korma and shared a side dish of aloo gobi and plain naan bread. The food was excellent. After two glasses of wine, Heather's worries were like the early morning mist that disappears as the sun's rays burn it off. She relaxed and found that she was feeling warmth deep down in her body.

Thoughts that she was unused to settled in her mind bringing visions of being intimate with this man that she was enjoying listening to. At times she missed hearing his words because she had such wayward thoughts.

It was nearly midnight when Stephen pulled up at Heather's front door and walked around the front of the car to open the passenger door. Heather thanked him for an enjoyable evening and was about to ask him to come in when he leaned forward, brushed his lips lightly against her cheek, then turned away and got back into his car. He waved his hand as he drove away, but he didn't look back. Heather was left feeling ridiculously forlorn, not knowing what she had expected or wanted from him. She knew that she would have said yes if he'd asked her out again, but he hadn't, and it hurt. She entered the silent house and crept up to her room, kicking herself for allowing him to get under her skin.

The following morning, she gave a potted version of their evening to satisfy her mother's curiosity, but the question that Yvonne wanted Heather to answer went unasked. She didn't allow her mother to voice it. As Yvonne began to say, 'And did he –?' Heather swiftly changed the subject and went to dress Sienna to go shopping.

When they arrived downstairs and were putting on their coats in the hall, Yvonne called Heather to come into the kitchen. As she walked in and looked at her mother's expectant face, Heather said, 'I don't want to talk about Stephen anymore, Mom.'

'I just wanted to say I'm sorry for being so nosy and ask if you'd like me to come to the shops with you. I won't mention Stephen's name again, honest.' Yvonne grinned engagingly at Heather's stern face making her laugh as usual.

'Okay, but please keep your word. Come on then, hurry up! I want to go into town before all the parking spaces are gone.'

On the drive in, Yvonne told Heather that her grandparents' house had sold, and the buyers wanted to move in before Christmas. 'I have to go up to Inverness Tuesday, so you'll have to manage without me for a while.'

'That's okay, Mom. Sienna isn't your responsibility. She is mine. I'm just grateful for all the times that you do mind her so willingly. I wish I could come with you and help, but I have to go to work. It's always busy at this time of the year.'

'I know, love. And Susan has so many orders on her books that she won't be able to help either. I thought about getting

Marge to come with me. I'm sure she'd be only too glad to do something different for a while.'

'Sounds like a good idea to me, Mom. How long do you think you'll be away?'

'Sorry, love, but I don't know how long it's going to take me to sort everything out and then dispose of all the items that your grandma's been hoarding for the last fifty-odd years. She's going to find it very difficult to part with some of her things, but we'll have to make some compromises – it won't be possible to accommodate all her treasures. Anyway, your granddad's a practical man. Hopefully, he will have started to sort things out already. I know he's looking forward to sharing the burden, well, he doesn't think she is a burden, but she's become ill enough to make both their lives very difficult at times. I'll ring Marge later and see if she's free.'

'Heather,' Stephen called her name quietly as he followed her along the corridor leading to the labour ward, 'hold on a minute.'

Against her better judgement, Heather stopped and waited. It was over two months since their evening out together, and, even though they'd worked the same shifts on two occasions, he'd not attempted to speak to her in a personal way. She was feeling rejected and not a little put out by the lack of communication between them.

'I just wondered, if perhaps you hadn't disliked our last date, whether you'd risk another evening together soon?' Stephen spoke casually with no explanation for his distant behaviour.

Heather shook her head. 'I don't think it's a very good idea. You haven't been in any rush to talk to me since the last one, have you?' She didn't know if she was hurt or annoyed at his neglect, but she felt wrong-footed. She began to continue on her way, leaving him to follow.

'Hold on! I thought you understood.' He ran his hand down his cheek and looked mystified. 'We've both been under a lot of pressure at work, and I've been waiting for a moment to ask you out again. All my free time has been with my mother. It's been touch and go as to whether she'd pull through or not.'

'Oh, I'm sorry – I didn't know. What's the matter with her?' Heather was quite annoyed with herself as she wondered if it had been part of the hospital gossip that she hadn't heard. Was she the only one in the hospital who didn't know what Stephen was going through?

'She had a water infection that she neglected, and it became a case of sepsis. She nearly died. We've all been so worried. I thought everyone knew.' He held his hands out towards her.

Heather frowned. 'I am so sorry; I didn't know. I thought that you'd been avoiding me. Is she out of the woods now?'

'Yes. Thank God. I don't know why you would think that I was avoiding you – I think about you all the time – I have since we first met.' He touched her hair lightly. 'Now shall we get over it and have another date?'

Heather flushed. 'Yes, but I must get on. We need to talk some other time.'

'Okay. Can you join me for a drink after work? We could meet at the main entrance.'

'Looking forward to it,' Heather said.

She felt as though she was floating as they went companionably into the postnatal ward. She found it hard to keep her mind on her work, especially after she caught a glimpse of Stephen as he hurried to assist with a difficult birth that was taking place on the labour ward.

When they met up after their shifts had finished, they walked over to the local pub and sat nursing soft drinks as they talked about their day. Then Stephen spoke seriously, 'Okay. So am I forgiven, and will you come out with me again?'

Heather rolled her eyes to the ceiling as her face coloured up. 'There's nothing to forgive. I was stupid not to ask you what was wrong instead of making my own story up. I'm sorry too, and of course, I will. But things are a bit difficult at the moment.'

'Oh, in what way?' A worried frown drew his bushy eyebrows together in a straight line.

Heather had never seen him look like that, and she began to laugh and purse her lips. 'My Mom has always told me not to go out with men whose eyebrows meet in the middle – as yours are doing right now.'

He grimaced at her making his brows appear even weirder. 'Stop avoiding the issue: why are things difficult?'

Heather told him about her mother being in Inverness and why she had to go there. Then she took a deep breath. 'Now Dad's gone to help as well, so once I pick Sienna up from her childminder, I'm on my own with her. I can't ask Susan and Sean again; they've babysat three times this week so that I could go to the gym and for a run. I can't ask Lucy to help either, she has flu, and Julie and Ben are so busy with their little Heather Jo. I suppose I could ask John and Sam, but ...'

Stephen took a drink of cider. 'Why don't we have a takeaway at your place. I promise I will go home when you kick me out, or perhaps you could bring Sienna, and we could have a takeaway at my place?' He looked anxious as Heather hesitated. 'It will be okay, Heather, whichever you choose. I suppose we could wait. I waited a long time for you to agree to go on a date with me. But we enjoyed each other's company, didn't we?'

Heather took time to answer; she was picturing an evening spent together with only her sleeping daughter in the house and wondered if she would be able to trust this man who she liked so much but knew so little about. She told herself not to be so stupid. It was she who had a dark secret, not him, and she would never be a victim again.

'I really did enjoy your company. I think I would like it if you came to my place. Sienna doesn't need to have her bedtime disrupted then. Yes, I'd like that.' She sat back in her chair feeling flattered as Stephen looked as though he'd won a lottery. They arranged their staying in date for the following Saturday, and both of them felt elated as they left the pub. It was pouring with rain, and they were soaked as they entered their cars back at the hospital – but neither seemed to mind.

Chapter 28

Heather tucked Sienna into bed and read her favourite story about Rapunzel, a princess that was rescued by a handsome prince. Sienna shuddered at the bits about the witch and clapped her hands as the prince rescued the princess. Heather never ceased to enjoy her daughter's reaction to the story and had read it to her so many times that they both knew it word for word.

As she kissed her goodnight, she began to feel that she shouldn't be entertaining Stephen while Sienna was in the house and picked up her phone to ring him and cry off, but there was no answer. Heather realised that he would, in all probability, be on his way. They'd arranged for him to pick up a takeaway from the Chinese restaurant near Heather's home. Accepting that it was too late to put him off, she decided she would try to make the evening as pleasant as possible without giving him any idea that she'd had reservations.

She changed into a pretty, pale lemon dress that she rarely wore, brushed her hair and then went downstairs. She paced about nervously, checking the table setting each time she passed. Not many minutes elapsed before she saw headlights sweep across the window as the car turned into the drive. She shut the blinds then went to the door to let him in.

She tried to remain calm as he stepped across the threshold and planted a kiss on her cheek while holding two brown paper bags out to the side so he wouldn't contaminate her clothes.

'Mm, that smells good.' Heather led the way into the kitchen, where they emptied the contents onto plates and then took them through to the table.

'I've brought some wine, too, but it's in the car. I'll just go and fetch it.' He started to leave, but Heather stopped him.

'I've already opened a bottle,' she gestured to the wine cooler on the table, 'and we can save yours until another time.' Stephen nodded and sat down, happy to go along with whatever she suggested. Heather followed suit but thought warily – always supposing there is a next time.

She felt hungry, even though the butterflies that she was becoming used to were making themselves felt once again. She tried breathing deeply to calm herself as she helped them both to fill their plates and poured cold Chardonnay into her mother's best glasses. They hadn't exchanged more than a few words since he'd arrived and ate while lost in their thoughts. Heather began to wonder how she could be sitting there calmly eating with a man who, on the one hand, she was strongly attracted to, but on the other, needed to keep at a distance.

'Penny for them?' Stephen had been watching Heather's face without her being aware and wondered what was making her look so preoccupied.

Heather's mind did a scrabble about as she tried to find a suitable but untrue reply. 'I was just thinking how nice of you to suggest this so that Sienna would be okay.' As the words left her mouth, she thought that she sounded foolish and could feel the blush spread across her cheeks.

'What were you thinking?' Stephen gave a small smile. 'I know that you were reluctant for us to be on our own like this, but nothing is going to happen that you wouldn't want to happen. So stop worrying and let's enjoy our meal together. These noodles are delicious, aren't they?' He laughed at his transparent remark and Heather's look of surprise. 'Well, that is what's worrying you isn't it?'

Heather nodded. 'I'm sorry – I think perhaps I like you a little too much.'

It was Stephen's turn to look surprised at her honesty; it was the last thing that he'd expected. He put down his chopsticks and gazed at her without speaking for what, to Heather, seemed like a very long time.

'You must know by now that I'm in love with you, Heather. It isn't possible for you to like me too much – I want you to love me.'

Heather got up from the table and left the room: she didn't know what to do. She was sure that she'd fallen in love with him, but her mind was dangling from the parapet of a bridge. She wanted to be loved and kissed and comforted and have all the hurt and anger that she felt towards most men soothed from her mind. But another task needed to bc complete before she could allow herself the luxury of being weak. As she thought about the last of the three that she had yet to find and dispose of, she could almost smell an odour of bleach and relived the sight of Driver's penis as he pushed it towards her mouth. The memory filled her head and made her feel sick. She wandered around the kitchen, touching familiar objects with her cold fingers and trying to ground the rising panic that threatened to engulf her. She didn't know what she could say to explain her behaviour to Stephen or how to respond to his revelation.

Stephen appeared in the kitchen doorway; both of his hands were full of plates and cutlery. He placed them carefully down onto the breakfast bar and stood still while gazing at her crestfallen face.

'Do you want me to go, love?' he asked. If she said yes, he thought that would be an end to any chance he had of forming a lasting relationship with her.

Heather shook her head. 'No. I don't want you to go. I don't think I can make you understand how much I want you to stay, but how frightened I am.'

Stephen took her in his arms and held her pliant body close. 'I don't know what you have to be frightened of; I would never hurt you – I love you, my darling.' He could feel that she was trembling as he kissed her forehead. Then as she gradually relaxed, he kissed her on her nose and proceeded to plant what she thought of as fairy kisses on her cheeks, eyelids and across her face until she began to laugh.

'Stop! Oh, please!' she begged.

Stephen obliged. 'Come on, let's take our glasses into the sitting room and perhaps you can tell me what's the matter.' He took her hand and led her into the next room, where he pulled her carefully down beside him onto the sofa.

After a few minutes of silence, Heather gulped wine from her glass and began to choke as she inhaled a few drops. Stephen took her glass and patted her firmly on her back until she stopped coughing. He handed her a tissue from a nearby box. His contrary sense of humour wanted to tease her, but he resisted the impulse.

Red in the face as she recovered her voice and composure, Heather said, 'I'm so sorry that was silly of me.'

Stephen smiled lovingly at her red-rimmed, watery eyes. He took her into his arms and began to kiss the small scars that were still visible on her face. Heather felt as though all her insides had melted. She felt loved and cared for whether she deserved to be or not. Memories of other male arms, holding and controlling her while they did unspeakable things, intruded, but Heather shoved them away and snuggled even closer into his chest. They stayed like this, and as time passed, tenderness flared into passion. Stephen kissed her on her lips, his tongue touching hers as she returned the kiss.

Heather felt ecstatic; she'd thought that she would never enjoy any sexual feelings again. She remembered gaining pleasure from boys that she'd dated before being raped but realised that those feelings had been immature. She knew that she wanted Stephen to make love to her.

Their kisses became more passionate, and Heather didn't protest as Stephen unbuttoned the top of her dress and pushed aside her bra. A moment later, although his hands covering her breasts were gentle as they stroked her nipples, they unleashed such deep-seated memories of the viciousness of Ugly's hands that she pushed him away, sat up and pulled the top of her dress together. Heather rose unsteadily to her feet and moved away from the sofa. She was immediately appalled at herself as she saw Stephen's hurt and embarrassed face – he could barely look at her.

'I'm sorry, Stephen. I don't know why I reacted in that way.' She knew perfectly well what had triggered her response to being made love to by him, but she couldn't even begin to come up with a reason for her behaviour that would sound plausible. She walked to the window and peered through one of the slats in the blinds. She felt mortified and knew that he'd never want anything to do with her again. He was aware that she had given birth to Sienna, so there should be no reason, as far as he would be able to fathom, why she should reject his advances in such a fashion.

'I'm sorry too, love. I thought that you cared enough about me, and I completely misread the invitation that I felt in your body. I think it's time I left. I do love you, Heather, but I feel pretty stupid about what just happened. I don't understand.' Stephen took a step towards her, but Heather moved a step away from him. He shrugged as he walked toward the sideboard where his keys were, picked them up and let himself out of the front door.

Heather watched through the blinds as his car reversed down the drive then disappeared, taking away the man that she knew she loved but had dealt such a blow. She sank to the floor and sobbed, wishing she could turn the clock back to when she was a teenager, safe within her family's love. But that would mean you wouldn't have Sienna, a small voice whispered. The aside didn't stop her dress from becoming soaked with her tears. Much later, as she cleared away the remains of their meal, she remembered that her mother had promised to phone her the next day with an update about the clearance of her grandparent's home. She missed her mom's sensible approach to misfortune, even if she was not aware of the reasons for the problem. She would tell her to put Stephen behind her and get on with her life; it was his loss. She could hear her saying those very words, but she wouldn't know that it was Heather that had caused the problem. I don't deserve to be happy, she thought.

Heather stayed awake that night, assaulted by her thoughts. How was she going to cope when she next saw Stephen at work? Her pillow was wet through by the time the first snowy November morning arrived.

Chapter 29

Heather and Susan ran out onto the drive as their father's car came to a halt. They took turns to hug and kiss him and then went to help their grandmother into the wheelchair that he unloaded from the car boot.

'Hello, my loves. I'm knackered, but I'm so pleased to be here at last.' Her strong Scottish accent sounded alien in her present setting, causing her granddaughters to grin childishly at each other. Yvonne had cautiously left the car and waved her fingers at her daughters as she ran into the house, causing them to give even wider grins. They kissed their grandfather before he hastily followed Bob into the house.

'Can't stop. It's been a while since our last watering hole.' Bob called as they disappeared indoors.

'See you later,' Susan said. She left for her own home, satisfied now that she'd seen her family were back safely.

Heather wheeled her grandmother through the garage and stopped at the recently installed toilet. After helping her to use the facility, she wheeled her up the fitted ramp that led into the kitchen.

'Here, hold your horses! Where's my great-granddaughter?' Rose said, 'What have you done with her? I haven't seen her since she was a baby.'

Heather called to Sienna, who flew down the stairs to see what all the noise was. She stopped in the kitchen doorway and gazed at Rose, then walked confidently up to her.

'Are you my grandma's mommy?' she asked.

'Oh aye, I am, and I'm your great-grandma, now gie me a kiss and a hug,' Rose said.

Heather picked her daughter up so that she could greet Rose. 'Why are your hands like claws?' Sienna asked as she kissed her wrinkled cheek.

'Hush now,' Yvonne said.

'It's because I have arthritis, and it's scrunched them up,' Rose said.

'Oh, okay, will they get better?'

Yvonne put Sienna onto the floor. 'I'll explain later, love, but your great-grandmother is tired now from the long journey.'

Rose smiled. 'I could murder a cuppa, our Yvonne. My mouth's like a parrot's cage.' She gave her daughter a cheeky smile, and Heather thought how much alike they were.

'Coming up, Mom. I think we could all do with one. Heather, would you take your grandma upstairs to have a look at her room and show her the layout of the rest of the house? It's been many years since she's been here.' Yvonne went into the kitchen and filled the kettle.

'Okay. Come on, Grandma, the stairlift's fun. I've used it a few times, and Sienna loves it. Dad's already put another wheelchair at the top, so getting to your room will be relatively easy.' She kissed the top of the frail lady's hair then wheeled her from the kitchen. They chatted away as Heather helped to manoeuvre her onto the stairlift, then walked beside her up the stairs. Rose gave chuckles of delight as the lift progressed.

Yvonne put the kettle on to boil and listened to the chorus of melodious voices that surrounded her. She could hear the deeper tones that were coming from the sitting room where Bob had taken Albert. Yvonne felt tired but so relieved to be home after all the hard work that had needed doing before they could return with her parents. She thought once again how kind her husband for sharing his home with his in-laws. A kindness that both Heather and Susan had inherited from him. Yvonne sliced some ginger cake and took the refreshments into the sitting room. Heather and Rose re-appeared in minutes, with Rose chortling gaily about the stairlift and what fun it was.

'All our things are already in place in our room,' Rose told her husband, 'just like the removal men promised they'd be. And Heather has volunteered to help us unpack later, haven't you, lovee?' Heather nodded.

'I'll help too. It'll get it done quickly, and you can settle in without any fuss. You must tell me, Mom, if everything isn't how you want it to be, you will, won't you?' Yvonne gazed with affection at her mother, who she'd been so worried about, and then at her father. She hoped that he would now be able to relax as some of the responsibility for his wife's welfare was shared.

'Now weesht up and stop your worrying,' Albert said. 'We're grateful that you are kind enough to have us here. Everything will be fine.' Yvonne could see the suggestion of an unshed tear in his eyes. She passed him a piece of his favourite cake, hoping to take his mind off the fact that he could no longer manage on his own.

Bob took a fork full of cake and then said, 'I think we'll all feel a lot better once we've had a good kip. Me, for one, I'm going to have an early night.' He looked at his Rolex and exclaimed in a silly voice, 'It's already four o'clock! Where did the day go?' Heather threw a cushion at him, much to everyone's amusement. 'Here, mind my cake,' he chuckled.

After the unpacking and dinner, Susan and Sean arrived and spent an hour while Rose and Albert got to know Sean. Just before they left, Susan said, 'Hey! Listen up, everyone! We have some news.' Her cheeks were flushed and her smile wide as she skipped over to her mother and whispered in her ear, 'Our baby is due the middle of June.' Yvonne gave a cry of joy, and Susan broadcast her news to everyone else and then said, 'I'm sorry, everyone, but I promised Mom that I'd tell her first.' She danced over to where Heather stood by their grandmother, who chuckled indulgently as the girls did a triumphant dance together, which included several whoops, swaying and raising their arms above their heads.

When the room became reasonably quiet again, and all the congratulations, kisses, and handshakes finished, Sienna asked her Mom again if she could have a little brother or sister.

'Perhaps one day, love, but you are enough for me. I love you so much.' Heather picked her smiling daughter up and danced around the room with her, making her chuckle as she danced out into the hall and then carried her up to bed after she had blown kisses to everyone.

By the time Heather returned to the sitting room, it was to find that Susan and Sean had gone home, and her parents and grandparents were getting themselves ready to go up to their rooms. 'It's been such a long day, love. We're all exhausted. I hope you won't mind us leaving you to your own devices. We'll have a long catch up in the morning,' Yvonne said. She yawned and then began to push her mother's wheelchair out into the hall, followed by her father and her husband.

'Night, everyone, sleep tight,' Heather said.

Once she was on her own, Heather wasn't sorry to be able to go into the kitchen and pour herself a glass of wine which she took into the conservatory. She then sat quietly looking out into the moonlit garden. The poplar trees that occupied the boundary between their neighbour's garden and their own were swaying quite violently. Must be quite windy out there, she thought, glad to be inside with her family. She sipped her wine and began to think about Susan, who was so excited at being pregnant. She wondered if she felt jealous but quickly dismissed the thought. She wasn't jealous, but she wished that Sienna's birth hadn't had a shadow over it. Damn Snake man, she thought, damn him to the hell that he deserved. She began to stroke her remaining bracelet as her mind turned to Driver, and she tried to devise a means of finding out where he now lived. She could think of nothing feasible, and there was no one that she could ask about him either. If she mentioned to anyone the fact that she wanted to find him, she could be implicated in his death. She had no idea what conclusion the police had reached regarding Ugly's murder. Other than the phone call from Lucy, she had heard nothing. She thought that she'd have to plan a different way to kill Driver when she eventually found him. She caught a glimpse, in the dark conservatory window, of her satisfied smile. At least she'd had her revenge on two of the bastards, and she no longer cried herself to sleep each night. Nor was she always expecting the police to arrest her.

Her thoughts turned to the fiasco of her last meeting with Stephen. She felt horrible about the way it had ended and desperately wanted to think of an explanation that would put things right. She was on nights for the next two shifts and wondered if he would be too. She knew she must have hurt him, but she wanted to see him even if he didn't forgive her.

She yawned, drained her glass and then went up to bed, trying to dispel all disquieting thoughts.

As she undressed and cleaned her teeth, she thought about her Grandma and hoped that Sienna wouldn't be too noisy for her. It might make it difficult for Yvonne to help with childcare arrangements. It took her a while to get off to sleep, even though she'd tried to read another Alex Cross Book called "Pop Goes the Weasel." She found herself reading the same paragraph over a few times before it sank in. She eventually fell asleep with the book still propped up on a pillow by her side.

Next morning, Heather wandered sleepily into the kitchen and poured herself a mug of coffee. 'Where is everyone?' She asked her mother, who arrived shortly after herself.

'Well, Sienna is in with Mom. She's taken a real shine to both of them. I told her not to wake you yet as you're on nights tonight. She's such a good, obedient little soul. I'll miss her when she goes to school full time.' Yvonne buttered a piece of toast and offered half to Heather, who took a bite and then put two more slices of thick white bread into the toaster.

'How much do you think things will alter now that Grandma and Granddad are here?' Heather asked.

Yvonne shook her head. 'I don't suppose things will change that much, certainly for the foreseeable future. Your granddad will still be looking after Mom – he just needs some help now and again – but he's promised me that he'll tell me when he needs me. I'll be doing the meals for us all though, and looking after Sienna as I always have. So, no. Nothing much will alter, love. Now tell me about Stephen. Did you go on any dates while I've been away?'

'We did have a date, but I blew it. I don't want to explain what I did, but I behaved badly, and I don't suppose he will ever ask me out again.' A tear rolled down Heather's cheek as she finished speaking, and Yvonne jumped to her feet and hugged her daughter.

'What do you mean, love? It's obviously affected you badly.' Yvonne felt guilty that she hadn't been there for Heather. It was hard to believe that she'd been through such a terrible time in the past, she'd always denied needing any help, but she needed her support now.

Heather mopped her face. 'It's okay, Mom. Don't worry; I'll get over it. And it's too personal to tell you the details, even though you are my mother. I just reacted badly when Stephen tried to get too close. He doesn't know what happened to me or why I have a daughter. He must have thought that I found him repulsive, and I just had no way of explaining. I'm sure he won't want anything else to do with a loony, and that's how I behaved, just like a loony. I don't know why because I really love him.'

Yvonne said nothing for a while and then asked, 'Would it help if I had a talk with him and explained? I'm sure he'd understand.'

It was Heather's turn to jump up. 'Please don't even think about it, Mom. I don't want him to ever know about those filthy bastards and what they did to me.'

'Alright, love, don't be upset. I won't say anything, but perhaps you need to talk to him, and soon. He could be just what you need.' Yvonne didn't know what else she could say to help and decided that she would have a chat with Susan as soon as she could.

Chapter 30

Heather left home early the following night in the hope that she would see Stephen and perhaps apologise. She wanted him to understand that it wasn't his fault, but she still hadn't thought of a plausible reason for her behaviour.

She needn't have racked her brains. It wasn't long before she found out that Stephen had taken some leave, and Bridget told her that he'd gone to visit his mother, who was still feeling under the weather. She felt lost and alone as she worked through the next two nights – sure that he'd decided to avoid her.

When she did see him a couple of weeks later and asked him to meet her after work, he smiled politely and declined. Heather walked away feeling mortified, he clearly wanted nothing more to do with her, and she'd lost him. She told herself to get some backbone and managed to allow her pride to be a barrier to her feelings. When it was necessary, she made sure that they only spoke in a professional capacity.

Later that week, John met Heather for a drink after work. 'Are you coming to the Christmas party?' he asked.

'No. I can't be bothered. I'm in no mood to be sociable, believe me,' Heather said.

'Look, I know you're upset over something, but it's just what you need. Why don't you come with me and Sam? We'll enjoy ourselves, and you don't have to stay too long if you don't want to.' He fell to his knees and put his hands out towards her. 'Go on, come with us. It might cheer you up, love. Go on, pretty please,' he said.

As usual, he made Heather laugh. 'Okay, but I'll meet you there and don't be annoyed if I don't stay.'

On the day of the party, Heather dressed in a smart red trouser suit and black sandals and met up with her friends in the car park. John knew that Heather didn't want to see Stephen, and he hoped he wouldn't be there. He'd seen her cry over him on a couple of occasions, although she hadn't confided what the problem was. John and Sam linked arms with her, and both men were determined to look after her.

The canteen was well decorated. A buffet was out on several tables that had were pushed together. As soon as they entered the already well-populated room, John found them a table to sit at, and then as the DJ began to play "Livin' La Vida Loca", he coaxed Heather onto the dance floor. She was soon unable to think as she whirled around. As the evening wore on, Heather found that she was having a good time. She was laughing happily with her friends between dances when she saw Stephen get up from a table across the other side of the room. He was holding onto the hand of an attractive woman who she recognised as one of the receptionists that worked in the antenatal clinic. Heather thought that they seemed to be on very familiar terms. Stephen held her close while they danced, and she gazed into his eyes.

A fierce pang of jealousy hit Heather – she began to feel dizzy – and became aware of how short of breath she was. She leaned forward to hide her face and tried to steady the uncomfortable, rapid beating of her heart.

'What's up? Are you okay?' John asked. He noticed that most of the colour had drained away from her face leaving two flushed patches at the top of her cheeks.

'I'm okay, but I need to get some fresh air. I'll see you tomorrow.' Heather picked up her coat and handbag and, without hearing John's offer to accompany her, pushed through the crowd around the entrance and hurried into the frosty night. As soon as the cold air entered her lungs, she began to recover and drove herself home while picturing the man that she loved holding the receptionist close. She felt that she couldn't bear to see him with anyone else. Her mind reeled about trying to find a solution. She wasn't usually impulsive, but by the time she arrived home, she'd decided that she would hand in her notice and apply for another midwifery vacancy. She felt that she needed to make a new start and stand on her own two feet. Perhaps then she would be able to sleep at night and not think about killing and being abused, and maybe she could forget Stephen.

Heather didn't discuss it with her parents before she gave in her notice, then applied for a job that she'd seen advertised at a teaching hospital in Wirral. Susan, Bob, Yvonne and all her friends tried hard to convince her not to leave, but it was too late. Just after Sienna's fourth birthday, Heather moved and began work at Arrowe Park, where she was made very welcome in their maternity unit. They were very short-staffed, and Heather was sorely needed. She took on extra shifts, which kept her from thinking about anything too deeply.

Until she found her feet, she stayed in a small hotel. Then she rented a two-bedroom bungalow in Liscard that overlooked Mariners Park, a retirement complex for seamen. It was lovely and had a great view across the park to the River Mersey. She knew when she saw how near they were to the beach at the mouth of the River Mersey that Sienna would love it. Perhaps here, Heather thought she could forget her past, and even though she now saw herself as a monster, she knew that given the opportunity, she would still kill Driver.

The bungalow was adequately furnished, so after she'd made arrangement for a nursery placement and found someone that she trusted to care for her daughter overnight when necessary, she fetched Sienna to live with her. Yvonne was distraught and wondered if having her parents come to live with them had any bearing on her daughter, leaving and moving so far away.

Wirral wasn't too far away, perhaps a couple of hours, but Yvonne felt that it might as well have been a different country. She knew that Heather had seen Stephen at the Christmas party and been quite devastated. She supposed that was the reason for the urgency with which Heather had decided to branch out on her own. John and Sam had joined them for the dawn of the Millennium, and while the world held its breath to see if midnight would bring forth the chaos predicted – John had told her about what he had witnessed at the party.

Yvonne missed her daughter and granddaughter more than she'd thought possible. She drove up to see them as often as she could, leaving Susan to help her grandfather with Rose when necessary.

Heather cried herself to sleep each night for the first two months, but gradually her life started to take on some familiarity, and she began to make friends. She missed her family, and Sienna often asked when they were going to go back home. Heather was unable to do more than say that perhaps one day they might – although she thought that they never would.

Fate had a different plan in mind, however, and on a sunny Sunday morning early in May when Heather and Sienna were planning to catch the ferry across to Liverpool to the Albert Dock, there was a knock on their front door. Heather couldn't believe who was standing there, holding an enormous bunch of red roses.

'Well, are you going to invite me in or tell me to bugger off?' Stephen asked and held the flowers out towards her.

Heather hesitated, then opened the door wider. She went into the open plan lounge and kitchen area, and Stephen closed the door and followed her. Perched on the arm of the sofa, Heather watched in amazement as Stephen placed the flowers on the counter then walked to the window where he stood admiring the view over the Mersey. She could smell his aftershave, and it brought all her loving feelings sharply to the fore.

He turned to her and said, 'I think we need to talk.' He then sat down opposite Heather.

'I'm sorry, Stephen, but this is a bad time. We were just getting ready to go out.' Heather said.

Sienna chose that moment to come from her room. She'd been dressing her favourite doll ready to accompany them on the ferry. She took one look at Stephen and ran over to him with a delighted chortle. She rested her head against his arm, kissed his cheek and plonked down beside him on a low pouffe. He stroked her shiny, black hair and said, 'You remember me then?'

Sienna nodded. 'Of course, I do, silly. You're my Uncle Stephen, and I've missed you. Mommy does too. She cries a lot.'

‘Do you think you could go and play in your room for a few more minutes, Sienna, while I talk to Uncle Stephen?’ Heather said.

Obedient as ever, Sienna went into her room, giving her mother a wink. Heather smiled inwardly at her knowing daughter, but her expression remained stern.

‘What do you want to talk about, Stephen?’ Heather asked. ‘I wasn’t lying. I promised Sienna that we’d go on the ferry, and I’m not going to disappoint her.’

‘We need to talk about what happened between us the last time that we were together, but I don’t think you should disappoint her either. I’ve booked into a small hotel just up from the front where I intend to stay until tomorrow. I know you don’t have work because your mother checked which shifts you were covering – perhaps tomorrow would be a better time?’ He put his head on one side, a familiar gesture that she had pictured on many nights as she’d allowed tears to dampen her pillow. It brought a lump to her throat.

Now that he was here, Heather didn’t want to let him out of her sight and said, ‘W... well, if you’re staying, you could come on the ferry with us. Have you ever been to Liverpool?’

‘No, I haven’t, and yes, I would love to come with you and Sienna. We could talk later when Sienna is in bed, or perhaps tomorrow. We could just enjoy ourselves today. What do you say?’ He lifted his eyebrows and smiled disarmingly.

‘Well, as I don’t know what you want to talk about, I say let’s go to Liverpool, we can at least be civil. We’ll see how the day goes because I don’t want to talk seriously in front of Sienna either.’

Stephen continued to smile at her, but Heather’s hurt feelings wouldn’t allow her to reciprocate. She thanked him for the flowers as she quickly arranged them in the only vase she owned. It was far too big, but it would have to do. She then went to fetch her daughter.

Sienna skipped excitedly between the two adults as they walked down the slope to the floating landing stage and stood behind the barrier while they waited for the ferry to dock. Ten minutes later, they were on their way upriver towards Woodside, and more people boarded. The boat then headed across the river to where they disembarked. Heather held onto Sienna's hand as they walked across an iron swing bridge and proceeded to roam past the shops and cafes that surrounded the dock where a few small boats moored. They later lunched at one of the café's outside tables where seagulls constantly stalked about, waiting for titbits that they could beg or steal, much to Sienna's amusement.

Replete, they continued to explore and entered a gem shop where Stephen bought some pretty stones that had caught Sienna's eye. He offered to buy some earrings and a necklace for Heather, but she politely refused.

She couldn't believe that he was here with them and occasionally allowed herself to watch him as he walked ahead through a narrow space or when he stood looking in a shop that sold seafaring merchandise. She still loved him – her body sang with it. She wondered what he wished to talk to her about and looked forward to being able to listen but dreaded it at the same time. Perhaps he'd come to tell her that he was marrying the woman she'd seen him dancing with, she speculated but laughed at the thought. Why would he come all this way to tell her something like that?

Her mind dared to hope that he still loved her, and she wondered if she could bear to tell him the real reason why she had reacted so badly to his lovemaking. She didn't know, and, as they ventured further into Liverpool, she ceased to puzzle about her feelings and enjoy being with two people that she loved. Stephen went out of his way to amuse Sienna, and, as they approached St. George's Hall, he pretended to be afraid of the lion statues that guarded the entrance. Sienna told him firmly not to be a baby as they weren't real and couldn't eat him. Heather laughed but felt very proud of her four-year-old daughter as Stephen thanked her for telling him that he was safe.

Sienna giggled and said, 'You didn't think that they could eat you, did you?'

When they returned home, after having their tea at the Queens Hotel on the front at New Brighton, Heather realised how much she'd enjoyed their day out. She knew that the stressful phase was coming and hoped that Stephen's departure wouldn't make her feel too sad or too much like returning to Birmingham. She'd grown to like her life just as it was, even though she missed her family and friends –especially him.

Chapter 31

Heather found it very difficult to settle Sienna down at bedtime. She read her a story as usual, but when it finished, Sienna sat up, leaned mutinously against her pink pillow, clasped her arms around Fred, and said that she needed Uncle Stephen to read her a story too. Heather realised that Sienna was trying to hold on to this man who represented their past life and asked Stephen if he would read to her. He agreed, and they both entered her room where he looked stern as he said, 'I'm not going to read you a story, young lady, but I will tell you one if you promise to settle down when I've finished.'

'Yes, I will. I promise, but what's it about?' She snuggled down further into her bed and watched Stephen intently as he began to talk.

'Once upon a time, there was a little boy who had two older brothers who were very unkind to him ...'

Heather listened for a moment, then went into the lounge and kicked off her shoes. She sat with her legs tucked under her on the sofa and watched a container ship manoeuvred by two tugs that were dwarfed by its enormous bulk. They guided it expertly into a lock that accessed the unloading dock. After five or ten minutes, Stephen came and stood beside her, surveying the movement on the river. 'She's fast asleep. I guess she found my story too boring.' He chuckled.

Heather smiled. ‘I’ve so enjoyed today, Stephen, but I think we need to get this over and done. What do you want to talk about?’ Heather’s speech was stilted as she attempted to take control of her feelings.

‘I’ve enjoyed myself, too. So thank you for letting me join the two of you.’ He let a long minute pass while Heather sat quietly appraising him. She knew that her attitude was off-putting, but she wasn’t about to help him out.

Stephen sat beside her. ‘I guess Julie phoned and told you that I would be coming to see you, did she? I had to work hard to get her to tell me where you’d disappeared to.’

‘No, so I’m sorry that you’ve come all this way – I could have been on holiday or anything. Anyway, what do you want with me? You made it pretty clear that we finished almost before we started. I know it was my fault, and I still can’t explain, so there’s little point in you being here unless you’ve come to tell me that you’re getting married, although I can’t think why you would think that I needed to know.’ Heather didn’t stop for breath.

‘If you stop going on a minute, I’ll tell you why I’m here – but what makes you think that I’d be getting married?’ Stephen looked utterly baffled.

‘What about the receptionist that I saw you with at the Christmas party? You seemed to be pretty close.’ Heather could feel herself becoming very warm as she remembered how she’d felt on that occasion – the memory of it had run on a loop in her mind for some time.

‘She was just a friend, and I suppose I was trying to make you feel jealous, and I’m sorry. It didn’t have the desired effect, did it? I just drove you away.’ Stephen sounded despondent.

‘This is all water under the bridge, Stephen. I’ve told you that I can’t explain what happened then, but I know I’m happy now. I like my job and living here, and so does Sienna. So, please just say what you came to say, then leave. Sienna gets up quite early, and so do I.’ While she spoke, Heather was trembling inside; she didn’t want him to go, but he had to stay out of her life. She couldn’t possibly be simply friends with him, and she couldn’t have a relationship either.

Stephen reached for her hands and held them loosely in his. ‘You don’t need to explain, my love – I know what happened to you before Sienna was born. Ben told me a story, he didn’t say it was about you, but I knew that it must have been. It explained everything. He said that I should give it another try if I loved you – and I do. I love you more than anything, Heather – please believe me.’

Minutes ticked by, then Heather tore her eyes from his face and gazed across the river. ‘I do believe you, Stephen, I love you too, but if you knew what happened to me, and no one knows what those bastards did to me, then you must realise that I don’t know if I could ever be comfortable having sex, even with someone that I love as much as I love you.’

‘Oh, my darling. It must have been terrible for you, and I don’t know how you can either, but I want to try to make up for all the things that they did to you. I would never want you to do anything that you didn’t want to do, and I promise that I will never touch you again in that way unless you ask me to and tell me it’s what you want. But I want to marry you and spend the rest of my life with you and look after Sienna, too. Please say that you’ll be my wife.’ Stephen hardly dared to breathe while his words sank in.

Heather started to cry bitterly, eventually stumbling over her reply. ‘I can’t marry you, Stephen. I want to, but I can’t.’

She mopped her eyes. 'You don't know my secrets, and I can never tell you – you might hate me if you knew.' Heather realised that Stephen would think she was talking about the rapes. He couldn't know that she meant being able to exact the revenge that she'd had and the murder that she was still planning.

'I would never hate you no matter what you told me, my love,' Stephen said. He held out his arms. Heather scrutinised his face as if to see deep into his soul and fathom if she could trust him. She swung her legs off the sofa and moved into his embrace. She stayed with her head on his shoulder until the shadows lengthened on the walls, and the evening became night.

After what seemed like a very long time, Heather broke the silence. 'I'm sorry, I truly am, but I don't think it would be fair to marry you, under those circumstances, my darling. I want to be by your side forever, but I just don't know about the intimacy –they really hurt me, you know.' She held his hand tightly. 'I've never been able to tell anyone what they did to me – perhaps one day I might be able to tell you.' She looked up to see tears on his cheeks and knew for certain that she could trust him enough to marry him.

'Alright, I will marry you if you think you can wait, but what if I'm never ready to have sex?' she frowned.

'Then we won't have sex, but we will have as much closeness and love as we can both manage. Now say it properly – I will marry you, Stephen.'

'I will marry you, Stephen.'

He laughed and then insisted that he went to the hotel that he had booked.

'But I'll expect you here for breakfast bright and early,' Heather said, 'and then we can spend the day together before you go back to Birmingham.' They kissed goodbye and spent another ten minutes hugging before Stephen finally managed to prise himself away. Heather was left to retire to her bed, where she had trouble sleeping and regretted telling him to go. She now had too much time to dwell on her doubts and fears.

Heather and Sienna were in night attire when Stephen arrived the next morning. But he was happy to cook breakfast, something he enjoyed doing, while Heather and her daughter showered and pulled on casual clothing.

'I know I said early,' Heather said as they sat down to scrambled eggs and toast, 'but what are we going to do with this lovely day?'

'We could play on the beach,' Sienna said.

'I'm sorry, poppet, but I would like to take you both to Manchester to the Arndale Centre. I haven't asked you yet, Heather, but I would like to buy you an engagement ring if that's okay?'

Heather blushed and said that she thought it was a lovely idea. 'I've never been to Manchester or had an engagement ring.' She chuckled, and Stephen proceeded to kiss her lingeringly on the lips, making Sienna whoop with joy.

'Does this mean that you are going to be my Daddy?' Sienna asked with a beaming smile.

'I sure am, little girl – will you be my daughter?'

'I sure will.' Sienna ran off to get her doll to take with them.

'Do you think we could visit the new Lowry Museum at Salford Quays?' Heather asked.

'I don't see why not. I don't have to be back until late, so we can spend the whole day up there if you wish.'

Heather had never been as happy as she was when they climbed into his shiny, black Audi. All thoughts of secrets and Driver went out of her head and stayed away as they drove along the M56, then parked in the retail centre. Sienna begged a ride on a mechanical horse that was set up just inside the entrance.

'Not stupid are they? This is just the place where most people will give in to their children's demands if they want a pleasant shopping trip,' Heather said. Stephen gave her a guilty look as he'd put the money into the slot as soon as Sienna had asked.

'Guess I'm an easy touch too, not that I think Sienna is the bratty sort of child that would play up if she didn't get her way.'

'No, but she does have her moments.' Heather held out her hands as the ride came to an end, but Sienna was helped off by Stephen. They both looked so happy that Heather's butterflies began to twirl in a way that had nothing to do with sex.

After browsing in several establishments and trying on three other engagement rings, Heather chose a princess cut, solitaire diamond. She couldn't stop looking at it and moving her fingers about to watch the sparkling stone as the overhead lights brought forth its rainbows. Sienna was so excited and kept on holding on to her mother's left hand and stroked the diamond gently. Stephen had insisted that she kept it on her finger when they left the shop.

Sienna's behaviour amused Stephen, and when they were passing the next jewellers, he asked Heather to wait outside on a bench. He took Sienna into the shop where he bought her a tiny ring that had some bright semi-precious stones set into a silver band. It wasn't expensive, and he didn't want there to be any upset if she lost it. Heather was very touched by his kindness. Sienna saw little else for an hour as she frequently waved her hand about to catch the light.

After lunch at Burger King, they looked around a few more shops, then went to Salford Quays and explored the complex before going into the Lowry Museum.

'I didn't know that he was an accomplished artist before he started painting matchstick people,' Heather said, as they stood before an impressive portrait he had painted. They wandered into the gift shop where Stephen bought a framed print entitled *Coming from the Mill* that Lowry had painted in 1930.

When they returned to the bungalow, Stephen stayed for a cup of coffee and then reluctantly left for Birmingham. Heather said goodbye with a light heart and promised that she would bring Sienna the following weekend to visit at her mother's, where they could meet up and start to make plans.

Chapter 32

Heather phoned her mother the following day and told her about Stephen's visit, but she omitted the fact that they had become engaged; she wanted to tell her face to face. Yvonne was delighted with the news as Heather sounded happier than she'd been since she left home.

'How long are you staying, love? For good?' she asked.

'No, mother,' Heather was amused, 'just for the weekend. I have work on Monday and Sienna is due to start school soon. I don't want to unsettle her.'

'What's made you decide to visit now, is it Stephen?'

'Well, I suppose it is, but I'll tell you all about it when I get home. How's everyone?' Heather asked. She already knew that they were okay; her mom had visited two weeks previously. She'd never been allowed to feel lonely; her family and friends had frequently been in touch.

'Everyone's fine and dandy. Oh, the family will be so excited that you're coming home – not as excited as I am, my love – I've missed you both so much. Okay, okay, I know you want to go so I'll just ring your sister and tell her the good news. Love to you both. Bye, my darling, see you soon, take care,' Yvonne said.

Having her mother and father living with them hadn't made a great deal of difference to Yvonne; it was her daughter and granddaughter's absence that troubled her. For the most part, Albert was capable of looking after Rose and asked for little help. Yvonne did all the cooking and cleaning and often took her mother shopping while her father had a break. The elderly couple spent most of their time in their bedsitting room watching television or in the conservatory reading and playing cribbage – unless Yvonne and Bob encouraged them to be in their company. Rose's condition didn't seem to be deteriorating, and her new medication was helping with her symptoms. They didn't say a lot about it, but Yvonne knew that they were happy and grateful for all the help to ease their lives. They were used to spending most of their time alone since Yvonne had left to go to University in Birmingham, so she tried not to intrude too much.

As soon as the phone conversation with Heather ended, Yvonne phoned Susan. She allowed the phone to ring several times before answering, and then she didn't wait for her daughter to speak before she dived in.

'Susan dear, what are you doing this weekend? Heather and Sienna are coming to visit, and I'm going to plan a surprise party on Sunday and invite all her friends, so you and Sean must be here.'

'Oh, wow! That's great! Okay, Mom, we hadn't planned anything, but I would have cancelled if we had. I can't believe she's decided to come. I wonder why she's changed her mind.'

'Well, I know that Stephen went up there last weekend to visit her, so I suppose that's it. Perhaps they've made up their differences, I hope so. I'm going to ring John and Sam now, so I'll speak to you soon. Bye, my love … oh, by the way, how are you feeling today?'

Susan roared with laughter as she said, 'I'm okay, Mom. Bye for now.'

By the time Yvonne had told most of Heather's friends the news, it was late evening before she phoned Julie and Ben.

'Hello, love, I just wanted you to know that Heather's coming to visit at the weekend and I'm arranging a little surprise party for her on Sunday, can you both make it?' Yvonne was tired of repeating herself. She took a rather large swig of her glass of wine as she waited for Julie to reply.

She didn't have to wait long before Julie nearly deafened her by shouting excitedly to Ben, 'Heather's coming home at the weekend. We need a babysitter.' Yvonne could hear Ben laughing in the background, and then he said something unintelligible.

Julie started to explain to Yvonne, who said, 'Oh, don't get a babysitter. We will all enjoy seeing Heather Jo, and it's been a while. I bet she's quite a handful now, isn't she?'

'She's a lot of hard work, but such a blessing. Exciting times eh? Are you sure we should bring her with us?' Julie asked.

'I'm positive. Heather will be surprised at how big she's grown.'

'Alright, we'll bring her. I'm longing to see Heather and catch up – I hope she isn't mad at me for telling Stephen where to find her.'

'Is that what you did? Well, she said that they'd enjoyed his visit, and she didn't sound annoyed at all. So we'll see you on Sunday then. I'll look forward to it, love. Bye for now.'

Yvonne sank into a chair in the hall and took another sip of wine. She wondered if she should set the food up in the conservatory. If the weather was beautiful, everyone could fill their plates and take them into the garden to eat. She began to plan the menu for the weekend, feeling as though her nest was filling up again. She'd missed both of her daughter's more than she could explain to anyone other than her husband. He knew how much she'd cried, after first Susan, then Heather left home within a few months of each other. Yvonne sat at the space under the stairs, which she always referred to as her office. Booting up the computer that Sam had set up, she began to enjoy herself typing up the guest list and the menu. Then she played a couple of games of Hearts before Bob arrived home and enticed her into the dining room to keep him company while he ate Mexican chicken and rice. He was just as pleased as his wife when she told him that Heather and Sienna were coming to visit.

'Perhaps they will make a go of it. After all, now he's been to see her. It's obviously his influence that has made her decide to visit us rather than have us visit there all the time.' Bob said. He smiled indulgently as Yvonne told him what she was planning, then said, 'Well, I haven't seen her since her birthday in April, so I'll try and make sure that I'm free this weekend. I know that there's at least one prison visit I should be making, but I'll cancel it until Monday. How are Mom and Dad?' Bob's parents had both been killed in a car crash when he was in his early twenties – now, he always referred to his in-laws as Mom and Dad.

'They're fine. Dad took Mom for an outing into Solihull earlier today, but they felt drained afterwards, and when I asked them if they would like to come down for tea, they said they'd prefer to eat in their room. I went up not long ago to fetch their dishes. Dad said they were going to have an early night, so I'll just leave them unless they phone down for any reason – time enough tomorrow to give them the news.'

'Okay, love. They've settled in well, considering the beautiful scenery in that part of Scotland? They've lived there all their lives, haven't they?' He paused and looked thoughtful.

‘I don’t suppose they will have been going out very much, though, since Mom’s been so unsteady.’

‘No. I think that they are happier than they’ve been for some time, and I love having them here. Now, do you want to watch a film or shall we have a quiet night?’ Yvonne asked. She cleared Bob’s plate away and went to fill the dishwasher.

When she returned to the dining room, it was to find that he’d already gone into the sitting room where he was choosing a film for them to watch.

Heather had promised that she’d phone her parents from Mere Park when they pulled in for a comfort break. She bought a small cactus plant for her mother to keep on the kitchen window ledge, along with two others that she already owned and then made the promised call.

‘Hi, Mom. We’ll be about another half an hour if we’re lucky.’

‘I’ve got the coffee pot on already, and your room’s all ready for you. I can’t wait for you to be here love, where’s Sienna?’

‘Grandma wants to know where you are.’ Heather passed the receiver to Sienna.

‘I’m here, Grandma, and we’ve bought you a present. And I’m very excited. Is Granddad home too?’

‘Hey, if you stay on the phone, we’ll never get there, say bye, bye, honey. I know everyone’s waiting to see us.’

Heather took the phone, and Sienna called, ‘See you soon, Grandma.’

‘Bye, Mom. We’ll see you shortly. We’re both excited now.’

It seemed to be no time at all before Heather pulled into the drive and gazed at the house where she’d been so happy and also desperately unhappy. Her Mom and Dad met them as they got out of the car. Sienna ran from one to the other, hugging, laughing and demanding kisses. Heather followed suit and had her share of hugs. Their happiness overflowed as Susan appeared at the window, waving and frantically gesturing for them to hurry into the house where she could hug them too. Sienna ran ahead while Heather took their overnight bag from the boot, then followed her into the living room. Susan had seated herself in a new rocking chair, and Rose and Albert were side by side on the sofa. Heather kissed them, then flopped into a chair as she stared around at their joyful faces. She'd missed them all and vowed that to find a vacancy in one of the maternity units back in Birmingham. Heather wanted to come home. She also needed to find Driver before marrying Stephen. There had been very few days when she hadn't racked her brains trying to think how to trace him. She wondered how she had prevented herself from becoming insane while living two lives. Perhaps you haven't whispered the persistent small voice.

An hour after they'd settled into their room, Stephen arrived. Heather flew into his outstretched arms, causing a few jaws to drop as the pair stood entwined.

'Can I tell them our secret now, Mommy?' Sienna pleaded and ran to her mother with her palm held out.

'You haven't told anyone yet?' Stephen said. His eyebrows nearly touched his hairline.

'No, I wanted you to be here.' She put her hand into the pocket of her jeans and handed Sienna her ring.

They both placed them back on their fingers, and before Heather or Stephen could say anything, Sienna shouted, 'Look, everyone, we're engaged!' She grasped her mother's hand and showed off the two rings. There was a moment of surprised silence, then congratulations and more hugs and kisses greeted the news.

‘When are you thinking of getting married? And don’t tell me it’s going to be a quick wedding at the registry office. I couldn’t bear it.’ Yvonne said.

Heather and Susan roared with mirth as their mother’s look of happiness changed to dismay at the prospect of yet another daughter cheating her of her dreams of being Mother of the Bride at a big wedding.

‘We’ll let you know, Mom, but it’ll be in church, so stop worrying,’ Heather said.

Chapter 33

Sunday dawned miserably. It was cloudy, and everywhere felt damp to the touch. Yvonne, more than anyone, felt disappointed as not only was she going to lose Heather and Sienna once again, but her plans for the party were now uncertain. Happily, towards one o'clock, the sun came out and gave Yvonne's world a boost. She and Heather cleared away their early lunch, then began to set up a trestle table in the conservatory.

Sienna was entertaining Rose and Albert as she recited a funny poem that she'd learned from her babysitter. It was written in a cockney accent and told the story of a "muvver who was barfin' her bebe one night." Sienna's rendition was so hilarious that Yvonne left her task and went into the sitting room to listen. Heather had heard it before and continued to load food onto the table, ready for later.

At three o'clock, Susan and Sean arrived, followed minutes later by Julie and Ben with their little one. Julie immediately noticed Heather's engagement ring and, after congratulating her, spent a short time telling her how insightful she'd been to send Stephen to the Wirral.

'Yes, Julie, I suppose you were, but I would have liked a little warning, but it did turn out for the best, so I forgive you.' Heather grinned at her friend's crestfallen face and then hurried to answer the doorbell and let Stephen, Lucy, John and Sam into the house. Everyone began talking at once; it sounded like a disturbed wasp's nest. After a little while, Heather indicated to Stephen that he should follow her. Mystified, he found himself in her room where, after greeting each other lovingly, he sat on Sienna's bed.

'Are you okay, my love? You don't seem to be all that cheerful,' he said.

Heather didn't hesitate. 'I want to leave Arrowe Park and come home – I've missed my family more than you could know.'

Stephen moved to sit beside her on the bed and clasped both her hands together in his. Heather took a deep breath; she didn't like being held like that; it reminded her of the way that Driver had held her. She slowly withdrew one hand and laid it gently on his cheek.

'Well, give your notice in and come home. No one will mind, and I'm sure that you'll soon get another job.' He looked pensive. 'You know, Heather, my apartmcnt has only one bedroom, but if we get married soon and buy a house, you wouldn't have to go to work unless you want to.'

'I'd like us to marry quickly, but I can't bear to disappoint Mom yet again. You know she was distraught when Susan and Sean married hastily. How about seeing if we can arrange it for just after New Year? You don't mind getting married in a church, do you? You're not a catholic, are you? Damn, I know so little about you.' Heather pulled a face.

Stephen laughed aloud. 'Heather, I'll marry you tomorrow, or I'll wait until you say, but please don't make it too long. Susan's baby is due soon, isn't it? I think that will probably be enough excitement for a while, and then it'll be Christmas and

New Year, so I suppose after that would be a good time. Meanwhile, we can find a house that we both like. And either move in together, or I will move in until after we are married. What do you think?' He studied her face intently.

'I love you very much, and I think you're wonderful.' They kissed, and when she could breathe, Heather asked, 'Shall we tell them it will be the second week in January then? We'd better go down; they'll be wondering what we're up to.'

'I love you too, very much, and yes, come on, let's go and tell them our news.' He took her hand, and they went down to join their guests who were sitting on wrought iron benches placed strategically around the sunken part of the gravelled garden that was warmed by the brilliant sunshine.

'We thought we'd have to send out a search party,' John teased, 'Where have you been hiding?'

'Leave them alone, nosey.' Sam reprimanded his partner with a grin.

Heather and Stephen sat down on a decorative concrete bench, and soon Sienna left her grandmother and wriggled between them. Nothing changes, Yvonne thought, remembering the way the girls had always wriggled in between her and Bob

'We had things to discuss. You can stop your teasing, and I'll tell you about it.' Everyone's eyes were on them. 'We're going to come back home to live, if you'll allow us to Mom, Dad?' she asked, and gazed serenely at her parents,

'Of course,' they chorused.

'I knew you'd say that,' she grinned, 'and Stephen and I want to buy a house as soon as we find one we like.'

'Not too far away, please,' Yvonne said. She waggled her crossed fingers, making everyone laugh.

Heather raised her voice. 'And we want to get married in a church with bridesmaids and a reception afterwards.'

Her mother's face became the colour of the red geraniums that were planted in the terracotta pot by her side.

'When do you mean?' Yvonne asked as everyone began to talk among themselves.

'Oh, shh,' Heather waved her hands excitedly. 'I forgot the most important bit. We want it to be the second Saturday in January, so please don't any of you book holidays for that weekend.'

Someone, Heather thought it was Sam, began to sing Congratulations, and everyone joined in at the top of their voice.

'Now all the neighbours will know!' Heather laughed and then dragged Stephen away to get some food. She was suddenly feeling famished.

Sienna talked nonstop for the first few miles on the M6 but, much to Heather's relief, as they passed Stoke-on-Trent, she fell asleep. It was the first time that she'd been aware of silence for the whole weekend. She began to think about Stephen and the plans they'd made and worried if they would be able to be happy together if she couldn't let the past go and they couldn't consummate their marriage. Her thoughts turned to Driver once again. If she could only find him and end his life, she just might be able to put the past behind her. But would you, the small voice in her head asked, are you just making an excuse not to be touched again, even by the man you love? Heather shook her head firmly and picked up a CD, which she pushed, rather too forcefully, into the player. She concentrated on the soothing sounds of Enya and the tiny snores that emanated from her sleeping daughter.

Heather gave notice at Arrowe Park and, as she had some holiday due to her, she was able, with her family and Stephen's help, to be back home before Susan made her an Aunt to baby, Gemma Rose, on the twenty-fifth of June.

Susan was in her own bed twelve hours after the birth, much to Yvonne's amazement and concern. As soon as she knew that her daughter was home, she hurried there with Heather and Sienna. She hugged Susan then quickly surveyed her new grandchild with adoration making her eyes shine.

'Are you sure that it's safe for you to be out of hospital this quickly?' she asked Susan. Worry for what she didn't know was written all over her face.

Heather groaned and then said, 'Things have changed, Mom, since we were born, even since Sienna was born. If mother and child are well, then there's no need for them to stay in, so stop worrying. Don't forget that there are enough doctors and midwives in and surrounding this family – she wouldn't be any better off in hospital!'

'I suppose you're right. I'm an old fusspot – she's beautiful, isn't she?' Yvonne picked her second grandchild from her crib and sat in the white, painted nursing chair with Sienna by her side.

Sienna couldn't take her eyes off her cousin, who, unlike herself, had blond hair, so fine it appeared to be non-existent. It was instant love, and when she was allowed to take her grandmother's place and hold Gemma on her lap for a couple of minutes, with a supporting arm from Heather, her face glowed with the wonder of it all.

Sean came into the room a short time later and said bluntly, 'I know you're all excited, but I'm throwing you out for now. Susan needs to rest, and so do I. Why not come back this evening with Bob, and I'll make us all some Bolognaise?'

'You don't have to do that,' Yvonne smiled and kissed his cheek, 'I'll make a meal and bring it with us. Will seven o'clock be okay?'

Sean nodded, and Susan gazed in awe at this normally mild-mannered man who was now being very assertive. She was grateful for his intervention. She just wanted to try and get the hang of feeding her daughter.

The casserole that Yvonne cooked smelled delicious and, after eating, they stayed for an hour admiring the new baby. Bob was overwhelmed to be a grandfather for the second time. He made everyone, except Susan, gasp in protest as he teased her. 'Well done, my darling. Now, when are you going to give us a grandson?'

'How about as soon as Gemma is two, will that do?' Susan gently slapped his grinning face.

Heather wondered if she would ever have another child as she glanced to where Sienna was standing with her index finger grasped firmly in Gemma's hand. She didn't expect to, but the thought brought her butterflies awake, and she hoped that perhaps one day she might.

The next day, when Susan and Sean brought Gemma to meet her great-grandparents, John and Sam arrived too. When Yvonne had answered the door chimes, she was pleasantly surprised to see them on the doorstep.

'We hoped you wouldn't mind us popping in without ringing, but we were passing and hoped for a peek at our newest friend.' John looked up at her with a winning smile.

'Come in. I know everyone will be pleased that you came. Would you like a coffee?'

'If it's not too much trouble – may we go through?' Sam said.

'Of course, make yourselves at home.' Yvonne went into the kitchen, and the two men joined the cooing group around Gemma, who was lying in her aunt's arms. Her eyes were closed as she contentedly sucked on her bottom lip, with Sienna paying close attention. Rose shed a few private tears.

Chapter 34

Yvonne had taken breakfast upstairs for her husband and parents, leaving Heather and Sienna to have theirs in the kitchen. Heather was admiring the orange and brown, paper-thin leaves swirling madly as they lost their hold on the trees and bushes in the garden when Sienna asked, ‘Why haven’t I got a daddy?’

Heather didn’t know what to say. She was so intent in the fact that Sienna was hers alone that she hadn’t worked out a story for her. Snake man's image flashed before her eyes. Her stomach clenched as she remembered the cold feel of the scalpel in her hand as it sliced across his bared throat. She smelled the iron in his blood again as she’d watched him die.

Heather turned from the peaceful garden. ‘Hold on a minute, love; I need the loo. We can talk about it when I come back. Make sure you drink all your juice up.’

Heather was panicking and very angry with herself for not anticipating her daughter’s question. She ran upstairs and vomited forcefully into the toilet. After mopping her mouth with a tissue, Heather sat on the edge of the bath, racking her brains for an answer that would satisfy her daughter’s curiosity. She thought that if she stayed upstairs for long enough, then Sienna might have found something to play with and forget that she’d asked the question. The urge to vomit threatened again but was controlled. She took the time to comb her hair and tidy the vanity unit while her brain worked feverishly to come up with a plausible lie.

'Mommy, I've finished. Are you coming down?' Sienna began to walk up the stairs. Heather hurried from the bathroom and went to meet her. As they walked hand in hand into the kitchen, Heather still hadn't decided what she should tell her daughter. Her stomach felt incredibly hot, and saliva spurted into her mouth. She spat discreetly into her handkerchief. She knew in her heart that Sienna wouldn't give up asking the question.

She tickled her daughter's neck, making her squirm and giggle. Heather managed a laugh too as she said, 'I'm sorry I took so long, chicky. If you go and play with your Lego in the conservatory, I'll make myself a cup of coffee, and then we'll see if we can build a house together.'

'Okay.' Sienna ran off, and Heather breathed a sigh of relief, hoping her daughter had forgotten all about the question she'd asked. But she knew that it would only be a reprieve; she had to be able to tell her something.

After a few minutes, Heather took her coffee into the conservatory where her daughter was colouring in her book of fairies. Sienna dropped her pencils, fetched her tin of Lego, and emptied it out onto the mottled green tiles.

'Do you think you should put your pencils away first before Grandma and perhaps Great-Grandma might come and be with us? You don't want them to slip on them, do you?' Sienna obediently cleared away, and Heather joined her on the floor, where they began to choose pieces of Lego and fit them together.

After a few moments, Sienna said thoughtfully, 'Gemma's Daddy is Sean, so who is my Daddy?' She held onto the red piece that she had just picked up and gazed intently at her mother.

Heather's heart sank – she had to answer. 'I'm afraid that your Daddy died before you were born, love.'

'What was his name?' Sienna said. She still held onto the same red piece of Lego, and her lip drooped. She understood what died meant.

'His name was David White, and he had a car accident. I'm afraid he didn't get better. I'm so sorry, my love, but you have all of us to love you, don't you? And Stephen is going to be your Daddy. You promised him that you'd be his daughter, remember?'

Heather had expected Sienna to cry, but she nodded and seemed satisfied as she continued to press her pieces onto the baseboard. Heather sighed with relief but swore under her breath. Why she had used the fucking name David when she could have said any name. It's too bloody late now, she thought. She needed to tell her parents and Susan the story that she'd fobbed Sienna off with in case she questioned them. She supposed that Sienna would ask for more details as she became older and began to sketch out a plausible story for when that happened. So many lies, too many lies, she thought sadly. Minutes later, as she completed the second wall of Lego, she could hear her mother coming slowly downstairs.

'You carry on, my love, while I go and make Grandma a cuppa.'

'Shall I come with you and help?' Sienna asked.

'No, thank you, darling. Why don't you see if you can finish that other wall off before I get back?' Heather rose and went into the kitchen, where she knew that Yvonne would already be making coffee. 'Mom,' she put her finger to her lips and said, 'shh …' then gestured towards the conservatory door, 'I need to tell you something.' She went on to tell her mother about her conversation with Sienna.

'Well, I don't know why you were surprised; she was bound to ask sometime. I'll tell your Dad and Susan, so don't worry, love, you did the right thing. Susan's coming round later on. I think Gemma will take Sienna's mind off any more questions. Anyway, we've lots of plans to make, haven't we ...? Christmas isn't too far away, and then January will be on us. I can't wait.' Yvonne looked blissful as she went on to talk about wedding cakes, dresses and venues. Heather was more than pleased that her mother was being allowed to make all the arrangements. She just wanted it to be a fait accompli and start her married life with the man that she fell deeper and deeper in love with each time she saw him and got to know his ways. As her mother prattled on about what should be the happiest day of her daughter's life, Heather wished with all her heart that she didn't have to think about finding and killing Driver. She felt that it was the only drawback to her happiness, but he was never far from her mind.

After the agent left, Heather said excitedly, 'This is the one – I love it. What do you think?'

Stephen considered the facade of the detached house with its mellow pink bricks that blushed in the rays of the late autumn sun. It was only two roads away from Heather's parent's house, and it had a good size driveway and well-tended gardens front and back.

'Well, it has got four decent size bedrooms, and the kitchen is refurbished, the boiler is in good working order and – '

'Stop being so practical; you know what I mean. Could we be happy here?'

'Well, why didn't you say so? Of course, we could. I'd live in a tent with you, but it wouldn't be very practical, would it?' He stepped back as Heather landed a punch on his arm. 'Hey, you strong woman, that hurt. I hope you aren't going to abuse me when we're married.'

'Be serious, Stephen. It's a big decision.' Heather tried to keep a straight face, but she couldn't prevent her lips from turning up at the corners.

'Well, I think we should put in an offer subject to a survey. We'll go back to the estate agent before they close and see if the owner accepts it. What do you reckon to a couple of thousand below the asking price?' Stephen grabbed her gloved hand and pretended to hurry her towards the car.

'Let go please, Stephen – I can walk on my own.' Heather had another flashback of the rapists as they had dragged her into the back of the white van. She spoke quietly and tugged at her arm. Stephen immediately let her go.

When they were in the car, Stephen said gently, 'You know, Heather, it might help if you could tell me about that day. It will probably always eat away at you unless you can talk about what happened, if not to me, then someone else.'

Heather's shoulders slumped. 'I can't.'

'That's okay, my love. I meant when you were ready, not this minute.' He quickly changed the subject as Heather had sounded so distressed. 'Hey, don't let's spoil our luck at finding this place. I'm a little fed up with house hunting, and this one seems perfect.' He leaned across and gave her a peck on the cheek as she started the engine.

Heather allowed the engine to idle as she looked at her husband to be, gave a tiny smile, and then nodded her agreement. She thought how well he seemed to understand her feelings and felt sure that he would keep the promise that he'd given to her, but she didn't see how she could ever be completely honest with him. Heather wondered for the hundredth time if marriage could succeed based on lies. But she knew that she was going to go ahead and marry him, even though she could never tell him the truth about herself.

The next two months were some of the happiest that Heather could remember. She was so busy with work, the new house and her daughter that she didn't have time to dwell on the need to find out where Driver had gone.

Just before Christmas, Stephen sold his apartment and moved into their new house with most of his furniture. Once her pink and white bedroom was ready, Sienna wanted to move in, but it had was decided that Heather and Sienna should stay where they were until after the wedding.

Yvonne thought that the house was lovely, especially as it was only five minutes' walk away. She spent a fair amount of time happily helping to strip paper from walls with Sienna dressed in an old shirt that belonged to Bob. She always took Sienna with her knowing that she was about to lose their everyday contact.

The wedding was all planned, and life seemed to be going along very smoothly for them all. Christmas was memorable, yet again as family time. It had always been special but, Heather thought with sadness, this was possibly the last one where the whole family would be sitting down to Christmas dinner together.

Bob gave his usual toast to absent friends and then said, 'I want you, girls, to know how proud I am to be a Grandfather, and I hope that there will be many more little ones to sit on my knee and puke down my jacket.'

Yvonne told him to be quiet, but they all laughed, and Heather thought how quickly things were changing. She shuddered because she understood how things could change in a devastating way for her whole family. It was unlikely that a third killing would go undetected. I could just let it go, she thought, but something screamed inside her that Driver deserved to meet the same fate as the other two.

‘What’s the matter, love?’ Stephen asked his fiancée. He’d been watching her as myriad expressions chased across her face. All eyes turned to Heather. Yvonne and Susan had become less worried about her over the years, but their fear for her re-surfaced.

‘Nothing. I was just thinking how lovely it was for us all to be together and how the family’s growing.’ Heather squirmed as she told yet another inevitable lie.

‘Mm, yes it is, and it’s wonderful.’ Yvonne said. She stood and topped up everyone’s glass, ‘I wonder what the New Year will bring?’ she laughed. ‘Well, I know there will be a wedding, and I hope that it will only bring nice things for us all. We deserve it.’ She sat down as everyone cheered. Heather’s cheer was a little less enthusiastic than the others, but it went unnoticed.

Chapter 35

Heather couldn't have been more content than when she walked down the aisle on her father's arm, followed by Sienna holding onto Susan's other hand, as she carried Heather Jo on her arm. They looked very proud as they were ushered into the first pew by Yvonne and Bob. Stephen spoke to Ben, his best man, and then turned to Heather as she reached his side. He carefully lifted her white, gossamer veil and gazed tenderly at her.

'You are beautiful, and I love you.' He whispered, his voice sounded deep with emotion. Heather blushed and smiled as she let her eyes tell him that she loved him too.

After the ceremony and the signing of the register, they walked back up the aisle to clapping and good wishes from family and friends as they passed. Heather didn't usually like being the centre of attention, but she blossomed under the eyes of everyone that she cared about and revelled in all the photos that were taken. She felt so much joy that she thought she might burst. After the pictures, they drove in style to the reception at a large hotel. It wasn't far from the church, but to Heather, it could have been a hundred miles away. She made the journey holding on tightly to Stephen's hand as if she was in a daydream where nothing untoward could ever happen.

There were more photographs taken on the steps leading up to the old weathered stone building. Once inside, Heather caught her breath. The tables were set out in the shape of a horseshoe and adorned with white linen trimmed with azure blue satin. They looked stunning. She felt proud of her family as she floated in her fairy tale white dress up to the top table. She manoeuvred her way along to the centre seats, where she kissed her husband and then sat down beside him. Their faces flushed with the excitement of it all, and Heather later told Stephen that she had indeed felt like a princess. She looked along the table to where her father looked very handsome and her mother like a queen, resplendent in a pretty, pale green dress and jacket. A matching wide-brimmed hat, which she was just in the process of taking off, completed her ensemble.

Stephen's mother, Vera, was a tiny woman when compared to Yvonne. She wore a cream suit with brown accessories that Heather thought an unfortunate choice, as it made her appear a tad pale. Then she remembered that Vera might still be feeling a trifle unwell and was possibly not as rosy as usual. She turned her head, and her eyes alighted on Sienna and Heather Jo, who were also in pale green dresses with cream sashes and a circle of flowers in their hair. They were talking animatedly as they sat at the next table with Susan and Sean. She smiled then reluctantly withdrew her eyes from the touching sight as Stephen brushed her arm.

'Have I told you lately that I love you, Mrs Gordon?' Stephen whispered as he leaned towards her.

'Not since we've been married – I love you, too, Mr Gordon.' Heather now only had eyes for her husband, who made her heart beat a little faster each time she caught sight of his handsome face or thought of his toned body.

After the wedding breakfast and the speeches were over, Heather looked around the room and felt incredibly loved to see all her friends and relatives gathered in one place. But none of you would like me if you knew I was a murderess, she screamed inside her head. Her face remained serene.

While the tables were cleared and the DJ began to set up on a raised dais in one corner of the large room, Heather tore herself away from her husband's side and went to talk to her sister. She introduced herself to Stephen's sister, Carol and her husband, Kevin, who was sitting with Susan and Sean. She'd never met them before as they lived in Devon and had been late arriving. Heather took to them straight away. Kevin was a quietly spoken man, and Carol resembled Stephen. They both spoke with a charming drawl, and like her brother, Carol proved to be fun.

About eleven o'clock, Heather and Stephen slipped away to spend their first night together in their own home. Yvonne had taken Sienna to stay with her for two weeks while the newlyweds honeymooned in a villa in Portugal. Heather wasn't too keen on flying, so it suited her to stay near to the British Isles. While they were in the air, Heather mentioned that she wouldn't have minded staying at home.

'Oh no, Mrs Gordon, I know just what would have happened. I'm not sure that your family would have stayed away for more than a day or so. I want you all to myself.' Stephen smiled while he spoke, but he meant it. He was hoping that perhaps being on their own, and sharing a bed, would lead Heather to want more than just a kiss and a cuddle. He intended to keep his word but thought that it didn't hurt to hope.

'I know you're right. I'm not sure I would have been able to resist going to see Sienna either. So let's enjoy our time together without any worries, eh?' Heather slipped her hand into his and told Driver to get out of her head. She intended to forget about him as far as she was able to while on honeymoon. Heather rarely thought about Snake man or Ugly now. She wished that she hadn't had to kill them, but she still didn't regret it. They had deserved to die, and so would Driver when the chance arose.

Heather and Stephen found that the two weeks flew by and were idyllic. They spent the whole fortnight exploring, taking long walks hand in hand, swimming, and eating in good restaurants. In the evening, they enjoyed the local entertainment. They gambled in one of the casinos and spent three evenings dancing in a local night club. During their whole time together, they were as close as two people could be without having sex. On their first night in their own house, Heather had asked Stephen if he minded if she slept in the spare room. He'd opened his mouth to agree but changed his mind and told her that he would like her to sleep in the same bed as himself. Stephen again promised that not to touch her unless she asked him to. Heather reluctantly complied with his wishes and was grateful that he kept his promise. He did nothing more than kiss her lingeringly, then turn away and shut his eyes. It took her a little while before she managed to nod off. Her brain wouldn't let go of thoughts that troubled her and images that she'd hoped would leave her alone on this night of all nights.

After the first night spent in a hotel bed, Heather found that she could trust Stephen, who slept in his shorts. She wore sensible pyjamas hoping that they would act like a wall preventing accidental contact with each other's bodies. They slept on either side of the bed and left space down the middle of the mattress. After a couple of nights, both Stephen and

Heather began to really relax with each other and inevitably woke one morning with their legs and arms entwined. Heather quickly untangled herself and went to have a shower leaving Stephen in bed. When they got into bed the following night, she felt comfortable enough to move onto his outstretched arm. She enjoyed the slightly personal smell that emanated from his recently showered body.

Stephen found it almost impossible to control his feelings. Feelings that sat like a hot lump of stone in his belly, but manage them, he did. Just having Heather cuddled up to him was enough for the time being. He didn't intend to break his promise. Some nights after Heather had fallen asleep, he went to the bathroom and relieved his frustration, but it did little to stop him wanting to make love to his wife. Night after night, he hoped that she would show him that she too wanted to consummate their marriage, but when he began stroking her back one night, she moved away from his embrace and closed her eyes. He felt dismissed and vowed not to move one finger if she turned back to him the following night.

Heather felt sad in the morning and promised herself that when he next began to stroke her arm, she would try her best to respond. She couldn't bear this man that she loved so much to be hurting on her account. She knew that he sometimes masturbated when he thought that she was asleep and hated herself for making this necessary. On the remaining nights of their honeymoon, Stephen held his wife but made no attempt to arouse her, and Heather didn't feel able to behave as the provocateur. They both often lay awake while pretending sleep had claimed them, but their days in each other's company were the happiest either had known.

Sienna ran down the stairs as she heard her mother greeting everyone in the sitting room. She flung herself at Heather and burst into tears.

'Hey, hey, what's this about? You've been okay with your grandma, haven't you? Did you miss us?' Heather picked her daughter up and walked into the conservatory with her.

When she stopped crying, Heather wiped the tears from her face that felt like a furnace; she'd cried so much. 'I thought you were never coming back for me. You've been gone so long.' She started to snivel again, and Heather remembered how long two weeks might seem to her child.

'Well, I'm sorry it's seemed such a long while, my darling, but stop crying because we're here now, and we've bought you some lovely presents from Portugal.'

Sienna sat up straight and said proudly, 'I know where Portugal is. Granddad showed me on the globe in the living room. Was it hot there? Granddad said it was, and that's why you had gone there for your honeymoon.' Sienna chuckled and kissed her mother fiercely on each cheek. 'May I have my presents now? I don't want you to go away again, please – I don't need any presents, really.'

Heather laughed and hugged her. 'Your presents are at home, honey. We only came to fetch you to come and live in your new home with us. What do you think? Would you like that?'

Sienna nodded and then became serious. 'I will be able to come and see Grandma and Granddad, won't I? And Great-Grandma and Great-Granddad, too? Because I love them, and I don't want to miss them either.'

'Your bedroom will still be here, darling, and you'll be spending time with us when Mommy and Stephen are at work,' Yvonne said.

'But he's not Stephen. He's my daddy now. We promised, didn't we Daddy?' Sienna laughed with excitement as Stephen threw her up into the air and caught her again.

'Yes, we did. And, yes, I am your Daddy, and I love you very much, my daughter. Now, let's go home. I need to put my slippers on.' Sienna looked pleased and hugged his leg.

'I think it's someone's birthday next Wednesday. I wonder who that could be?' said Yvonne.

'Me, me, me! I'll be five,' Sienna stood up on tiptoes, 'I go to proper school now, don't I, Mommy?'

After her daughter's fears were put to rest and goodbyes said, Heather and Stephen left with Sienna to start their married life in earnest.

They quickly settled into a routine, many of their shift patterns coincided, and, with Yvonne and Susan's help, childcare wasn't a problem. There were only two things that caused Heather to lose sleep – both were of equal importance to her. She thought that solving one may solve the other and became more determined than ever to find Driver and end his life. Then hopefully start her married life properly. She had looked in the Birmingham phone book briefly before for Carl Patel but found nothing concrete to go on, and then other things had prevented her from continuing her search.

When she was alone the following Monday, she picked up the book again and found three people named K. Patel and two people named C. Patel. The listing for the address in Greet, where she already knew he had lived, was for K. Patel. She immediately dismissed the two with the initial C. The other two listed under K. Patel had addresses in Sparkhill.

She hadn't been to Sparkhill since she'd killed Snake man and was very reluctant to return there, but she had to find out which one it was. The thought of again spending endless hours sitting in her car outside a house was hateful to her. She also had Stephen to think of now. She wouldn't be able to slip away without question as she was used to doing. She couldn't think of an answer. She sat by the phone, twisting her bracelet round and round until she realised what she was doing and stopped. She felt desperate; she had to find him.

Chapter 36

Heather ran her fingers over the granite work surfaces in her kitchen and looked appreciatively at the bright red, shiny appliances. They had been living in their own home for two months, and the novelty hadn't yet worn off. She loved being married to Stephen and spent every day when she wasn't at work, ensuring that their space was as comfortable and pleasant for them to come home to as she was able.

Sienna's fifth birthday had come and gone, with all the love and fun that her family could imagine for her. She enjoyed being at school and spending her time mainly between her grandparent's house and her home. The high spot of her life was to be alone with her Mom when they would stay in their pyjamas until the afternoon and have what her mother called a slob day. She never told anyone about these days as it was their secret. She felt immensely grown up to have a special secret that no one else could share.

At the end of May, Stephen and Heather organised a house-warming and invited all their friends and relatives. The weather was warm and sunny, so they were able to spill over into the garden as the house was becoming full of people wandering around and talking enthusiastically. The constant movement reminded Heather of bees collecting pollen.

Julie and Ben were playing with Heather, Jo and Gemma. Susan, who was pregnant again and blooming with happiness now that the morning sickness had ceased, was squashed into a corner of the conservatory enjoying the children's antics. Lucy and John were chatting in the garden by the small fishpond, and Heather went to join them. She was a little unsteady on her feet and kept blaming Stephen, who had mixed her last drink into what he called a cocktail without a name. The music and the laughter are intoxicating enough, she'd said when he handed her a second glass containing a bright pink mixture, but she drank it willingly and asked him for another. As the evening wore on, Heather lost track of time and was surprised at ten o'clock when John and Sam kissed her on her cheek, thanked her for a lovely time, and then left. She had almost no recollection of anyone else going, but as she sank into a conservatory chair feeling slightly sick, she realised that the party was over, and Stephen was collecting glasses and taking them through to the kitchen.

'Where's everyone gone?' she asked her husband as he leaned over the sofa and picked up a forgotten coat.

'They've all deserted us,' he said and laughed, seeing her crestfallen face.

'But I was enjoying myself,' Heather said. 'Where's Sienna? Is she in bed?'

'Your Mom has taken her home with her so you can have a lie-in. It went well, didn't it? The house is well and truly warmed – and so are you.' He laughed indulgently and pulled her up by her hand. 'Come on, let's get you to bed, you tipsy woman, you.'

Heather walked unsteadily as though she were on board a ship as she made her way upstairs and into the bathroom. She made a lousy job of brushing her teeth, let her clothes fall onto the floor then climbed into bed, shut her eyes and drifted away.

When Stephen climbed into bed beside her, he couldn't believe that she hadn't donned her pyjamas as she always did. He leaned across and brushed her hair from her forehead, and lay watching her sleep. She was beautiful, and he desired her more than he was able to let her know. He snuggled his way closer to her sleeping form, eased his arm under her, and pulled her gently to him. He traced his finger along one of her scars and felt such fury towards the perpetrators. He didn't understand how any man could treat a woman so horrifically. He wanted to find them and have them punished, but Heather didn't want anything more to happen. She told him that she no longer thought about it, but at times he knew differently.

As he stroked her arm, she suddenly opened her eyes and looked up adoringly at him. 'Make love to me, please,' she asked softly.

Stephen couldn't believe that she was properly awake – he leaned upon his free elbow. 'What did you say, my love?' His heart began to pound; its drumming filled his ears.

'Make love to me, Stephen, I'm not too drunk; I know what I'm saying, and I want you so much.' She raised her head from his arm and kissed him passionately on his lips. Her hand began to travel the length of his body, pushed aside his shorts, and grasped his penis. She stroked it with butterfly touches. She'd wanted to do this many times but had never been able to allow herself to make the first move.

Stephen made love to her gently at first, but as the passion grew between them, they both forgot what time it was or which planet they were on. They eventually lay satiated, and as dawn coloured the sky, they slept in each other's arms.

The next few months passed in a whirl of new experiences for Heather. Every moment that she and Stephen were apart seemed wasted. She still loved being a midwife – but her work became a real inconvenience.

They spent time in Devon with Stephen's family, who Heather and Sienna came to like very much. But it was the time they spent in a four-star hotel when they went away for a weekend in Kent that stayed in her memory. They visited Canterbury Cathedral, and after about an hour exploring the beautiful building, they found their way into the chapel that was a shrine to commemorate the medieval murder of Thomas Becket. Heather read the plaque that told the story of his death and touched the remaining copper bracelet on her wrist as she began thinking about the murders that she'd committed. She went very quiet, and Stephen said that he'd had enough of history and persuaded her to leave what he considered to be morbid veneration. She was happy to wander along the quaint cobbled streets and later return for their evening meal to the hotel with their tired daughter.

The next day after breakfast, they visited Whitstable, where they ate a lunch of whitebait at the Crab and Winkle. They sat at flimsy aluminium tables placed on the edge of the docks where some fishing boats moored. Heather was fascinated as she watched a lorry tipping a load of whelks onto a mountain of them on the dock opposite where they sat.

'Yuk, who eats those things?' she asked Stephen, wrinkling her nose in disgust. He shrugged and pinched his nose together. The smell surrounding them was pungent, but they thought it was a fantastic place to mingle with the other holidaymakers. They bought waxed paper cups of tea, sticks of brightly coloured rock for each member of the family and candy floss for Sienna from the wooden shack village that had grown up at the end of the harbour. They made their way to a bench next to a wharf where a crane was scooping various grades of gravel into big heavy-duty bags. As each one became full, it was loaded onto a blue and white painted ship that already lay low in the water. Sienna swung her legs happily as she ate the pink candy floss by pulling chunks from the stick with her hands and sticking it to her nose when she missed her mouth. They laughed at her and the seagulls as they swooped and swirled. A small group was wheeling noisily around one of the newly painted fishing boats as it calmly put out to sea; its red and white hull rapidly becoming smaller and smaller. They watched its radio mast shimmering in the strong sunlight for a few minutes, and then it was gone, as if by magic.

The sun was scorching hot as Heather rubbed sun cream onto her daughter's exposed skin for the third time that day, insisting that she replace her sunhat. Sienna looked about to rebel but did as she was told, and, hand in hand with Stephen, they walked back to the car between weird-looking, small, wooden houses that were painted black and built following the line of the shingle.

'I think that this could be one of my favourite places – do you think we could spend a week here sometime?' Heather asked Stephen. 'I know its shingle, but I think that Sienna would love it and the green sea looks very inviting. What do you think? Would you like to spend more time here?'

'I don't see why not. I think this area of the country is lovely. Perhaps we should see what accommodation is available for next year. I believe that Hyde is worth a visit, too. But we should probably be on our way home now. We can stop in Oxford and have a meal.'

Heather offered to share the driving, but both she and Sienna nodded off before they reached Oxford and Stephen chose to drive home without stopping. They woke as he pulled into their driveway and switched the engine off.

'Oh dear, I'm so sorry, love,' Heather said. She looked contrite as she lifted Sienna from her car seat. 'I'll just give her something to eat and then pop her into bed. Would you order us a takeaway please – I don't mind what you choose.'

'Okay, love, I think I fancy Chinese,' Stephen said. He stood and stamped his feet before visually checking the tyres and then entering the house.

Sienna held on to her cousin's hand, and they both gave little skips between walking sedately with Heather and Susan around the houses by where Susan lived. The girls were dressed in orange and black witch costumes, and Susan and Heather had on long green cloaks and pointed black hats that they'd made themselves. Both the girls looked frightened as they knocked on the first door. When a pleasant woman answered, they were too scared to say trick or treat, but she knew what they meant and kindly held out a basket of sweets for them to take one each. By the time they were onto their third house, they were shouting the words out as each door opened.

'It's begging, really,' Heather said.

'Oh, go on! We're just having a bit of fun, don't be such a wimp.' Susan replied. Heather felt as though she'd been punched in her stomach; it was like being back in the white van again as her sister used the phrase having a bit of fun. She twisted her bracelet round and round; for her, the pleasure of Halloween had disappeared. She was glad when they called it a night and took the two tired but happy children home. It would be several years before Heather began to see Halloween for what it was and could hear the words a bit of fun without having the same upsetting sensation.

In November, all the growing extended family got together and went out for a meal to celebrate Stephen's birthday. While they were eating, Heather was able to announce that she was pregnant and the baby was due the following May. Susan, whose baby was due in a couple of weeks and frequently cried at anything sentimental, burst into tears.

'I'm so happy we'll have little ones together, won't we?' She got up awkwardly and went to hug her sister.

'Go on, you soppy 'apporth!' Heather whispered, but she shed a tear herself.

After everyone had congratulated them, Heather glanced at her mother's face. She was sobbing quietly into a table napkin. Heather ceased to cry and looked horrified. 'What's the matter, Mom?'

'I'm just so happy; I love being a grandma,' Yvonne said.

She ceased crying as Bob gave her arm a rub and said, 'Go on, you soppy 'apporth!' As usual, everyone laughed as they hugged each other and excited chatter once again filled the pub room with their noise.

Chapter 37

Grinning widely, Stephen said, 'He's beautiful, isn't he, Gemma? Do you love him?' She looked very serious as she held onto her tiny brother's fingers and gazed at him while he lay placidly in his crib.

'Yes, I do. He's my bruvva.' Gemma said.

'She rarely lets him out of her sight, but he is beautiful, isn't he?' Susan looked around at her family, who were seated at the dinner table, waiting for Heather to bring in the Christmas pudding.

Heather heard a chorus of agreement as she pushed open the kitchen door with her hip, then placed the large pudding on the table, poured brandy over it and stood back while Sean set it on fire. She sat down and allowed Sean to cut the pudding and pour brandy sauce into the dish of everyone who wanted it. Heather felt tired but had enjoyed hosting the family Christmas dinner. Her mother and sister had helped with the preparation, and she knew that the men would clear away. It was becoming a family tradition and one that she applauded.

Heather went to check on Gary, her baby nephew, who was named after Sean's father. He was asleep, and she tried to persuade Gemma to return to the table, but Gemma said that she was full up and patted her stomach to prove it. Sienna asked if she too could leave the table to play with her new doll that she'd put to bed in the sitting room. Heather told her that she could, and Gemma quickly followed her, forgetting for the moment that she had a brother. Heather and Susan looked across the table into each other's eyes and grinned as if to acknowledge how clever they both were to produce lovely children.

Heather and Stephen couldn't wait until their other daughter was born. They decorate the nursery in pink and white, but once they'd settled on a name, they kept it secret until after she was born.

Time was flying past for them all. Heather had ceased to dwell on her need to find and kill Driver. It was her healthy life that was paramount, and the rapes and the killings were pushed to the back of her mind. Sienna's sixth birthday was celebrated as usual at her grandmother's house. Then at the beginning of March, Heather was glad to finish work and put her feet up occasionally until the birth was imminent.

Poppy weighed in at eight pounds six ounces, bang on time, on the twenty-seventh of May. She was the complete opposite of Sienna; she had very light skin and fair hair. Heather hadn't thought that she could love any other child as much as she loved Sienna, but she had a lot to learn about love. The sight of her second child filled her with just as much joy as her firstborn. Although Stephen loved Sienna, he hadn't been there when she was born, and he was completely bowled over by Poppy. He'd delivered hundreds of babies, but he confessed to Heather that the love he felt for this baby was totally different.

Yvonne had been present at the birth and had been allowed to cut the cord, separating her grandchild from her child, not such an easy thing to do. A few months later, she told Heather that it was one of the best moments of her life, but it felt as though she was cutting through a piece of tough rubber.

Heather had almost forgotten that she had the third copper bracelet on her wrist. She was so used to it being there, but two weeks after Poppy's birth, as she placed her onto the changing mat – Driver loomed big in her consciousness. It was like a wake-up punch to her contented mind. How could she be happy when the third bastard was still walking the earth? The memory of her vow to kill them all surfaced again and burnt into her heart.

It was some time since the voice in her head had argued with her, but it sounded now, telling her to forget her vow. She had other responsibilities. You can wait, and you need to become stronger and fitter again, it told her. She nodded her head as though it had spoken out loud. She then smiled at her baby daughter and assured herself that she could wait; her family were more important. But once again, fate was about to take a hand.

At the beginning of August, Sienna told Heather about a friend at school who'd been to a place called Drayton Manor Park. She spoke so longingly about it that when Heather told Stephen, he suggested that they go the following weekend if the weather was kind. They invited Susan and Sean to join them, but they had other plans.

'You're like a big kid.' Heather teased her husband as he took Sienna on their fourth ride of the day while she stayed with Poppy on a bench in the shade of a giant oak tree.

'They all are. They never grow up really, do they?' The woman, who looked lovely in a blue and yellow sari, smiled. 'My husband is over there with our daughter. They're on their third ride. They're on that big ship,' she pointed, 'It looks dangerous to me, but I can't bear that sort of thing anyway. I just hope he is holding on to our daughter tightly enough,' she laughed. 'I shouldn't worry – he's a perfect father and wouldn't let anything happen to her. We visit here often.'

'Do you live near here, then?' Heather asked, just for something to say.

'Yes, not far. Do you know Amington?' Heather shook her head. 'We moved from Birmingham to be by the Crown pub where my husband works. Are you from around here?'

'No, we're from Birmingham. We're just here for the day.' Heather looked up, 'Here's my husband now with our other daughter, Sienna.' She held out her arms, and Sienna ran into them then peered into the pushchair. 'Hello there, you two. Was that fun, Sienna? You look very hot.'

Sienna began to speak too loudly but placed her finger across her lips and calmed down when she remembered that Poppy was asleep. 'It was great, Mom. I'd like to go on that one again, but Daddy said it's too scary.'

Heather glanced over at the woman she'd been enjoying having a conversation with before Sienna had sat down on the bench. Her husband and daughter had arrived back, and her daughter was hopping about with her legs crossed while her husband leaned forward and kissed his wife tenderly on her cheek.

'That was fun, but I need the loo, Mommy,' the little girl, who was about five years old, said and continued to hop.

'I need the loo, too,' Sienna said.

The woman got up from the bench, and her husband took over rocking the pram.

Stephen had disappeared to buy cold drinks for them, and Heather began to collect her things together in preparation to take her daughter to the toilet when the Asian woman asked,

'Would you like me to take your daughter with Amina?' Heather hesitated, but she couldn't see any reason why not and felt that it would be rude to refuse. 'Would you mind?' The woman shook her head. 'That's very kind of you,' Heather said with a smile. Sienna had already joined hands with Amina, and they skipped off in the direction of the toilets.

Heather watched them for a long moment, then turned her head to look at the man sitting a couple of feet away from her. He was bending forward, adjusting the coverlet on his son's feet. As he straightened up, Heather recognised his face: it was Driver. Her heart stopped in mid beat. She almost fled from the seat, but her legs would not obey. I'm not ready, I'm not ready, she thought. Then her mind became coldly calm, and she continued to consider his profile as his eyes followed his wife and the children. He began to drum his fingers on the handle of the pram, keeping time with the calliope music from the fair while watching the crowds of people milling about. He turned towards Heather: his dark skin paled, and his hand faltered then lost its rhythm. He looked away in the hope that she hadn't recognised him.

'Hello Karl,' Heather said. Her voice was hard and sharp – a shard of granite.

His head shot round, and his eyes met hers. 'How do you know my name?' he asked with a familiar tremor in his voice that made Heather's stomach churn.

'I think you already know the answer, don't you, Karl? I'm glad that I no longer need to look for you. Your wife told me where you live and where you work.' Heather could feel herself becoming calmer as she twisted her bracelet round and round on her arm.

'Yes, I do,' he said simply. His shoulders slumped, and his head fell forward into his hands. His voice continued to shake s he said, 'I've had this hanging over me for the last seven ears – I'm sorry, so very, very sorry for the way I treated you hen. I've no excuse, but I'm not a bad person. I've hated nyself and the other two ever since.' He removed his hands nd looked directly at her as he asked, 'Did you kill them?'

Heather didn't answer, just continued to stare at this man who she'd obsessed about killing. Suddenly she knew that seven years' worth of tears had washed away every vestige of hate for him. She no longer felt anything; it was as though she was a different person, and he was, too.

'Are you going to kill me now you know where I live?' Karl asked, the timbre of his voice becoming lower.

'Do you love your wife? She seems like a very nice person,' Heather said.

'More than anything, and I would never behave as I did then, please, please, believe me,' he said.

Heather did believe him; she remembered that he hadn't actually raped her, although that had been his intention. Suddenly this man seemed more like a stranger, and her need for revenge disappeared as she said calmly, 'No, I am not going to kill you – you have your wife and family to thank – I don't think anything should be allowed to destroy their lives. I hope I never have any regrets'

Heather stood up and, holding on to the pushchair, walked to meet her daughter, who was skipping along, still holding Amina's hand. She thanked Karl's wife and then watched as she joined her husband. They began to murmur as they walked away from the bench. Heather could see Stephen hurrying from the queue towards her carrying three bottles of water. She felt strangely unreal; it was over – it was really over. She'd had all the revenge that she needed. At that moment, the old Heather died, and a new, free woman took her place. As she walked along with her family, she slipped the third copp bracelet from her wrist and unobtrusively dropped it into th first waste bin that appeared.

The End

Acknowledgements

Although I began to write a novel in my early twenties, li with all its ups and downs left no room for me to pursue m dream of becoming an author. I feel certain that this boo would never have come to fruition if not for the help an encouragement I have received in my later years.

With this in mind, I would like to thank my wonderful wife, Susan Elliot, for her help and guidance every step of the way. Sometimes I listened. Thank you, Susie.

I am lucky enough to have a very loving and close family network who have cared for and been there whenever I've needed them. Special thanks go to my son-in-law, Gary Williams, a man who has a wealth of life experience, for taking the time to explain police methods and routines when asked. And an even bigger thank you for being my chauffeur and friend on many occasions when I have had hospital appointments to go to on a regular basis. Thank you for listening to me too.

I have been very needy on occasions where technology is concerned and feel very grateful to my soon to be grandson-in-law, Adam Throssell, who has readily given his knowledge and time to patiently explain and assist practically. Thank you for being so kind.

A big thank you to Dr Gladys Mary Coles, my tutor in creative writing at Ness Gardens, which is part of Liverpool University. Thank you for your wise words and your belief in my ability to write this book.

I can't end without thanking my friend, Janet Hill, for her editing skills and freely given time and encouragement. Thanks Jan, you've paid me back for introducing you to Kevin.

My love and thanks also go to my friend and niece, Mary Mooney, for reading my first draft and giving both critical and positive feedback. She also brings us M & S goodies on occasions, so thank you for those too, Mary, aka Lisa.

Last but not least, thank you for purchasing this book. I know you could have picked any number of books to read, but you chose one of mine, and for that, I am incredibly grateful. Your feedback and support will help me significantly, so I hope you can take some time to post a review on Amazon or maybe share with your family and friends on social media.

By the Same Author:

Sally-Secrets and Lies

Happiness can be hard to find and even harder to hold on to. In February 1916, when Sally Brooks is twenty-five months old, a family argument changes her life forever. Lied to since childhood and unaware of secrets that will cause her heartbreak, will she ever be able to make sense of past events and gain the happiness she deserves? Follow Sally's family life and relationships as she grows from naïve child to protective mother, learning about betrayal and loss, friendship and love on the way.

One Child Too Many

Sara Caldicot has an uncomplicated life that she shares wit her close-knit family. Her younger sister, Lyn, is spoilt an self-centred, but she has always been loved and protectec When Lyn becomes disruptive at home, Sara's mom asks he: for support. Sara tries her best to help, but in the process, she uncovers a secret. A secret so dreadful that it threatens to tear the family apart. Can Lyn be made to see sense, or will her selfish actions end up destroying more than just relationships?

Love and Beyond

Stella is special, but she doesn't find that out until she dies and arrives at the Waystation. There she is given the opportunity to return to her life with the woman that she loves if she agrees to carry out a mission. Find and intervene in the lives of four people to safeguard one who is significant to the future of the world. But there is a problem. If anybody discovers her secret, the deal is off. Stakes are so high that failure is not an option, but even being an angel does not convince Stella that she has the power to succeed.

All of the above books are available for purchase, in both paperback and e-book format, at www.Amazon.co.uk.

For more information about the author, please visit www.lesleyelliot.co.uk

Printed in Great Britain
by Amazon